Advance praise for

# THE RABBI'S HUSBAND By Brenda Barrie

I0654152

---

Brenda Barrie does it again. Engagingly and with the deepest compassion, *The Rabbi's Husband* explores the intricate connections that bind us together as families and communities. Barrie treats each of her characters with dignity and with such an open heart that I couldn't help but be moved by every one of them. Their love is as palpable as is their pain, and I turned the pages eagerly, rooting for things to come out well for one and all. This is a truly fine novel.

> **David Haynes**, author of *The Full Matilda, Somebody Else's Mama,* and others.

The prenuptial counseling offered by most rabbis includes plenty of advice on the importance of communication. How strange, then, that the lead characters in *The Rabbi's Husband* – who clearly love each other very well - are such poor communicators! This very flaw is the catalyst for Brenda Barrie's riveting, well-told and cautionary tale.

> **Rabbi Cheryl Rosenstein**, Temple Beth El, Bakersfield, CA

## Praise for THE BINDING

---

In *The Binding*, Brenda Barrie has nailed the psyche of the son of Holocaust survivors. I know, because I am one of them. I see myself (in each one of her major characters)... *The Binding* may be a work of fiction, but it is one of the truest stories I have ever experienced.

> **Charles Adler**, radio talk show host, newspaper columnist, news commentator, & analyst for the Global Television Network

Praise for **THE BINDING** and **THE RABBI'S HUSBAND**

[*The Binding*] is a thought-provoking book about a second generation still affected by The Holocaust...with the pacing of a mystery and the sweetness of a romance....Thank goodness we need not say goodbye to [these characters] but meet them again, in far more detail, in Barrie's second novel, *The Rabbi's Husband.*

**Carol Matas**, author of *Sworn Enemies, Code Name Kris, Lisa's War, The Garden,* and others

# THE RABBI'S HUSBAND

a novel

Gray Matter Imprints, Irvine, California

Also by Brenda Barrie

# THE BINDING, a novel

Poetry

*Full Speed. Full Stop*

# THE RABBI'S HUSBAND

a novel by
*Brenda Barrie*

GRAY MATTER IMPRINT EDITION

*Library of Congress Cataloging-in-Publication Data*
Barrie, Brenda
The Rabbi's Husband, a novel / Brenda Barrie
      Fiction, Novel, Contemporary Jewish, Women Rabbis, Rabbis
      ISBN 978-0-9835921-1-2)
      ISBN-10: 098359211X
      1. Novel 2. Fiction 3. Contemporary Jewish 4. Women Rabbis 5. Rabbis
      Library of Congress Control Number: 2011938837

Original artwork on book cover of *The Rabbi's Husband* is entitled *Searching* by Ruth Rosen

Published by Gray Matter Imprints™, division of Gray Matter Consultants LLC, P.O. Box 50278 Irvine, CA 92619


10 9 8 7 6 5 4 3 2 1

Printed in the United States of America

Gray Matter accepts queries only.at:
      Gray Matter Imprints
      P.O. Box 50278
      Irvine, CA 92619

Publisher's Note: This novel is a work of fiction. The names, characters, organizations, places and incidents are either the product of the author's imagination or, as in the case of Minneapolis and Orange County, are used fictitiously, and any resemblance to actual persons (living or dead), events or locales is entirely coincidental.

*For my Grandchildren*

*It would take many lifetimes to write the books
worthy of each of them individually:
Simon, Aliza, Maks, Elisheva, Benjamin,
Ariela, Shulamit, Yaakov, Ezra*

# ACKNOWLEDGEMENTS

The publishing world is in the throes of change. So, who to thank in this acknowledgement? Traditionally, it would be an agent and a major publishing house editor.

But today, and for me, it is far more relevant to thank independent small publishers, new technologies and the individuals who taught me, and who, I hope, will continue to teach me all I need to know.

Having now sold two books to small presses I need to thank both RockWay Press and Gray Matter who brought my novels to their audiences. I have had conventional agents and despite some reasonable efforts I doubt my books would ever have made it to market or found their audience in this tough traditional publishing environment. Small, responsive publishing houses and thoughtful self-publishing are the way to go.

I would like to thank my readers, who loved *The Binding*, and who will, I hope, find something equally valuable in *The Rabbi's Husband* and *An Unorthodox Romance,* to be published next year.

Special thanks to friends who are the most patient readers of various drafts. This book took longer than most, and Rena Konheim, Virginia Sheff and Joan Kaye stayed with me.

My biggest thanks go to my teachers, authors all, who generously share what they know.

First, Louella Nelson, teacher extraordinaire, who was the first to say "Bingo," when I managed to drop the first three chapters a book and start where the story really began. Lou's dictum, "come in late and leave early," is true. And, she taught me how to do that.

Even before I met Lou, my mentor and dear friend was the late Carol Shields, who helped publish my first poetry and was always willing to listen to new ideas

She was intrigued that the subject matter for my books was contemporary Jewish life.

"I'm a Presbyterian," she once said. "That's good for about ten minutes of thought a week." Thus, a time-saving benefit of being part of some majority; which Carol also understood.

"Don't compare your book to my tenth novel," she said. "Read my first few books."

Well, I've read them all and Carol was not only a Pulitzer Prize winner (for *The Stone Diaries*, 1995), but a very classy lady, and, so giving and so wonderfully normal and stable, that the thought that I could be "like" her, gave me, and continues to give me, something to aspire to.

I also want to thank Carol's husband, Don Shields, who encourages me to keep Carol's memory fresh and to continue to see her influence in my work.

My thanks to teachers must also include Alexandria Szeman, the creator of RockWayPress who taught me more about editing a book than I thought possible. She is now laboring to publish more new writers and to make *The Binding* an e-book. Her understanding of what makes a novel – read her award winning novel *The Kommandant's Mistress* (under the name Sherri Szeman) to find out – exceeds the knowledge of most people in the field. She was also one of the first to understand how the new technologies make book publishing much more available.

In addition to RockWay, my adventure continues with the much newer Gray Matter Imprints which, in being willing to move from business publishing to fiction, has made possible *The Rabbi's Husband*, and the upcoming *An Unorthodox Romance*.

Writing *The Rabbi's Husband* began in Orange County, then continued in Baltimore and was finally completed in Orange County once again. Carving time from a hectic work schedule was part of the delay. *The Rabbi's Husband* progressed first with the support of my writing groups in Baltimore: Jill Morrow, Sherry Morrow, Emily Levitt, Shawn Sapp-Nocher and Nora Frankiel.

Likewise, the book might never have been finished without Lou Nelson's classes and my present critique group in Orange: Janet Simcic, who keeps us in line; Dennis Phinney, who keeps us inspired; Ed Kaufman, who exemplifies what can be done with a story and a thoughtful consideration of a personal life; Ron Hoefer, for his willingness to confront; John Gray for the beauty of his prose (there ought to be a book, John); and Ana Arellano, who I hope will soon finish the wonderful book she is now working on, thereby writing her first book in her twenties and getting about a thirty-year jump on the schedule of many in our group.

One of the most important thanks goes to my husband, Sid Bursten, who always stands beside me – and sometimes just a little behind, where he can deliver a small push or two. When I met Sid 50 years ago, he was the very cute guy I wanted to impress. Sid taught me about typography then, and in subsequent years (and decades, now that I think about it) continued to teach as we worked together on newspaper and magazine publishing projects that brought me to where I am today. One way or another, and willingly or sometimes needing one of those little pushes, I've been learning from Sid ever since (and teaching too) in a marriage that is a rare partnership and my bedrock.

Thanks too, to my daughters, Renata Bursten and Aviva Cohen, advance readers and supporters, and to their children, who fortunately think a grandmother who writes books is "cool." I hope these grandchildren understand how "cool" it is for me to be able to dedicate this book to all of them.

The circumstances and characters of *The Rabbi's Husband* are purely fictional.

Along the way I've taken some liberties with the geography of the cities where this novel is set, up to and including dropping a synagogue into Dana Point, Orange County, where some residents have said it would be welcome.

# PROLOGUE

## *Late December, 1994*

It was Dan's night to clean up. Tovah had cooked and was now putting leftovers away.

"Will you go grocery shopping tonight?" she asked, putting a damp paper towel and then plastic wrap over the salad.

Any child of Hadas Feldner knew how to store a salad so it would hold one more day.

He had been daydreaming at the sink. If asked, Dan might have said his thoughts centered on how nice if their rented house had a dishwasher.

Really, though, his secret plan was on his mind. A chance to talk to his wife was more important than anything else. He turned quickly.

Too late. Tovah had moved on. She was mentally checking off where everyone ought to be tonight.

- Kids in bed.
- Chores for Dan to keep him occupied.
- She could go and hide in her study. Again.

"You could go shopping right after the kids are in bed. You don't have to wait. The stores might not be as quiet as later, but you'd be back earlier. Or, do you still have something to do in your work shop?"

Tovah didn't stop for his answers. She never did these days. Because she knew what he was going to say, or because she didn't care?

"Nice job," she said surveying the clean counters and the dishes, rinsed in such hot water that they steamed in the dish drainer. Tovah was great on compliments, on 'please' and 'thank you.' She knew about positive reinforcement.

Dan turned, squeezed dry the sponge he was using and put it in the special plastic holder he'd suction-cupped to the inside of the sink.

It looked like he'd have to go ahead without telling Tovah. One finger of his still-damp hand went to the pocket of his brown cords. The note he'd already written crackled a little. Tovah wouldn't hear that small sound.

Should he just leave it? Where to leave it?

Tovah looked at him, waiting for an answer, a comment, something. What had she said last? Right. Grocery shopping.

"Tovah." Maybe he could still tell her what he needed to do, instead of just going ahead.

But, he couldn't manage to get her full attention. It had been months. It was good she was so sure of him. God knows he loved her. She was the best thing that had ever happened to him; but he couldn't manage to talk to her anymore. Loving her wasn't enough right now.

Tovah was too busy figuring out how to love her goddamn job. Obviously she planned to do that by carrying it out perfectly. Otherwise, why would she disappear into her study to write sermons she'd probably never give and keep daily committee and work notes so exact they could be subpoenaed by Congress to show exactly what the most junior of four rabbis in a large congregation did all day, and half the night.

Rabbis – especially those working directly with families and their problems – were expected to keep an accurate day timer, but you would have thought Tovah had a job like their lawyer friend Michael Bregman, in Madison.

Michael, an associate in a major law firm, had to make sure his firm knew his exact number of billable hours. When Dan heard what it took to produce those hours, he knew he'd done the right thing dropping out of law school years ago, just after he'd met Michael.

Tovah didn't have to be so exact in her reporting, but she recorded everything as though she did.

True, Temple Isaiah was one of the biggest Reform Temples in the Midwest. Also true, when Tovah landed this job three years ago, the plum placement available after ordination, her classmates and her professors had been impressed. But, Tovah didn't belong at Temple Isaiah. He'd let it go and let it go, but he finally realized she was never going to figure it out.

Tovah rubbed her hand along the thick, old, but very clean ceramic counter tiles, laughing when they squeaked under her fingers.

"Perfect, as usual." She always said that about any job Dan took on.

Just as she did every evening, Tovah reached up on tiptoes, and kissed him. He moved to catch her by the shoulders, but he wasn't quick enough. Sometimes he wanted to shake her, make her listen, but his wife was a small, curly-haired dervish. Her kiss, like all the kisses lately, slipped either to his cheek or chin.

Kiss delivered, Tovah was on to a whole new subject.

"Right. I forgot. You want to repair Leah's chair and finally paint it red to match the rest of the kitchen."

She waved one hand around the black, white and red room where he'd put her soft drink memorabilia on display.

"I guess it's the workshop first, and then the groceries. Don't worry about me. I'd like to get one or two sermons ahead for the New Year. I think Rabbi G. will let me deliver more of them if I have a couple in the bag. Don't you?"

When he felt like this – when his old nemesis, his personal gray cloud descended – he could not keep up. Tovah didn't seem to realize he was at least a half step behind all the time. He'd been unable to share his plan, again.

As long as the kids were well looked after during the day, by Dan, the househusband, with Leah's physical therapy and most of the household chores in his expert hands, Tovah felt she was free to concentrate wholly on her job.

How long could she concentrate on a job she hated?

No matter. Dan couldn't wait any longer.

# CHAPTER ONE

The high–pitched voice of a child filled her ears. Bright white light reflected into the room from the snow piled outside the house. The light gleamed right through Rabbi Tovah Feldner's closed eyelids. Resisting the voice, she pulled the quilt up over her head and tried to roll up into a ball, compressing her normal five feet four inches into something approaching half that length.

*"Eemma. Eemma."* The voice definitely became that of her five-year-old son, Ari. It penetrated right through her heavy blanket. Tovah groaned. She counted on the extra sleep she got on Wednesday, her official day off. She was definitely not ready to get up.

"Mommy. Mommy. Do I go to school today?" Ari switched to English, since he didn't get her attention in Hebrew.

Could she answer a question and still stay asleep? Definitely worth a try. She pushed the blanket down far enough so her reply wouldn't be muffled. "Of course

you go to school today, Ari. That's your job. It's my day
to sleep in. Go find *Abba* and he'll get you ready."

"I can't find Daddy! Leah wants to get out of her crib.
We're both hungry."

It really was unusually bright in the bedroom for an
early December morning in Minneapolis. The sun didn't
reach over the horizon until around eight. Reluctantly,
Tovah opened one eye and focused on the digital alarm
clock beside the bed: Nine-fourteen.

Nine-fourteen! She bolted upright, suddenly panicky.
Except for the usual turmoil of bedding on her side of
the king-size bed, the rest of the red and black plaid
quilt was smooth.

"Ari! Where's Daddy? Where's Leah?"

Her small son, still in fuzzy, footed, one-piece pajamas,
looked aggravated.

"I told you. I can't find him. And Leah's in her crib. I
told you already. She wants to come out. And we both
want breakfast."

Before she fed the children, before washing up,
without even finger-combing her flaring black curls into
some semblance of order, Tovah checked the whole
house, even listening for the sound of Dan's power tools
in case he was already in his workshop in the basement.
She hurried outside, first stuffing her bare feet into her
warmly lined winter boots and throwing her down jacket
over the extra-large t-shirt she slept in.

For some reason it was a garment Dan actually found
sexy, bright red, with 'Harvard' written across it in Hebrew.
Once she'd complained, saying he didn't take nearly as

much interest in her more enticing lingerie. In Hebrew he said he liked to imagine the riches underneath the shirt. That had sounded like the Song of Songs to Tovah; the nicest description ever of what she thought might be her somewhat overabundant body, although with a struggle she kept herself near a size ten.

Thinking of Dan put her in danger of crying, but she held herself rigid. Not one tear; not yet. She pushed the moment when she would allow herself to cry far into the future.

Dan had taken the Escort when he'd gone shopping late the night before. Despite her notion that he might have gone earlier, he'd bundled up and gone out shortly before eleven p.m. Tovah had worked until close to midnight, then gone to bed. Normally Dan would have come to bed about a half hour after her.

Before he'd gone, Dan had parked the van for her in the garage off the back alley. The snow in front of the garage door lay pristine. Light snow had been falling since early morning, but there were only very old filled-in tire tracks in the alley, and no visible trail at all from their garage or driveway. He hadn't come in late and then gone out again early in the morning. He hadn't come home at all. Something awful had happened to him.

Tovah stood outside for a long moment, her arms wrapped around her body, against the cold, against her mounting panic within. *First you must look after the children,* she told herself.

A few minutes later, with Ari and Leah in the kitchen eating their hasty breakfast of Cheerios, Tovah called the police from her study.

"This is Rabbi Feldner," she said. Even distracted and upset, she knew identifying herself as a rabbi helped.

Dan's usual joke – like a doctor she'd have used her title to make dinner reservations if she'd thought it would speed things up – had never been truer. The short tether of the telephone cord almost drove her mad. She tugged at it as though she could lengthen it or free herself.

"I think my husband's been in a bad accident. Or he's been mugged, or robbed, or something even worse. He likes to shop at the all-night supermarkets to save time. He went out about eleven and he hasn't come home."

It only took Tovah a few minutes to realize the two police officers who'd responded to her call assumed Dan had deserted her and the children. She'd seen it before in her work, when she assisted families at Temple Isaiah who were reporting runaways. Everyone thought their missing person had been mugged or killed. The police rarely believed it.

She kept the police in the front hall at first, because allowing them to penetrate deeper into the house seemed like clearing the way for bad news.

It was the kind of team usually sent to cover routine domestic complaints in Minneapolis: one man, one woman, both young, basically still rookies.

"Ma'am, the sergeant had us check the hospital accident sheets before we left the station," the man said. "No one answering your husband's description."

"You've checked all the hospitals and the morgue too?" Tovah demanded, knowing she had to stay firmly in the mind set of 'rabbi' if the only other option was 'victim.'

Her candor surprised them. Both officers looked up from their notebooks. "Yes ma'am."

No wonder the police department sent at least one woman. Even in her dark blue uniform, with a stern visored cap and an equipment-laden black leather belt, the female officer looked sympathetic. All Tovah could see in the face of the young male police officer was boredom.

The look of sympathy in the eyes of the police woman confirmed the authorities considered this another case of a deserted wife and children.

"No," she blurted out, denying their assumption even before it was stated. "No. He didn't leave me. You don't understand. He…we love each other…and the children."

They'd already insisted she check the downstairs coat closet. None of Dan's outdoor gear was there; not his ski jacket and boots, not the dark red cap, scarf and gloves, her recent Chanukah gift to him. He'd probably been wearing those when he left the house, so that didn't prove a thing.

She couldn't bear what the officers were thinking. She took a few steps back, pushing at the swinging door separating the front hall from the kitchen. "The children; you see we have two children."

She flashed a wobbly smile at Leah and Ari, then let the door swing shut again. She dropped her voice.

"Our daughter has some physical problems. My husband handles all her therapy. He would never leave her. He would never leave!"

When did she first believe it?

Not when the two police officers insisted she see if any of Dan's other possessions were missing.

They accompanied her upstairs and planted themselves in the narrow second floor hall, where they somehow managed to stay out of her way as she ran from the deep closet in the master bedroom to the smallest room, Leah's therapy room, where all the suitcases were stored on shelves Dan had built under the low eaves.

"It's so hard to tell," she insisted to the police officers and to herself. Truthfully, it wasn't difficult. The brown cords Dan had been wearing, his favorite jeans, a pair of gray pants and several shirts. Empty spaces in the dresser drawers indicated several of Dan's sweaters, plus underwear and socks, were missing. That must all be in the laundry. She couldn't find Dan's old duffel bag or his backpack at the moment, but that didn't prove anything. She could not be a deserted wife.

After more than an hour the police were gone, taking along her denials and a recent picture of Dan.

"Handsome," the young woman officer had said. "Exotic."

Tovah had to smile. Everyone said that. But it hurt too. In the picture she'd given them, Dan's smile had seemed to be especially for her.

The moment she shut the front door she had to call her parents. It was suddenly as essential as breathing. She took just one minute – she couldn't have survived more than one more minute – to check on the children.

She had them settled in front of the television set in the living room. The rare treat of daytime cartoons would keep them occupied. They smiled at her, a little confused, but still willing to watch television instead of asking questions. She found a smile for them somehow, before fleeing to her study to call her parents from a spot where the children couldn't hear.

She couldn't expose Leah and Ari to her paralyzing anxiety. It permeated every syllable coming out of her mouth. She might fall apart; she might break down completely. Then who would look after the children? Who would look after her?

Her tears fell even before the speed dial connected. Her father answered. As soon as he realized who was on the line he had his wife pick up an extension.

Tovah's mother could remain calm in the face of almost any tragedy. She managed to soothe and question at the same time. Rabbi Eliezer Feldner, like his daughter, was always far more excitable at first. He kept repeating whatever she said, adding his own questions, one piling up on another. With no punctuating answers from Tovah that made sense, his voice scaled higher and higher.

Her knuckles clutching the phone had gone white with her effort to explain. Her whole body, like her voice, shook. She could hardly get the words out. "Dad, I'm trying to tell you! I don't know! He said goodbye. He went out. He didn't come back. It's like he's dead. Or, like one of those awful jokes: the husband who goes out to get a paper or cigarettes and doesn't come back for thirty years."

There was a pause. At the other end of the line, her father's voice suddenly dropped several octaves, flattening to a calming murmur, as though he'd suddenly become a different person. Dan had labeled such a moment "shifting into rabbi mode." He said his father-in-law did the best version in the world, with Tovah close behind.

"Tovah," her father said. In rabbi mode he spoke softly. "The police are gone, so you will go and get some lunch together for the children, something easy, something they like. Then, when they go for their naps you will sit down and think. Did something happen? Did you have a fight? Did something happen in the last week, in the last few days, a shock to Dan? You'll call the bank, too. Is any of your money gone?"

"How would I know? Money? How would I know what he's been thinking?"

"Did I say you know? I only said you will give the children lunch. You will sit with them and try to eat something too. It doesn't have to be fancy, soup, a sandwich, a piece of fruit. Then they will nap and you will make a cup of tea and sit quietly and think. Perhaps you do know something, but it hasn't occurred to you yet. Perhaps you know absolutely nothing. Whatever has happened may have nothing to do with you."

"Dad, it's probably robbery or kidnapping. He's just gone. What if he's dead?"

"Likely, we would know already. We won't borrow such problems. Right now you will do as I've asked. Yes? And before the children get up, you will call us back. At two-thirty, in less than two hours, you will call us back. We will be in my study, at work."

His voice faded for a moment as he turned to speak to his wife, forgetting she was also on the phone. "Hadas? Just before two-thirty can you walk over to the *shul*? Good."

He returned to the telephone. "So, now tell me what you're going to do?"

Tovah knew this technique. In a crisis her father often gave people a task: something simple, linear. She had used this technique with others.

She parroted back her father's directions, grasping at them like the lifeline they were meant to be. "I'll look after the children. I'll give them lunch, and they will both take naps. I'll make some tea, and try to think about what might have happened. I'll call you back at two-thirty."

How could anyone believe Dan would desert them?

Whatever awful thing had happened, she appreciated neither of her parents trying to provide false comfort. Neither said, "It'll be fine. Don't worry." They each said, "I love you. We'll talk at two-thirty this afternoon."

Just then, lunch for the children and naps loomed like the biggest job in the world: barely manageable, but finally accomplished. She was momentarily proud she'd managed a few spoonfuls of soup and even nibbled on the crusts of Ari's sandwich. Eating was a mistake. The children were in bed only seconds before her body utterly rejected the food. She managed to make it downstairs to the bathroom near the back door, so neither Ari nor Leah heard her retching.

# CHAPTER TWO

Since they'd soon figure out he'd abandoned the Escort at the airport, they'll find Tovah, thought Dan. Then she'll know....

No. She'll know before. She'll find my note.

He probably should have left the note in the kitchen, but the workshop was his special space. If he'd gone back to move the note to some other spot, he'd never have been able to leave the house again.

Even if I get back and know who my mother is, even if Tovah eventually understands what I'm doing...No, not if. She'll understand. We love each other. I'll be able to make her understand...it's not as if she's been paying a lot of attention to me lately.

He was sitting in a small commuter plane, fourteen rows of seats, single seats on one side of the aisle and two on the other side. All the singles were full and the doubles, where Dan had taken a widow seat, were rapidly filling. Who would guess so many people would want to leave the Midwest for Detroit or Newark, his destination, in the middle of the night? Tovah would think he'd taken the car at first. Instead he'd left the car at the airport and taken this flight, the Midwestern version of a Red-Eye. Taking a plane should slow her down. If she cares at all; if she looks for me.

He'd hoped to be well away by now but the snow, the cold, had delayed the flight. By the time they got the airplanes wings de-iced and the snow in the motors blown clear it would be closer to three a.m. than the scheduled departure time of one-thirty.

In the meantime the door to the stairway had been open all the time people were struggling out to the plane, fighting the wind on the tarmac. There were no jetways for flights like this. It was so cold the air in the plane glittered with suspended ice crystals.

A woman, one of the last passengers to board, came down the aisle, inching sideways, *shlepping* a suitcase behind her while she gripped two large shopping bags, Dayton's and Target, in her other hand. Dan's mother-in-law tended to travel loaded down like that, which is why Tovah's father always said the only way to travel with her was in an automobile, preferably the Feldner's roomy old station wagon. Hadas Feldner usually responded tartly by saying she'd only developed the habit of multiple bundles because for years they had traveled with six children, five of them boys. With luck, Tovah would be just like her mother when she was older.

He winced as the woman passed by. She probably had a seat in the rear and surely someone back there would give her a hand. No, she'd backed up and stopped next to the aisle seat of his row, trying to check her seat number by attempting to look cross-eyed through her glasses at the ticket she held clamped in her teeth.

There was no way he could watch a woman struggle. He stood up, ducking his head so he could get to the aisle without smashing into the bulkhead.

"Do you belong in this row?" he asked the woman, who nodded violently in agreement, unable to say anything because of the ticket in her mouth.

"Let me help," Dan took her small roller suitcase first and then the two shopping bags and placed them in an overhead compartment compressing them as much as possible. She smiled at him, took off her parka and added it the tiny space overhead, tucking in the trailing ends of the garment, then waited while Dan also took off his parka, gloves and hat, leaving the scarf wrapped around his neck like an embrace. The lone flight attendant edged down the aisle and pushed the bin shut. Dan climbed back into his window seat while the woman sat down next to the aisle. Why had he opened himself to a seatmate's conversation? She was obviously a nice woman who'd now want to say 'thank you' and maybe even chat, and he couldn't imagine speaking to anyone tonight. At the same time he certainly could not ignore a woman, barely five feet tall, struggling with a suitcase. 'No good deed...' he thought, not quite finishing. He certainly didn't need any more punishment.

His flight companion reached over and touched his arm. "Thank you," she said. Then she pulled out a pocket book, Laurie King, one of Tovah's favorites, and seemed content to leave him with his thoughts.

Momentary relief flooded through Dan. Then he felt ever more terrible. How sad, only the beginning of his travels and he already felt so isolated. He'd never make the contacts he'd need in New York feeling this way. Maybe if his neighbor had wanted to talk he could have explained...

How could you explain to a stranger what you didn't fully understand yourself? Would telling a stranger clarify thing in his own mind?

His plans were pathetic he thought. There is no chance Tovah would already be looking for him. She'd work on those sermons, and then she'd go up to bed. She wouldn't even know he was gone yet. Probably she wouldn't even care.

She might not even search. Not ever. If she got angry with him she might not. Whether he came to bed or not, Tovah would sleep through the night. Then she'd find his note and understand that his task was urgent. Even if she didn't know exactly what it was.

The tap on his arm just then was such a shock he started up, banging his head on the low bulkhead.

"Sorry," his neighbor said. "I didn't think you were asleep. I just thought you might like a piece of this." She offered him a Hershey bar she'd just unwrapped. Dan smiled and broke off a piece. He'd have to learn not to react violently, just because he happened to be thinking about Tovah or the children.

"I would tell my kids not to snack on a plane, or anywhere else, in the middle of the night. I'd say it would give them indigestion," the woman said. She smiled and broke off a piece of chocolate for herself.

"Me too," Dan said. Normal everyday conversation was comforting.

"How old are yours?" the woman said.

"Mine?"

"Your kids," she said, looking surprised that he'd lost the thread of their conversation so quickly. "Mine are almost grown, in college. I really can't tell them anything." She laughed ruefully.

How would she react, Dan wondered, what if he were to ask if any of her children were adopted? If she was an adoptive parent, she might understand his plight. Or perhaps she had been adopted herself. Lots of people were.

You could hardly ask a stranger such a question. You couldn't bring up adoption with most people. Except in cases where the adoptee was an obvious genetic mismatch to the adoptive parents. But, even that wasn't true for him. People didn't look at him and say, 'hmmm, Vietnamese and Caucasian, maybe with a soupcon of...' They just thought Dan's appearance was 'exotic.' If you were racially mixed you ought to look the part. Dan loathed the word 'exotic.'

"I could still tell my kids something," Dan said. "They wouldn't be up this late though. They're only three and five."

"So you're traveling at night so they won't miss you during the day. That's good," the woman said. "The only reason I'm on this plane is I need to get to my mother in New York. She's in the hospital. They told me, 'There's a flight at one-thirty.' One-thirty a.m. of course. So, here I am. Traveling at this time of night certainly wouldn't be my first choice."

"Mine either," Dan said. Let her believe he was traveling through the night so the children wouldn't miss him. Let her assume he was a good father. He'd never be able to explain why he had to make this trip; that he knew his wife, Tovah, would never have stood for it, so he'd just left.

He couldn't really explain his search, without talking about Leah, which made things really complex. Should you leave a child who still had some physical problems, even if the quest was to help her? Everything had seemed so reasonable when he'd planned it all out, although he hadn't talked to anyone in Minneapolis. He had called ahead to New York, talking to the priests in the New York churches his mother was supposed to have frequented while she'd hidden herself away, waiting for him to be born.

He could imagine what this woman would say as Tovah's stand-in. "You're looking for a woman who gave you up more than 35 years ago? You don't know her real name, just that she called herself Adele. You don't know what her plans were for after your birth? She might have been leaving for France, where she had family. You say she was originally from Vietnam, so she could have gone anywhere. Why do you think you can find her now?"

Of course his companion hadn't said anything at all. She was smiling and offering him another piece of chocolate. In a few minutes they would take off and then the flight attendants would be around with coffee and some sort of snack to help time pass. He doubted he would sleep, but at least by the time the new day really began he'd be in New York.

When a light tap on his arm came again, he realized he had slept. He was so uncomfortable he could only be on an airplane.

"You said you'd like the snack when it came around," said the lady of the luggage and the chocolate bars. "They're bringing around what I guess you could call breakfast."

"Thanks for waking me," Dan said. He meant it. He'd either been dreaming or reliving Leah's last medical appointment, where the doctor had suddenly decided Leah's problems might be even more than the Cerebral Palsy caused by her extremely premature birth.

"You know, maybe this young lady has Dystonia," the doctor had said. "You've cleared up so many of her original problems. As long as you continue with her therapy, C.P. isn't much of an issue any more. But I wonder about the involuntary movement. Could still be the C.P. of course, but there might also be a familial Dystonia. It would have been hard to tease it out so early, if you hadn't eradicated most of the C.P. symptoms. What do you think?"

Dan hadn't put so much effort into Leah's therapy program to have doctors wonder what he was thinking. They were supposed to think, to tell him what was wrong, and let him fix it. He'd made himself an expert of sorts, but only on one small subset of medicine, the symptoms affecting children born prematurely, who had Cerebral Palsy, and who could be helped to overcome that condition. He hadn't been willing to have Leah subjected to the surgery some doctors wanted. He'd designed just what he'd wanted; a safe exercise regimen rigorously followed every single day of three-year-old Leah's life. He could fight what he knew, what he had researched. He had never heard of Dystonia.

Odd, he thought, even though he'd been told all this several weeks ago, he hadn't actually researched Dystonia. Maybe he should have. He had written to the Dystonia Foundation in Chicago, but that was all he'd done. What would Tovah think when material arrived in the mail? Let her wonder for once. She'd call Leah's doctor and then she'd know about their last appointment. She'd listen to the doctor.

One thing he knew. When a doctor said, 'familial' it was code for a genetic disorder. It had never occurred to him that in eradicating Leah's birth-related problems he might have left the field open for an even-worse diagnosis. If Leah had that kind of problem it had to be his fault. He didn't know his birth family at all. He only had a tiny bit of information about his mother, and he knew nothing about his father at all. Anything genetic the children might suffer from had to come from his side. Tovah always denied her immigrant parents had any real in-depth background knowledge about their families, but her parents would have said if there had been such a problem.

Dan had no family history at all. Not an uncommon outcome of the private adoptions of the 1960's, but still a problem. He'd been so shocked at the mention of Dystonia. It meant that what he'd worked so hard to eradicate, C.P., had only been a distraction. It had caused him to waste time, rather than undertaking the search for his mother. He should have searched before he'd dared father any children. Even when Ari was born, so healthy, it had felt like a near escape. He should have looked then. But Tovah had been so happy and his reaction to Ari's birth, his depression, had seemed a passing problem.

At Leah's last medical appointment, when the doctor mused about 'familial Dystonia,' Dan wanted to grab the medical man by his immaculate white jacket and pull him a nose-length away. He should have made the doctor look him straight in the eye.

"Can't you see I'm adopted, part Asian, part Caucasian, part who knows what? If you'd read the file in front of you, or if you'd think about things for more than two minutes, you'd see I have no idea about my family. How would I know anything about a familial condition?"

Of course he hadn't done any such thing. He'd put his arm around Leah, who was exhausted from all the tests and the day-long series of appointments they went through every three months, and he'd said, very quietly, "I don't know of any problems in my wife's family. She'd have mentioned anything she knew about, I'm sure."

"I don't suppose it matters very much," the doctor had said. "Just a thought, you know. It's early for Dystonia to manifest. We've got time. For the moment you can just continue with her physical therapy program. Things are going so well. Her walking is great and her fine finger movements, too. We'll give her eyes a little longer because there seems to quite an improvement there. Quite amazing. I didn't think an exercise program could do it all, but it has. Dystonia varies so much, anyway. Just go on as before. Next time we'll talk about some other ideas."

The doctor had leaned back in his bright blue leather chair and smiled. This doctor always smiled. How could you tell what a doctor was thinking, what he knew, if he smiled all the time. What if he waited until you dropped your guard, because your child seemed so much better, then suddenly punched you in the stomach with the idea there was a much greater enemy out there, one that could definitely be traced to your family? Dystonia? Certainly, if there had been anything like Dystonia in Tovah's family, she'd have known. Dan would never know unless he could find his mother.

# CHAPTER THREE

On her first afternoon alone, only the activities her father required kept Tovah functioning. She'd become incapable of independent thought. Her brain filled with scenarios of what might have happened to Dan, but any logic she possessed had fled.

The bank's automated telephone system stymied her. "For your bank balance, press three. For help on other matters, press four."

What other matters? What else could matter? What were those numbers? Three? Four?

She settled for what seemed an eternity on hold, with the telephone cord knotting around her, tangled from her restless movements. Bland, cheerful Christmas music tormented her as she waited. The bank employee who finally responded clearly thought she was an idiot since she hadn't armed herself with her account number or her checkbook.

She started to explain. "My husband always looks after..." Then she didn't bother. How could anyone understand if she didn't?

Someone had been into their money. Someone had taken a carefully measured amount. Dan would never … or, maybe she only thought they had six thousand dollars saved. The bank records indicated two thousand dollars had been withdrawn the day before.

The young bank employee had surely never known the kind of fear now lodged in Tovah's belly. If he had any idea he would have been kinder. Once he'd found the necessary information he never would have tried to explain how much faster she could get the same information, "any moment you want it, just by dialing in on our new system."

Who would want news like this any faster? Slower would have been preferable. Never would have been perfect.

Normally, Tovah bristled at any implication of incompetence, but this time she just muttered thank you and hung up.

Dan couldn't have taken the money. He would never … The date and time of the withdrawal had to be a mistake. Someone had stopped him at the bank's new ATM machine late last night, forced him to withdraw money, and then snatched him away.

Even though Dan usually handled their money, Tovah really knew you couldn't withdraw two thousand dollars from a machine. Not in the daytime, and certainly not in the middle of the night.

"I think two thousand dollars, a third of our money, might be gone." Saying those words when she spoke to her parents again should have been proof to her. But, she still did not believe it.

"The police are already treating him as an actual missing person," she said with something like pride.

Just then, the fact the police seemed to take Dan's disappearance seriously provided the only validation she could find for her suffering. She knew the authorities usually waited forty-eight hours before taking any action.

"They know me from the Temple. I'm the one assigned to help with family crises. They're working very hard on this," she told her parents. It was hard to tell if she wanted to convince them or herself.

Being alone in the house all day Wednesday and Thursday seemed reasonable to Tovah. As a rabbi she expected to provide comfort, not require it. She didn't talk to anyone except her parents during those two days, not one person at work, except to call in sick at Temple Isaiah, as she had at Ari's kindergarten. She didn't even phone her neighbor and good friend, Robin.

Dan would have been her normal bulwark against bad news. She had never imagined a circumstance where he would be the bad news.

At mid-day on Thursday her parents announced they would drive in from Madison in the evening. They would leave right after an early dinner, her mother said. Tovah should expect them to be in Minneapolis somewhere between nine and ten. Tovah made only a token protest, asking in a whisper, "Can you really come, just leave everything?"

Hadas Feldner wouldn't enter into any kind of discussion. "You cannot be alone, certainly not all of *Shabbat*. Something even worse might happen."

Tovah couldn't imagine worse.

# CHAPTER FOUR

It took until bedtime on Thursday, just before Tovah's parents were to arrive, for Ari to finally figure out how to ask about his father. Clearly, he'd had questions since the morning he couldn't find Dan. As Tovah was taking the children upstairs, Ari stopped short in the hall, right in front of the closed door to their tiny physical therapy room.

"I bet Daddy is hiding in there," Ari said. "'Cause he's mad at us. 'Cause we haven't done Leah's exercises for two whole days."

Tovah couldn't say the first thing she thought of, "Then where the hell is he?"

She had to deal with the turmoil behind Ari's question. She'd hoped to have a little more time before facing this kind of thing with the children. She made herself stop and sit down right there, on the floor. It had never been harder to meet Ari's direct gaze. She pulled Leah down on to her lap and put an arm around each child.

How awful! Ari had to search for a way to even mention his father. Leah had no way to ask such a complex question, but she must be feeling even more desperate than her brother.

"Ari. Leah. Let me try to explain. As I said before, we think Daddy had to suddenly go far away, in the middle of the night. Just like *Baba* and *Zaida* have to come here tonight to be with us. Daddy won't be mad about the exercises. I promise you. He'll understand. We'll start them again soon. We'll start on Sunday, right after *Shabbat*. Okay Lolli-Pop?"

She jiggled Leah up and down a little on her lap, using Dan's favorite nickname. Usually it wasn't difficult to draw Leah into a conversation. Trying to limit her chatter and giggles had sometimes been their goal. "Lolli" or "Lolli-Pop" almost always made Leah smile; nicknames that had evolved from the lollipops doctors handed out at the end of office visits. Tonight Leah just twisted around and looked steadily at her mother, her changeable hazel eyes gleaming dark.

Leah had been blessed with a softer, more feminine version of Dan's good looks. Her skin tone was soft ivory, not Dan's olive, and her hair was a rare shade, more taupe, more silvered than a true brown. Tovah tried to return Leah's steady gaze without flinching and without tears. Dan often said children who dealt with serious medical problems could look right through you, all the way to the truth.

"Is Sunday tomorrow?" When worried, Ari looked even more like Tovah than usual. His face became a small mirror of hers, an identical furrow showing between the same emphatic black eyebrows.

"No. Tomorrow is Friday, then *Shabbat*, Saturday. Sunday is the next day."

"It's too many days of no exercises. When Daddy comes back home he'll be dis-dis-pointed."

"I know. I know. We'll explain. I promise."

Ari's face smoothed out the next morning when he found his grandparents in the kitchen making French toast for breakfast. It also smoothed out when he watched television. The TV had been on, flickering images across the living room at the children almost all of their waking hours. Normally Tovah hated the vacant stare of a TV-sedated child. These days it was a gift.

The deep ridge between her eyebrows felt permanent now. She envied her children the oblivion of television. And then, just as her mother had feared, things did get worse.

A Special Delivery letter from Dan arrived late Friday afternoon, just before the Sabbath began. Tovah heard the door bell, but knew her parents were on duty. They would handle any problems.

Then she heard her father mounting the stairs. Tovah hadn't left the bedroom all day, hadn't talked to anyone, except for moment or two when her mother came upstairs to confer about their Sabbath dinner. Other than that, she'd stayed in bed, only slipping down the hall to the bathroom when she was certain no one was on the second floor.

If she'd been thinking, instead of just huddling under the quilt in bed, she might have anticipated bad news from the sound of her father's footsteps. He was a vigorous man in his late sixties, tall and slim. Usually he moved easily, but now he clumped up the stairs as though they were suddenly too much for him. His knock on the bedroom door was gentle, his softly-voiced "Tovah?" a tentative request to enter.

Eliezer Feldner could discourse on many learned subjects in several languages. Regarding the letter in his hand, all he said were a few isolated words of Yiddish, using one loving word to address her, *"tochter,"* daughter.

Offering her the letter, he added, "a *briev* from Dan."

Fearfully, she eyed the envelope he held out to her. Her father had fanciful theories about the languages Jews had spoken all over the world. Ladino, a Spanish-Portuguese dialect, was for lovemaking, for ecstasy. Hebrew, *loshen kadosh*, the Holy Language, was for prayer. Yiddish was the language for either very good or very bad news. Hard pain suddenly flaring inside, warning Tovah of what kind of news was coming.

Dan's letter was formal, a resignation.

> *Dear Tovah,*
>
> *I'm sorry I didn't say anything more than 'good bye,' before. You'll also know by now that I had to go, until I find the answer to some important questions. I know you will be able to manage. Ari is busy with school now and Leah is no trouble. Hire someone if you need extra help.*
>
> *There are things I obviously must do, but the way we had things arranged made that impossible.*
>
> *By now you know I left most of our savings in the bank. So, you'll have some extra money if you need it.*
>
> *I'm sorry I couldn't explain more fully.*
>
> *I love you all.*
>
> *Dan*

The words she spoke to her father seemed to emerge from the pain in her stomach, a pain always her companion.

"He's gone. He left." Her voice was matter of fact, a computer voice without emotion. She didn't understand a lot of Dan's letter. Did it matter? She had no idea of what was going on anyway.

She couldn't bear her father's eyes. "I'll be down in a few minutes," was all she could manage as an escape.

He nodded. The concern on his face told her he would have much preferred to stay, but he turned and left as quietly as he'd entered.

She read the letter again, still not understanding. What did Dan need to do so badly? Finally, she left the letter lying on the wide bed and went down the hall to wash her face.

She and her parents had decided on an early Sabbath dinner. She felt almost paralyzed by her inner tangle: anger, sadness, disbelief. But, she had to tackle the stairs. Perhaps her mother needed some help.

The kitchen was fragrant with the meal Hadas had prepared. Her mother greeted Tovah without a word, simply hugging her hard. Keeping her arm around Tovah's shoulders, Hadas escorted her into the dining room. This small woman was the strongest woman Tovah knew.

Hadas had been extremely flexible this evening. Normally she prided herself on lighting Sabbath candles at the precise moment required. Tonight Hadas had interpreted the tradition broadly, as Tovah might have.

She had waited to light the Sabbath candles until everyone gathered in the dining room. Hadas tried to hand the matches to her daughter, but when Tovah shook her head, refusing, Hadas performed the ritual herself, chanting the blessing.

Watching while her mother took a few moments for private prayers after the blessing, Tovah momentarily pretended she was back in Madison, the youngest of six, all gathered at the Sabbath table, all safe. As the only girl, she'd always felt a special link to her mother during candle lighting. It didn't matter she and her mother didn't look alike, other than sharing the same dark curls.

Tonight Hadas' hair seemed to have more gray mixed with the black than usual. Her gentle, round face looked worn and worried. Tovah's face, far more angular, would never seem so gentle. As always, the candles highlighted the unique color of Hadas' eyes, clear golden amber.

Even though there were only five at the table, Hadas had set out six candles for this Sabbath. The sixth candle was for Dan. Dan had always been charmed by his mother-in-law's custom of lighting one Sabbath candle for each member of the family and for each guest at the table. The very first time he'd visited the Feldners there had been a candle for him.

Eliezer Feldner went on with the *Shabbat* table ritual without asking. He led them in singing *Shalom Aleichem* to welcome the Sabbath. Tovah was grateful her father hadn't asked her how she wanted things done. She didn't want to be called on for any decision. Every moment she didn't have to think was one more instant of blessed oblivion.

Tovah and Dan had considered the dining room the most important room in the house and they'd paid more attention to furnishing it than to any other room. They'd consciously tried to make it look something like her parent's dining room in Madison. They'd found a second-hand mahogany dining room set, slightly beat up but dignified. They had touched it up, covering every scratch. With Tovah's white and silver dishes on a white and silver tablecloth, everything looked just the way a Sabbath table should, as though the world was still a rational place.

Tovah's silver candlesticks stood on the sideboard. Her collection had started with Dan's engagement gift. Instead of giving Tovah a diamond ring Dan had commissioned a unique pair of sterling silver candlesticks, the design based on tall oak trees, a commemoration of how they had met.

Dan had always thought of the dining room as the appropriate place to display all his work. The prototypes he had created as models for his award-winning children's program, *Torah and Tools*, were displayed there. He'd made a representation of a Torah Scroll, the rollers beautifully carved. He'd also crafted a model of Solomon's Temple, and built his own version of the Ark of the Covenant that stood in the Holy of Holies, within the Temple.

Those classes had been Dan's favorite part-time job, developed and run for the Jewish Community Center in Cincinnati, while Tovah attended Seminary.

His program taught kids how to use hand and power tools, while teaching them about Jewish history. It reinforced academic skills, too. The children learned to read and interpret plans, to measure, and to understand scale as they made their own versions of Dan's models.

Dan had built the scale models of synagogues for his own pleasure. He'd created them, or modified existing buildings. Dan had treated those completed models like fine art, housing them in clear acrylic cases, set up on pedestals.

Both Dan and Tovah had assumed he would continue to develop his programs for children once they were settled in Minneapolis. But, there had never been time. Dealing with Leah's problems and their home had taken every minute.

Her father was just beginning the blessing over the wine. She stood with every one else, knowing her mind could float free for a few more precious minutes. She knew the folk tradition: on the Sabbath you gain *neshama yetarah* 'an extra soul.' She would have welcomed any renewal of strength; although to her the term 'extra soul' had always meant you might receive extra clarity if you could open yourself to the special peace of the Sabbath.

Ideally, clarity would come the way a solution to a problem sometimes presented itself, as a gift from a place outside.

Tovah had experienced a few special Sabbaths, Sabbaths with an extra dimension. One of them had been the night she and Dan had become engaged. The very first place Dan had ever celebrated a "real" Sabbath had been at her parents' home. He'd fallen in love with the ritual. It had been a crucial part of their falling in love with each other.

This evening clarity came to Tovah again, even though she didn't want it. Concentrating on the candles, she suddenly realized not only had Dan deliberately left her, he had planned his departure very carefully and over some period of time.

She must have gasped at her realization. Both her parents looked at her with alarm. Her father, in the middle of singing the long *Kiddush*, the Sabbath blessing, held the beautiful silver wine goblet aloft in one hand. His open prayer book was in his other hand. He didn't stop chanting as he moved behind her. Briefly putting his *siddur* down on the table, he continued from memory, while his arm around Tovah urged her to sit down if she felt faint.

She did sit down, but what had come over her was far more than light-headedness. Knowledge had come like a blow. How long had Dan been thinking about leaving them?

Her parents would have left her sitting at the dining room table when they took the children into the kitchen for hand-washing. But, Tovah followed them, the automatic response the only thing animating her. The Sabbath ritual provided the reason and the method to go on. Without it she would have been frozen forever in a hellish moment of full realization.

Since her family followed the tradition of not speaking during the brief period between washing hands and the blessing over the bread, there was total silence when everyone returned to the table. As Tovah waited, the flames of the six Sabbath candles seemed to twinkle and whirl, surrounding her. Each flame was multiplied again and again by the startled tears in her dark eyes.

Dan gone! All planned in advance! He knew there would be no service at the Temple this Friday. *Chanukah* had been earlier in December, so the big concert and the other celebrations were complete. It was almost the end of the year. There was a clear space, more than two weeks when Tovah had few responsibilities. There was nothing one of the other rabbis at Temple Isaiah couldn't pick up. Dan had chosen a moment when he believed she would somehow pull her life back together, once she realized what had happened.

Dan always planned carefully. He tried to anticipate everything. He'd insisted on a savings plan when Tovah would have spent more of her salary on a better place to live, or on a newer car. He'd said they had to have savings. You never knew what might happen.

He'd been right. Leah's premature birth and the medical problems following had convinced Tovah it was smart to be cautious. Could Dan have been planning to leave so long ago, way back when they first started to save? When had he begun to use his careful planning to fool her?

She remained motionless at the Sabbath table. She couldn't touch the food her mother put on her plate. But, racing back to the seclusion of her bedroom was not an option. Sabbath took precedence over everything. In a house where there had been a death, even *shiva* – the seven days of mourning – stopped for the Sabbath.

This Sabbath was exactly as if there had been a death. Something in her own home had died, and she had not known.

# CHAPTER FIVE

I t's *Shabbat*, Dan thought. I can make *Shabbat* here, on my own. There must be a million Jews here and hundreds of synagogues. But, despite this lecture it wasn't *Shabbat* for him. It was just Friday evening.

Did Tovah have to be there for it to be *Shabbat*?

All the good things of the Sabbath had come into his life with Tovah. There was a link in his mind: Tovah, meaningful Judaism, the Sabbath. Was that why he had let Tovah take charge of the spiritual aspect of his life, of so much of their life together?

During one Sabbath visit, even before they were officially engaged, Tovah's father had come around the table to bless Tovah, his only child present. With no formality at all, without comment, he had blessed Tovah, his hands on her head. Then he'd blessed Dan, too. Dan always felt his father's-in-law blessing had really joined him to Tovah. Their marriage a few months later was a formality and an excuse for a good party.

The night of the blessing Tovah had come quietly up the stairs to her brothers' old third floor dormitory room, now a guest room. The two of them had made love before, but it had never been in her parents' home. Nor had it ever been so meaningful.

When it was over he held her tight against him and she whispered something he'd seemed to know anyway. The words went right to his heart and mind, forever adding a spiritual element to their lovemaking. "It's a special *mitzvah* to make love on *Shabbat*," she said.

Tovah had brought intensity and meaning – no – she would deny it. Not the person. That was like idol worship.

Judaism had brought intensity and meaning to every aspect of their life. He loved the traditions. He should have told her the additional rigor of Conservative practices wouldn't bother him. Maybe if he'd told her, it would have helped her make a change. But, she'd never asked how he felt about moving from one branch of Judaism to another.

How could she not instinctively know that he'd found the various disciplines: keeping kosher, walking on Sabbath when they could, avoiding normal chores, went a long way toward keeping his world orderly? Those practices helped keep away the gray world he'd known before he and Tovah met. How could she not know?

The last few months in Minneapolis, his world turned gray again. Tovah turned all her energy away from him and he couldn't seem to generate his own.

Maybe finding energy within was really what he'd set out to accomplish on this trip. More than finding his mother, maybe it was some internal thing he needed? No. He shook the idea away, at least for the moment.

He needed to find his mother! The two were linked. His family was at risk if he didn't find her.

His marriage, his family; those were sweetest part of life, beginning with those first real Sabbaths at her parents' home. He'd never been a self-conscious guest. Right from the beginning Tovah's mother had handed out pre-Sabbath chores to him, just as she did to her own children.

Right after he and Tovah met, he began to study with her. He'd have studied anything she found interesting: needlepoint, bird watching. It wouldn't have mattered, anything guaranteeing hours of her undivided attention would have served. But, it had been Judaism.

"Are you trying to save my soul?" he'd said after one session. He'd only known her a few weeks, but already he would have willingly made her a gift of his soul.

They were in love. He'd already visited Madison and met her parents and some of her brothers. It wasn't Tovah, his girlfriend, who answered his teasing question. It was a rabbi.

"Your soul is your own business," she'd said. "I'm just trying to catch you up a little. If you want to know your own soul, you need a few tools."

She'd expressed her thought in terms of tools. To her it was just a figure of speech, but to him it was reality. The right tools could make a difficult job possible, a good job perfect.

Before he knew Tovah he used work to keep the gray away, to generate energy. Hard, physical work helped a lot. People thought of hard work as using up energy, but they had it backwards.

He'd been doing just that kind of job when he met Tovah. He'd just dropped out of graduate school for the second time. The only thing he had done before he left school was to make sure he had a job waiting for him.

If he hadn't found a job he might have stayed on at school, even though he knew right away that he had no real need for two years of pointless courses for an M.B.A. It would soon be out of date, as far as he could tell. He didn't even bother to withdraw from school properly, as he had when he'd left law school many years before. This time he'd just thrown a few belongings into his car and driven away.

He'd worked for so many people in so many parts of the country it had only taken a few phone calls to find a job in Stratton, Indiana. A company headquartered there had a state and county contract for extensive tree work. They were looking for an experienced foreman. The job would last at least six months.

It was just his kind of thing: a demanding job, a project with a beginning and an end. With a job like that he knew where he stood in the world, what he had to accomplish. There'd be something to show for it at the end, even if it was only a pile of downed trees.

In fact, at the end of the six months, with the tree job finished, he'd had a lot more than a heap of lumber. He had Tovah.

That whole six months had been a time of surprises. The first surprise had come during his getaway trip from school to Indiana. A state trooper had stopped him. Someone at the school he'd just left had reported him missing. Who cared enough? He'd only been gone two days, but already the whole experience seemed remote, as though those events had happened to someone else, and he'd been told about it.

"I suppose I should have left a note," Dan had said to mollify the state trooper.

"You should have; no supposing." The cop was clearly unimpressed with Dan's response. He handed back his identification. "I don't imagine you've let your parents know, either. If my boy wandered off, I'd be plenty upset."

"I've been on my own for years," Dan said. "I'm in touch with my parents regularly. They won't mind about my leaving school."

"Probably they'll never let you know how they really feel," the policeman said. He'd walked away shaking his head.

Once Dan and his tree crew began work in and around Stratton, the surprises were usually emergency calls. A round of powerful early spring storms downed trees all over the area. One day an historical building in the center of Stratton was threatened.

Dan's boss described the location, giving him the kind of directions common in a small town. "It's over to the square. You know; that schoolhouse."

Dan didn't know, so his boss added a few more details. "The one-room brick schoolhouse they moved to the center of town. You can't miss it. There's only one, and it's right there, on the square."

"Why did they move an old schoolhouse?" Dan wanted to know.

"Hell, I've got no idea. There was a big fuss when they did it. Made a church of it, I think. They probably damaged some of the tree roots when they did the job. Now it's our job to get it out of there safely." The boss clearly didn't care about the why of things.

"The danger notice was posted yesterday, so no one will be inside," he said. "They need the building for the weekend, so get it done tomorrow."

The next morning a single glance told Dan the tree had come within inches of demolishing what the town of Stratton had worked so hard to preserve. Somebody really cared about the old brick building. They'd sited it beautifully, placing it on a newly built basement, with careful landscaping to hide the raw-looking concrete. The brick had been re-pointed, and the trim had been painted a rich dark green.

The building was set in a grove of oak trees, obviously planted when the town was first settled. The oaks were much taller than the building, giving the old schoolhouse the look of a cozy cottage.

A lightening strike had caused the top of one the trees to break away. The upper part of the main trunk, and several branches almost as thick as the trunk, now hung inches above the small building. Only a single section of splintery wood and the strength of the old, gnarled bark had kept it from falling directly through the roof.

By seven a.m. Dan had deployed his crew for the day, giving them instructions in English and Spanish. "Get the generator up and running. Over there." He pointed to a sheltered spot near the back wall of the one-time schoolhouse. "We'll need power most of the day."

They were lucky. Working conditions were perfect. For the moment the storms had passed. There wasn't a breath of wind. It would be safe enough, as long as they were careful.

Amazingly the tree had remained stable throughout the night. They had hours of work with a sling and winch ahead of them, before he could guarantee nothing would fall.

They'd been at work less than an hour when a girl dressed in a real power suit swept down on them. He hadn't seen anything like it since he'd left New York. She was even wearing high heels. Despite the wet and uneven ground the shoes didn't slow her down much. She navigated across the rough lawn and began firing questions. How long would they be there? Couldn't they work faster, quieter? When would they be done?

Dan had no idea his destiny had just arrived, all dressed up, wearing a pair of ridiculous but sexy, high heels; five feet four inches of attitude in a purple suit.

He'd known she wouldn't get any answers from his men. Even the workmen who understood English wouldn't talk. They were all men who wanted no contact with officialdom.

He'd waited, continuing to work, but keeping an eye on her. He should have immediately demanded she put on a yellow hard hat, just to complete her ensemble.

By the time she got to him, she thought not speaking Spanish was the problem. She began by using her own unique brand of sign language.

"How long?" she said, tapping her wristwatch. Then she stepped back, hands on her hips, waiting for his answer.

At first he deliberately pretended he didn't understand. He'd already decided to let her sweat a little, no matter what. He stood up as straight as possible, glad to be so much taller.

They stared at each other. She tried again. This time she pointed to the tree, saying 'how long,' in a drawn out manner, as though her action would make things clear. She also spread her arms. He wanted to tell her the gesture indicated width, not length of time, but why bother? He was busy noticing she had a very nice body. The purple suit fit perfectly.

She was still speaking when he made the hand gesture his crew always watched for and obeyed instantly;

a quick stroke above his head, visible from every angle. They cut the generator, cut the saw. There was sudden, total, silence.

The silence was so complete her very loud voice seemed to ricochet between them. "Can't you tell me when you will be ...?" She heard herself, and stopped.

"Lady, this is going to take as long as the tree is long. Plus any time we waste answering pointless questions."

He hated when people came and checked up on him. He always did the best job possible, whether someone was watching or not.

She'd looked at him, started to say something else, then she clearly changed her mind. She spun around on those now somewhat muddy high heels and stalked away. Too bad he had to send such a cute girl on her way, but he had a tough crew to supervise. He had to keep his authority absolute. When he signaled his crew to start up again he saw respect on every face.

At the end of that day, as they were packing up, he was surprised to see the girl, in her unmistakable suit, through one of the rear windows of the building. The tree was down, so she was safe. Did she really have the nerve to spend the whole day inside, watching them work; probably taking notes? Would she dare take up a post in the very building he was supposed to save, one with the most explicit sign on the front door: DANGER NO ADMITTANCE.

He strode into the building with the sign in his hand. "Don't you people pay any attention to rules?" he demanded.

She sat in front of one of the newest laptops. At least she'd brought some work along. She spun her desk chair around. "What do you mean, 'you people?'" she shot back.

She still harbored resentment from their first meeting, he could tell. She looked at him through narrowed eyes.

"The kind of people who think someone needs to spend an entire day checking up on me and my crew."

"I've been trying to do my own work, despite the wretched noise going on all day long. No one sent me to watch you. You're not very interesting. You just disturb the peace."

He realized she was nowhere as tough as she seemed. Her words and the look on her face seemed dismissive, but there were tears in her eyes.

Her beautiful, large dark eyes swam with unshed tears, tears he'd caused. She was very pale. He felt terrible.

"Look, miss, I didn't mean to make you cry."

He got a crisp, no-nonsense reply. "Relax. You didn't. The noise did. It gave me a migraine. That makes my eyes tear."

Then she looked away quickly, so quickly he didn't believe her.

She spun her chair back to her work but continued their conversation. "So, by 'you people,' you just mean civil service types."

"I mean bureaucrats. They have nothing better to do than watch other people work."

"You know this through your many years of personal experience with bureaucracies?"

"I sure do. But, why would you care?"

"Actually, I don't care now; not at all."

How could he get her to turn around again? He felt silly, holding the now-irrelevant sign in his hand like a de-commissioned flag. He took a single step closer and put the sign on her desk. "You certainly cared a few minutes ago."

She responded to his challenge, turning halfway around and looking up at him. She was very pale and very pretty. No, she had a striking face, a face from an Egyptian wall painting. Better than just pretty. She had the most wonderful, abundant, dark curls.

"I thought you meant Jews when you said 'you people.'"

"Who in the hell would mean something like that in this day and age?"

"Oh, come on. If you were Jewish, you wouldn't be so relaxed about the possibility."

"I am Jewish."

"You are?" She surveyed him up and down. Obviously he didn't measure up to her standards, because she turned away again. Who did she think she was?

"So, in addition to telling me how and when my crew ought to do their work, you're also righting all wrongs, like anti-Semitism. You must have some job description."

"Well, Rabbi covers it pretty well. This is a synagogue"

"It is? Really? Here? Anyway you can't be a rabbi."

"Yes, I can. Or, rather I will. I'm a student rabbi. I'm here for the weekend to try out for this synagogue's summer job. They sent me the garage door opener and a key to the back door."

"Sorry, I didn't see your sign." She didn't turn to look at him, but she did flash a couple of keys and a garage opener on a large metal ring. Then she said, "Look, I have work to do. Please. And, try to keep the noise down when you leave."

As he walked out of the building the door slammed behind him. He hadn't meant to let it slam, but she'd never believe it.

Sure enough, a discreet brass plaque on the front corner of the building said: Temple Shalom of Southern

Indiana. He stood there a few minutes, trying to think of a reason to go back inside and talk to her again. He reentered the building. "Is this operation of yours Jews for Jesus?"

This time she swiveled around quickly. At least her office chair was getting a work out.

"Now, why would you assume Jews for Jesus? Do you see Jesus here in any way, shape, or cross?" she said. She had high color in her cheeks now. He guessed her skin was usually barely pink and very smooth.

"You said you will be a rabbi. Girls aren't rabbis. I'd know. We're members of Temple Emmanuel in New York. There are no girl rabbis."

"Of course there are women rabbis. How long since you've been in a Temple? The Reform movement has been ordaining girls ... I mean women, for years."

She was right. He hadn't been in a Temple for decades. He hadn't known any other part-Asian, part who-knows-what people like himself, Jewish or otherwise, when he was growing up. Most of his life he'd wondered how someone like him could be Jewish. As soon as he was old enough, he'd just stayed away from organized religion. Staying away was the best way to resolve conflicts.

He went on as quickly as possible. "So, you've been here all day, because you're trying out for this job?"

"Not just all day. I was here all night, too. I slept up there." She pointed to a mezzanine, a structure obviously added to the building's original interior.

"Why would you have slept up there? You could have been killed."

"I slept there because the rabbi's apartment is located there. I got in last night. I'll sleep up there tonight, and the next night too. I didn't see your sign. I'm sorry. Aren't you just a little overly dramatic about all this? As I said, they only sent me the key to the back door, the one closest to the garage."

He didn't mind shaking her equanimity. "Then you've got damn little to complain about, even if the noise we made meant you didn't get a thing done today, or if it gave you a headache. No one should have been in this building. The tree was hanging by a twig, by a shred of bark. It wouldn't even have taken the whole tree falling to kill you. Any one of the branches could have done it."

He left feeling a certain satisfaction. She looked a lot more concerned than she had before, even though now the building was perfectly safe.

He couldn't let things rest there, even though he'd finished the job and saved her life. He wanted to see her again, even if she wasn't properly grateful.

By the end of the weekend Dan had been to Sabbath services for the first time since his Bar Mitzvah year. He'd experienced Tovah leading services. Once he'd seen her in action he had no trouble believing one day she would be Rabbi Tovah Feldner. Tovah. He loved that name. He even went to the 'meet the rabbi' event Sunday afternoon at Temple Shalom.

He had no standing with the congregation, but he'd have hired her in a minute.

He waited until he knew she had been selected – how could they have done otherwise? Then he'd called his parents. His news about school didn't surprise them. He'd dropped enough hints. They much preferred hearing he was in Indiana, not Bali or Rio, places he'd called from before under similar circumstances.

He told them about Tovah. "I met the girl I'm going to marry. I saved her from being crushed by a falling tree," he said.

Dan's father, Allan, didn't take what Dan said very seriously. Dan had never before mentioned anything as sensible as getting married. Since his father didn't want to jinx any impulse Dan had toward settling down, he made what Dan thought was a poor joke out of his enthusiasm for Tovah. "If saving her made you want to marry her, it's a good thing she's going to be a rabbi, not a nun."

# CHAPTER SIX

One evening, a full week after Dan disappeared, Tovah heard someone at the door. Her heart leaped for just a moment. He'd come home! It just might be, because earlier that day her mother, Hadas, had found a note Dan had left her, on the bench in his workroom. Tovah was angry and embarrassed, because she had never checked his work room. She remembered listening for the sound of Dan's power tools from the head of the stairs. She should have gone downstairs. Why would he leave a note there? The note hadn't said anything helpful, anyway.

So, even as she went to pull open the door she squelched the idea of Dan coming home. It was probably just the paperboy.

Instead of the paperboy her good friend and next-door neighbor, Robin McDonald, stood on the landing at the top of the outside stairs. Robin had pulled her blue and yellow ski jacket tight around her, not bothering to zip it for the short run across their two front yards.

Although Robin was in the early months of pregnancy, no one could tell by looking at her. She was as slim as ever. A few crystals of fresh snow gleamed on her short blond hair.

"I thought I'd just drop over and say Happy New Year in person. Even though it's a little bit early," Robin said, smiling.

Tovah couldn't respond. Her mouth couldn't shape those three words. Happy New Year was too much of a lie.

Still out on the landing, Robin clutched her jacket more tightly. "I saw your parents' car. Where's Dan? How is everything?"

Tovah had to answer. If she didn't, Robin would know something was wrong. Still, she couldn't find a single word.

The two women looked into each other's eyes, uncharacteristic silence between them.

"Am I coming in, or what?" Robin said. "Are you all right?"

Tovah backed away from the front door so her friend could enter her home.

Robin brushed snow from her jacket, took it off, and handed it to Tovah. She held down the heel of one snow boot with the toe of the other and pulled out her foot. As she bent down to pull off her second boot, Tovah's mind raced. What to say to Robin? What not to say?

Hadas Feldner came through the short hall from the kitchen carrying a small stack of clean laundry. Her husband had gone home, but Hadas had stayed on with her daughter and grandchildren.

Tovah looked from her mother to Robin and realized that in just a few seconds someone outside her immediate family would know her secret. She hung on to Robin's jacket as though it offered protection or might delay things. But, that wasn't possible. She might as well run outside and try to stop the snowflakes from landing.

Her mother had been saying Tovah should talk to her friends and enlist their support. She'd wanted Tovah to call all her brothers and their families, too. So far Tovah hadn't found it possible to do anything so complex and revealing. She'd barely found enough energy to call her oldest brothers, Ben and Hillel, in Chicago, and her oldest friend in the world, Ilana, who still lived in Madison. The conversation with Ilana had been bad. When Michael, Ilana's husband and Dan's friend from his law school days, took the phone, she'd almost wept. Michael had been furious with Dan; just as she wanted to be.

"Damn Dan," Michael said. "I thought he'd given up the disappearing act." Michael would have to be angry for her. Tovah couldn't find the energy for feeling that way.

As bad as those conversations had been, she had not been able to see her friends' faces. The telephone had provided some protection against Ilana's tender concern and Michael's anger. Robin was right here in front of her.

Hadas set her stack of laundry down on one of the lower steps. She ran her fingers through her short graying hair as though harnessing the energy of her springing curls.

She smiled at Robin. "So nice to see you." Hadas and Robin hugged. They had come to know each other well as Robin and Tovah's friendship had grown.

"How is your family?" Hadas said.

When Robin finished saying her daughter, Sunny, and her partner, Dave, were both well, Hadas said, "I'm just exhausted. But, here you are visiting, so Tovah won't be alone. I can just follow the children upstairs and make this an early night."

Hadas retrieved the clean laundry and went up the stairs, not even glancing back.

As her mother disappeared, Tovah took a deep breath and turned back to her friend. Robin stood, her arms folded across her chest, weighing what had just happened.

"There's something important you're supposed to tell me," she observed.

Tovah couldn't meet her friend's gaze. When she managed a response, her voice was at least an octave higher than usual. "You could say that."

Silence again.

"I can wait right here until you're ready," Robin said.

Tovah took a second or two more. "No, you don't have to wait. Do you want to sit in the kitchen or in the living room?"

"Kitchen," Robin said, leading the way toward the back of the house. "There's more truth told in kitchens than in any other room in a house."

Dan's handiwork was evident all around the kitchen. He'd worked hard to make the old house they were renting less shabby, more to Tovah's taste.

Dan had always referred to Tovah's various collections as her dowry and he'd created ingenious ways to display them. He used to say there would eventually be more money in Tovah's *tchotchkes* than in anything the two of them might do to make a living. He'd converted the square, awkward kitchen at the back of the house into a lively red, black, and white room by repainting cupboards and changing hardware. He'd showcased Tovah's best collection, Coca-Cola memorabilia, on shelves and the walls all around the room.

Tovah delayed her explanation to Robin several more minutes, taking her time getting together hot tea and cookies. Robin, sitting in the small booth Dan had installed in front of a window, was certainly aware of Tovah's delaying tactics.

Obviously trying to make it easier for Tovah, Robin said, "I love this room. It was so clever of you to pick up this Coca-Cola stuff when you were a kid, to collect it before it got fashionable … and expensive."

Usually Tovah loved to talk home décor and almost-antique collectibles, minor passions of hers. But the two of them had exhausted the kitchen as a topic long ago.

"Okay, I can see its bad news," Robin said when Tovah finally sat down opposite her. "We can handle bad news. We've handled bad news before. But, you have to tell me what it is."

Tovah burst into tears.

Two hours later the two women were still sitting in the kitchen. Tovah was no longer crying. Both of Dan's letters lay on the table between them in the clutter of cookie crumbs and empty mugs.

Robin poked at the most recent letter. "He says here 'for now,' as if he means to come back."

Tovah sputtered angrily. "Do you think I'd let him come back? Would you let him come back? Do you think I should let him just wander in and out, no questions asked? I couldn't! I'll never do it. Sometimes I think it would have been better if he'd actually died."

"Tovah, you don't mean it. You don't!"

"Why not? If he'd died it would be over. People would come; I'd sit *shiva*. I'd be sad, but not so ... so, embarrassed."

"You don't mean it. You don't wish him dead. You wouldn't wish anyone dead. You won't die from being embarrassed. Besides, you haven't done anything to be embarrassed about. He did."

"I know. But, he's not here, and I am. And, if that's true, why do I feel this way?"

"Boy, the sixty-four thousand dollar question. Why do women feel bad when someone else does something horrible?"

They looked at each other, both with tears in their eyes, but laughing a little, too.

Robin collected herself first. "Look, you can't imagine how this will end. You're usually in charge. So it's much harder for you to suddenly lose control. If you ever find out exactly what the problem was, exactly why he left, you might feel you could give him another chance."

She turned sideways in the booth as she spoke, so she could sit with her knees drawn up. "Anyway, we can solve one problem right now. You've got to get back to work. I need a job. I'm your new baby sitter."

"Robin, you don't have to baby sit. I'm trying to find someone. They're asking around at the Temple."

"Nope, I need a job. The doctor doesn't want me teaching aerobics while I'm pregnant. But, it's better for Dave and Sunny if I have a job."

"It's really nice of you. I'll be so much less worried if Ari and Leah are with you."

"I'm going to do some of Leah's exercises. No, we'll do them together. You need to learn the routine."

"I know Leah's exercises," Tovah objected.

"Not as well as you should. I've been through Dan's material. We'll do them together."

Tovah didn't bother to protest. She wasn't as comfortable with Leah's therapy as she ought to be, and both women knew it.

"Robin, this is so good of you. You're such a nice person. No man would ever leave you."

Rare anger heightened Robin's color. She was normally so easy-going. "No, I'm not! Don't say that. It isn't what you really mean. You just mean I'm a wimp."

Despite everything, Tovah had to smile.

"I certainly don't think you're a wimp. A wimp would have married Dave the minute he asked."

"Well, he didn't mention it when I was pregnant with Sunny, and now I don't know if I'm ready."

"But, Dave never left you. He didn't tell you about his family, and his problems with being Jewish. But, he stuck around."

"It doesn't look like Dan just chose to do what he did. He must have been desperate. Look at what he says in his letter: he had things to work out and couldn't. He says 'the way we had things arranged.' What could have stopped him from doing something essential? Why didn't he say what it is?"

"How should I know? He didn't want to tell me." Tovah said. "I thought I knew what he considered essential. I thought I was essential, and Ari, too. Leah and her exercises were essential. Obviously, Dan could leave the essential behind."

Then, as her own words made her situation fresh once more, Tovah began to cry again.

# CHAPTER SEVEN

Despite Tovah's best intentions she only managed to get through Leah's physical therapy routine a few times in the first weeks on her own. Ari, Dan's assistant in all things related to his sister's exercises, had turned into Tovah's personal, pint-sized saboteur.

"We can't do exercises right before bedtime," Ari insisted one night as the three of them trailed upstairs. It was nearly eight o'clock. "Daddy says the exercises are too stim … stim … ulated for Leah at night. She's too tired. It has to be after nap or maybe right after supper, but not now."

"Ari," Tovah tried to be diplomatic with her son. "Until we get used to Daddy being away, we'll have to do things a little differently."

Ari persisted. "It's too late. You mustn't do them now. Daddy won't like it when he comes home."

Tovah didn't want to win an argument with a five-year-old by intimidation. But, balancing on the stairs, holding Leah on her hip and trying to reason with Ari was too much.

"Well, Daddy isn't here!" she snapped.

"You're mean," Ari said, and he ran to his room.

He came into the exercise room when Leah and Tovah were halfway through the forty-five minute routine. Physical therapy was going badly.

Ari looked as though he'd settled down, so Tovah gave him a great big phony smile of welcome.

Ari stood beside the exercise table watching his mother continue the reciprocal motion exercise she'd been trying to do with Leah.

"You're not doing that exactly right," Ari said. "The doctor won't be happy. If you don't do it right, it doesn't help."

"Ari, give it a rest."

He glowered at her, obviously deeply offended. Tovah had been trying to keep her daughter interested by playing "bicycle" during the reciprocal exercises. Leah really was too tired. She was like a bird fallen from its nest, fluttering nervously. Her hazel eyes were at their most changeable just then, shifting between green, gray and brown. Even her hair, usually flying like spun silk, hung limp, its rare color dulled. Leah was tiny for her age. When she chattered away she looked more like a precocious two-year-old than a child already past her third birthday. Tonight she didn't say a word, always a bad sign.

Tovah was tired. Leah was tired. Ari was heckling. It was the end of a perfect day.

"How long will Daddy be gone?" Ari asked this question an average of a dozen times a day.

Without any extra editorializing, Tovah answered him again. "It could be a very long time."

She always said the same thing. She wanted to be truthful. She couldn't set a time limit, and she didn't want to say 'never.'

Between moments of listlessness and squirming, Leah kept trying to get her thumb in her mouth. She hadn't sucked her thumb for months. She might nod off to sleep right on the table. Dan would never have allowed it, but Tovah had already decided; if it happened this time she would just scoop her daughter up and deposit her in her crib.

Ari had given up commenting on Tovah's exercise technique. Instead he focused on exactly how long a 'long time' might be.

His questions pinged against Tovah's brain like sharp pebbles.

"How many sleeps are in a long time?"

"How many more times will it snow before Daddy gets home?"

Clearly Tovah's answers didn't satisfy Ari.

Tovah didn't notice when her son switched from time and weather to a more personal scale of measurement.

"Will I have a birthday before Daddy comes home?"

"Will I be able to tie my shoes before Daddy comes home?"

"Will I be as big as him when he comes home?"

Just then Tovah was trying to focus on one exercise she particularly disliked. It required the perfect alignment of Leah's hip, knee and ankle joints, straight and smooth, while the little girl lay on her side.

"Will you be dead before Daddy gets home?"

Ari's question hung in the air, the word 'dead' shimmering, actually visible to her. The ancient mystics of Safed in Israel had reported seeing letters of fire burning in the air, but Tovah had never thought it likely she would have a mystical experience. But there it was:

DEAD ... DEAD ... DEAD

She had the overwhelming need to raise her hand, as though to push away the word. However, she was still holding Leah's leg. Leah didn't like having her leg dragged about. She started to cry.

Leah never cried during therapy. Dan had made Leah's program a period of fierce concentration lightened with his special nicknames, with songs and jokes, with plans for the future. There were never tears. You don't cry over your job, Dan said. You do your job.

Ari's horrible word still shimmered in front of Tovah, but she tried to compose herself enough to answer her son's impossible question. She also had to keep a firm hold on the crying Leah. Which child to attend to first?

She tried for a smile as she turned toward Ari. The attempted smile was definitely a mistake. Her attempt got all tangled up with her true feelings. She wanted to cry too, just like Leah. The resulting grimace frightened both children. Leah got a side view of Tovah's face and her ordinary crying turned into a shriek.

Ari bolted from the room.

This time he didn't run to his room, the first place Tovah looked after she'd lifted Leah from the table. She called after Ari repeatedly, checked every closet and corner where she thought he might hide, stopping for a moment only when Leah's wailing demanded all her attention.

Ari had disappeared. At least he couldn't have left the house. She had snapped the deadbolts on the front and back doors before they'd come upstairs.

By the time she'd re-checked the doors and searched the house several times, Tovah had lost control too. Her own sobbing made her breath ragged. She couldn't quiet Leah, either. The little girl had gone rigid in her arms. She couldn't comfort her daughter, nor could she put her down, nor find Ari.

The idea of calling 911 flashed through her brain, but what could she report: a small child crying, a mischievous older brother, an upset mother. If every woman with such problems called 911, they'd jam the switchboard.

She dashed around the house again and again, searching for Ari under beds and in the closets, carrying Leah every moment. When she couldn't manage her daughter's weight one more second, she collapsed into the rocking chair in Leah's room. The little girl fell asleep. Tovah wouldn't have believed it possible, but she dozed briefly.

She awoke stiff and cold from her short nap. Almost a whole hour had passed since their aborted exercise session. She had to find Ari! Leah slept on as Tovah placed her in her crib, bypassing pajamas or a nighttime diaper.

Where do you hide if you're a five-year-old boy? Why don't you answer your mother if she's calling for you? After scouring the house again, Tovah started to wonder if Ari was devious enough to keep shifting his hiding place. Then, perhaps in response to desperation, her mind suddenly cleared. She knew! Of course she knew where Ari was. She'd almost made the same mistake with Ari she'd made with Dan. The first note Dan had left was the clue to where Ari would be. After weeks her brain was suddenly alert once more. In response to a crisis affecting her children, her imagination had re-engaged.

Purposefully, she headed down the basement stairs again, this time going straight to Dan's workroom. She'd finally stopped thinking about herself and where she would go to hide. She knew where Ari would go. He would go where his father used to go to think.

Ari was in Dan's shop under the workbench. He'd hidden behind the big, hand-lettered sign Dan had made to introduce Leah's therapy program. The sign said Leah's Reconstruction Project and listed everyone involved.

Ari had crawled under the bottom shelf of Dan's workbench behind the sign, rolling himself in one of the canvas drop cloths stored there. Then he'd fallen asleep. Dan's yellow hard hat stood sentinel beside Ari, like a favorite toy.

Ari didn't wake up, even when Tovah slid him out of his hiding place, his comfort spot, as near to his Dad as he could get these days. He remained bedded in paint-spattered canvas.

Tovah sank down on a corner of Ari's bunched up drop cloth. How could she not have known immediately where Ari would go? Was it the same as not knowing where Dan had left her a note?

Had her not knowing been part of what drove Dan away?

Every fiber within her wished Dan had not gone. How could he? He had to know how devastated they were. If he didn't know, why was that? Should she have understood he had something to do?

Damn him!! Was this some kind of a contest?

At least her brain was in gear again. Dan had chosen his course. She had to choose, too. She would have wanted to see Dan either in school or working on his classes and his design ideas long before this. It had seemed to both of them the children came first. Dan seemed to understand even better than she did. His devotion to Leah had been absolute. He'd never mentioned work of his own.

One thing was certain. She would not subject the children to any more trauma.

Before Dan left, she'd been on the verge of finally raising the subject of looking for a new rabbinical position. It had to be more than just a new job. The kind of change she had in mind meant a re-envisioning of their religious life, a shift in form and habit. There would have to be a move to the type of synagogue she should have chosen in the first place, a place much smaller than Temple Isaiah, with it's hierarchy of senior, assistant, and associate rabbis. Most important; she needed to return to the Conservative wing of Judaism.

Conservative practice was so different from Reform. She was tired of being told to choose: to cover your head in synagogue or not, to wear a prayer shawl or not, to keep kosher or not. No one in Reform Judaism even considered attending a daily *minyan*. Where would they find one, anyway?

True, not all Conservative Jews did these things, but many of the Rabbis did, and no one thought it was antiquated. She needed room in her life for these traditions and *mitzvot*. She needed to know she was commanded to do these things, that they were expected of her. Those commandments deepened her Judaism, and all aspects of her life.

If she was ever going to be an effective rabbi she had to return to a more strict observation of the Sabbath, to keeping kosher in a strict way, to daily prayer at set times.

She should have shared all this with Dan long ago, but what if he had been unwilling? For her it would be a comfortable return to the practices of her childhood, but what if Dan found it alien?

Also true, it would be very hard to admit she'd made a basic error in her life choices. When was the last time she'd admitted to such an error?

Now, with Ari asleep beside her in his canvas nest and Leah safe in her crib, she had to admit her mistakes. If she were going to make a new life for her children, she had to be truthful, at least to herself.

She couldn't imagine exactly what course of action to take, but it would come. Somehow she would find enough faith in her own abilities, enough energy, to make the necessary changes.

Tovah finally unwrapped Ari, and, cradling him in her arms, carried him upstairs. She took Dan's hard hat along, whimsically placing it on her own head. When she put Ari to bed, she left the hardhat beside him on his night table. It would stay there until they packed up to move.

# CHAPTER EIGHT

Okay. He'd wrenched himself away from Tovah and the children. He was in New York but he couldn't get his search started. What was wrong?

Even staying in the cheapest hotel cost too much. He didn't know what else he could do. He didn't want to get a job. He'd have no time to search if he had a job. But, he wasn't searching. He was wandering, as though he was a new student at Columbia or the Jewish Theological Seminary right next door.

He should be at Holy Family, St. Michael's, or the Cathedral Church of St. John the Divine right now. He should be at the churches where he would be interviewing anyone who would speak to him, priests, old-time parishioners, anyone he could find. Had he done any of those things yet? No. He skirted close to the churches, but never quite dared enter those alien places where his birth mother had apparently felt so at home.

He had to do something! Eventually he had to go home and explain to Tovah why he'd left. Still, for days, surrounded by a miasma of indecision, he did nothing.

Then he found the right place to live. That was it! The right place would make all the difference. The hand-printed sign leaped out at him from one of the many bulletin boards in the area:

*Sublet – Studio Apartment*
*directly across Holy Family.*

A row of phone-number tabs flapped off the sheet of paper. Dan tore down the whole sign so no one else would get the apartment. This was what he'd been waiting for.

Clearly the room wasn't anything special to the current tenant. As though from a great distance, Dan heard the young man, a student, say he was leaving graduate school before he flunked out. Who cared why he was leaving? Dan's compulsion to walk over to the two dust-streaked high windows in the room and peer out was overwhelming. This was the vantage point he must have. The two windows faced Holy Family, framing the whole complex: the church, the school, and a third building, once a residence for unwed mothers.

The apartment was one room, tiny, maybe twelve feet by twelve feet, with a minuscule kitchenette along part of one interior wall. Next to the kitchen a very narrow door led to the smallest bathroom Dan had ever seen. He'd realized immediately that once the Murphy bed was pulled down from its plywood cabinet the room would be wall-to-wall mattress, but he didn't care.

Somewhere in his brain, Dan knew living across the street from where his mother used to live made no difference. But, from this room, the young woman who had called herself Adele seemed very real to him. He could imagine her standing at a window in the third building at Holy Family. Maybe her room had been on the second floor too. Any apartment, even this grungy little room, probably represented freedom to her. Could she have imagined a time when her son would stand at a second-floor apartment window across the way, and stare at where she'd lived?

He'd never shared his need to search for his mother with Tovah because it seemed so preposterous. He had so little real information. It had all happened years before. In the thirty-six years since his birth, this Riverside Drive neighborhood had been transformed more than once, from a safe middle-class enclave to a drug-ridden slum. Now a renaissance blossomed with new shops and restaurants lining the two main thoroughfares, Amsterdam and Broadway.

The preliminary phone calls Dan had made to New York before leaving Minneapolis seemed purposeless now, even though he'd spoken to people in the churches he intended to visit. One of the priests at Holy Family had been particularly helpful. The priest knew the history of the area. Holy Family had been run by the Diocese of New York. Lately the Franciscan Order had taken over. The priest had confirmed there had once been a residence for unwed mothers attached to the church. Later it had been home to a community of nuns. Now it held administrative offices and some classrooms, filling needs created by a new, successful, Church school. The complex no longer had any use for a residence or a convent.

Dan had actually been in this area once before, while a teenager. Then he had worried the area had been too dangerous for Adele. His mother, Elaine, had assured him it had been a much safer place around the time of his birth, and Adele had been uncommonly cautious, staying in the residence except for essential shopping, her doctor appointments and church visits.

He had expected to be relentless once he was in the new apartment; looking for Adele constantly. Instead he spent hours staring out at the buildings of Holy Family, as though, if he really concentrated, he would actually see her.

Sometimes he'd turn from the window and peer at the drawing, his only real clue to his mother, a sketch of Adele as she'd appeared near the time of his birth. It had been a gift from the artist, the wife of his father's law partner. These days he kept the sketch protected by a clear plastic sleeve and propped up on the high narrow dresser next to the Murphy bed, leaning against the smeary mirror. When he looked into the mirror to examine his own face as compared to hers, a third face, Leah's, seemed to float between.

Leah would resemble his mother when she grew up. The delicate jaw and chin, the shape of the eyes and cheekbones were similar. Did that make Leah even more vulnerable?

Ari resembled Tovah so strongly, always a comfort to Dan. It suggested his son would have the confidence of the Feldners.

He tried to tell himself Adele had her own kind of strength. Her strength could also serve his children. Adele had found the nerve to leave her job at the U.N. when she had to. Did she have to go on welfare? Had she cut herself off from her friends because she was embarrassed to be pregnant? The man involved must have been unwilling to marry her, or even support her. What if there had been so many men she didn't know which one was his father?

He left the window to look at Adele's picture again, but he couldn't hold eye contact, even under her penciled gaze. He returned to his post at the window. He'd left his children, too.

With the New Year, 1995, Dan finally took some initiative. Part of every day he walked the grid of streets in the neighborhood as though he had made an appointment to meet Adele, but couldn't remember the right street corner. He'd come home from those walks his mind teeming with images having nothing to do with Adele. Rather, they were all incidents in his life with Tovah, when they had been so happy.

He'd have liked to stop during those walks and make some sketches, but he didn't allow himself. Drawing and building were indulgences he didn't deserve any more.

He had been so happy to find a place in Judaism for things like drawing and building. There was a whole holiday, *Sukkot*, having to do with building. The first time Tovah had shown him a *Sukkah*, Dan discovered he could be of real use to her.

He loved to retell their *Sukkot* story, always saying the sight of his first *sukkah* had him praying – praying it didn't fall in on someone – especially not on Tovah and one of her Sunday School classes.

The little hut was supposed to be flimsy, symbolic of where the Jewish people had sheltered, waiting for Moses to come down from Sinai with the Ten Commandments and the whole Torah. The problem was no one in Tovah's third year student congregation, in Michigan, had any idea about construction. He doubted there was one straight-driven nail in the whole structure. As for *skakh,* roofing material, they'd used huge pine boughs. The minute he'd found a ladder he started removing the boughs, even though Tovah was about to lead the youngest Sunday School class inside.

This *sukkah* didn't fulfill any commandment, as far as he was concerned. When he saw it, he couldn't believe anyone would actually venture in long enough to say a blessing, let alone to eat a meal.

"Dan Goldin, what are you doing?" Tovah demanded when Dan's face appeared in the one of the openings in the roof. At night you were supposed to be able to see the stars through the roof.

As he balanced on the ladder, trying not to put any extra weight on the building while lifting boughs off, he said, "You can't roof a rickety *sukkah* with heavy pine boughs. You've got to use lightweight stuff: slim bare branches, corn stalks, dried fern fronds, wheat stalks."

"Or palm fronds. But they aren't common in Michigan," Tovah said, annoyed. Dan was interrupting her class. She was also laughing at him.

"These things weigh a ton and it's worse because they're wet," he said. "It just snowed, for God's sake. One of these drops on someone and it'll be a fractured skull, not a holiday."

His tone of voice, the expression on his face, had stopped any argument from Tovah. She'd shepherded her class out of the *sukkah,* promising they would all come back later. By the time she came back, Dan had scrounged enough dried-out bulrushes and tall grasses from a nearby creek bed to serve as roofing material. He'd also hammered two dozen nails into the building at crucial points.

From then, any place Tovah served as a rabbi had a *sukkah*, a thing of beauty and absolutely safe.

These memories, sacred to him, seemed to forbid doing the things he loved while in New York, a self-inflicted penance.

He was recalling these kinds of events when he found himself standing by the windows in his room. There had been a sketch pad on the window ledge. Without being aware, he had been ghost drawing. He hadn't drawn a *sukkah* or any other memory. He had made a detailed drawing of one of the second floor windows at Holy Family where Adele might once have lived. All the stonework around the window was meticulously represented. In his sketch Adele stood at the window, Tovah beside her, with Ari and Leah in front of the two women. All four looked across at him.

Very slowly Dan put down the sketch pad. Something would shatter if he moved too quickly. He had to get away from the picture he'd just created. It seemed urgent he accomplish something. If he left the apartment right away there was still time today.

Dan put on his jacket and snatched up the precious picture of his mother he always kept with him. Carefully he slid it into his backpack. Then, quickly slinging the pack over his shoulder, he left his apartment.

It had become a day without continuity. All he knew was some time later he found himself at a corner of 112th Street. Some special quality of light made him stop.

The setting sun was at the perfect angle to magically highlight the huge jewel-toned rose window on the front portico of the Cathedral Church of St. John the Divine. His mother had spent a great deal of time there. He'd been avoiding this church above all others.

He reached over his shoulder to get into the pocket of his backpack, searching until his fingers met the slick surface of his all-important portrait. He pulled it out and peered at it, as though he feared some other drawing had been substituted.

It was just as usual: a black and white sketch of a young woman, slightly Asian in appearance, her straight dark hair looped back over her small, close-set ears.

When he'd first seen the drawing, as a teenager, the face in the picture had seemed so old, a woman in her twenties. As he'd grown older, she seemed young. There had been a period of time after Ari's birth when he'd given little thought to the picture. Who his real mother was hadn't seemed very important. Sometime during those years the drawing had been put away, folded in thirds like a letter. The folds had left creases falling at Adele's neck and at her eyes. The paper had been handled a great deal over the years. Now it had a soft, crumpled finish. The marks of wear added up to the effective aging of Adele's face. What had once been the likeness of a woman in her twenties now gave a good idea of what the same woman would look like more than thirty years later.

After one more confirming glance at the picture, Dan continued to hold it, a talisman. The church a block away claimed his real attention.

It was risky to stand still on a New York sidewalk at such a busy time of day. Dan shouldn't have been surprised when one of the people brushing past him almost dislodged the picture. He closed his fingers gently on its surface. Protecting the drawing was instinctive to him, like sheltering a person. He did it now, even while studying the building a block away. The people brushing past him disappeared. In the whole world there was only Dan, the glorious building and the drawing of his mother.

Dan began walking toward the Church.

# CHAPTER NINE

The morning after the exercise fiasco, trauma still fresh in her mind, Tovah arrived at her office at Temple Isaiah. Never again would she subject her children, or herself, to such emotional chaos. Damn Dan. She could manage on her own, in Minneapolis, or wherever her work took her.

It ought to be someplace new. She wasn't doing anyone a favor staying at Temple Isaiah. If and when Dan came back, they'd be gone. Then he would know how it felt to be the one left behind.

She didn't pause when she entered her office. The room was a 'leftover,' a long narrow room on the synagogue's third floor that had been created when the building's lone elevator had been installed decades before. She never used the elevator. Bad enough to hear it wheezing up and down like an asthmatic.

Probably because she'd been months late in starting work, Tovah had never taken the time to add any personal touches her office, except for a couple of family pictures.

She'd never really felt at home in the space.

This morning she didn't even take the time to hang up her heavy coat, tossing it over one of her two mismatched visitors' chairs. She phoned her father for a no-nonsense, business-like conversation.

"Good morning," she said. ""Do you still get the monthly list of all the job openings available in Conservative synagogues? If you do, could you send it to me right away?"

"Who is calling, please?"

"Okay, okay." She had to laugh. "How are you? And, how is mom?"

"Aha, so this is Tovah. Good morning, Rabbi. How are you?"

At least he didn't make her go through the entire litany, inquiring about each member of the family. Once he'd made his point, he let her set the agenda. "Yes, of course I get the list. You must know there aren't many choices in January."

"Right, that's what I'd expect. "Only the jobs left unfilled from last year, or the placements that didn't work out. Or, there might be a couple of new synagogues looking for their first rabbi. Those are the places most likely to hire a Reform renegade anyway. So it's perfect time for me to apply. I have to work in some Conservative *shul* for two years before the Rabbinical Assembly will accept me."

Her rapid-fire, can-do delivery didn't deflect her father. "You have a contract. Will your board let you go?"

"Why not? How valuable, how necessary, is the most junior of four rabbis?"

"You know every job has value."

Her father would never let her remark about their work go unchallenged. Without a doubt, Tovah's comment had brought him to his feet, pulled him out of his venerable brown leather desk chair.

Tovah was on her feet, too. It was good to be able to talk about this, to debate. What good was a decision you couldn't justify?

"Well, okay," she conceded. "There's an intrinsic value. But, four rabbis are way too many. There should be a rule. Not more than six hundred families tops, four hundred would be better; with two rabbis at most. We're too big, too specialized here."

"Temple Isaiah is a good place. Rabbi Greenlough is a good man. You've said so yourself."

"He's born for his job," Tovah agreed, pacing back and forth, sidestepping her few pieces of office furniture. "Anyway, he'll let me go. He wouldn't hold me. He's not the type. The board does what he wants, especially when it comes to the rabbinical staff, his own *minyan* of rabbis."

"You, as a rabbi, would know a *minyan* is ten, not four," her father said dryly.

"Okay. Okay. Not a *minyan*. But, he's certainly got a quorum, more than enough rabbis. Enough so each of us has a specialized area. All the social action issues are on one desk. It's what they call it too: social action, not *tikkun olam*. It's not repairing the world, it's just politics. All the family problems on another desk, unfortunately mine. When I was interviewed they asked me if I enjoyed working with families. Of course I said yes. It's just I didn't expect to end up doing social work."

Her father considered what she'd just said. "I know you're not saying these families shouldn't be served. Or, that you're too important to serve them. Also, does it really matter if you call it social action or *tikkun olam*?

Either way it is repair of the world, the job God left us. Good pastoral work is part of it."

Tovah had considered these questions a great deal in the weeks since Dan had left, as she'd tried to figure out where she'd gone wrong.

"Dad, I understand what you're trying to say. Of course the families should be served. I'd be happy to serve them. But, there's no balance. I'm not their rabbi. All I see are their problems."

Her father's silence suggested he agreed with her. It gave her the confidence to go on. If only Dan could hear her too. She should have said all this to him long ago.

"As to what words we use, I think those choices are important. When we know an action as *tikkun olam*, it becomes religious in nature, a *mitzvah*. As "social action" it's not the same."

What would Dan have said if she'd told him all this. Would he have left?

Imagining Dan undid her. She'd veer into even more intensely personal territory unless she was careful. It wasn't fair to her father, and it hurt too much.

There was only silence. Her father knew when to listen. It was a good silence, giving her the strength to acknowledge some of the errors she'd finally recognized.

"Do you remember some of the things I said when I made my decision about what kind of rabbi to be, which seminary to attend, and why? I was talking politics, not spiritual choices. I made a mistake."

There, she'd finally admitted it, said it aloud. No thunder shook her office, no lightening lit the sky. Her father didn't gasp in surprise.

"Look, let's say it. I'll say it. I made my decision about which seminary to attend on the basis of feminist politics and hurt feelings. It was partly those damn extra years it took the Conservative movement to ordain women. Plus, they were so unbelievably ungracious about it when they did act. However, I made the mistake. I ended up in the wrong seminary, wrong for me. It would have been better if I'd gone to JTS in New York and tried to change things from inside."

She'd avoiding saying those words for several years, even though deep inside she'd known they were true. Had she been afraid her world would crumble? She could have made Dan understand. Why she been so unwilling to admit to error?

There hadn't been a sound from her father. "Dad," Tovah said.

"I'm still here," he said. "Waiting to be surprised, shocked, by something you say."

"I'm always the last to know, I suppose."

"It's often that way," he agreed.

Her world had crumbled – maybe Dan had left – because she been unwilling to admit her errors? The thought brought a muffled sob trying to emerge from the back of her throat. For several seconds she could not speak.

But, she had to speak. She had to hear her nasty little secret told. Keeping something secret meant it didn't exist.

She sat down heavily in her desk chair before she went on. "I compounded the error. I took the wrong job. Because I thought … I guess because I could get it. It was the fast-track job. Fast track to what, exactly, I didn't consider. I didn't think whether I really wanted it or not, or whether I was suited to it. It was the very best job offered to my class, so it should be mine. It seemed to make sense at the time."

"And now?" Her father's short, intense question gusted into her ear, as though he'd been holding his breath as he'd listened.

"Now nothing makes sense. And, I've got to wonder. If I was unwilling to face this before and it cost me Dan, in good conscience, should I go ahead?"

Then she really couldn't say another word. The sob she'd swallowed threatened to erupt as tears. If she could hear it in her voice, her father could too.

Her father waited, giving her time to recover. Then his voice came, a shade or two more gentle than before, but asking the same question. "And now?"

"Now? You could also say if I've already paid the price, why not go ahead?"

"And, when Dan comes back?"

"If he returns, well … if that happens I don't know what I'll do. How could I know? I know it's only been a month, but Ari, Leah, and I need to go forward."

She couldn't say much more. Even just thinking about Dan made her feel especially weak and vulnerable.

She just managed to get the words out. "I guess no matter what happens, I need to make a change. I have to, if my career is going to mean anything. If Dan comes back, I hope he'll understand."

How could something seemingly so difficult suddenly be so clear? The truth made her squirm. How she had ducked and dodged. She'd never wanted to face Dan and admit to a fundamental error.

"If I'm going to do anything now," she continued, "It will have to be a big change. Right from how I get the job. This time I'm even willing to use the *yichus* of being your daughter. Your reputation alone will probably get me a job."

"You always rejected any help from me. You would do it yourself, you said, without connections."

"That sounds like I'm Leah's age. 'I do it mine-self.' The truth is I never could. I needed Dan. I've always needed your help, your advice. I'm older now. Hopefully I'm also a little smarter. The special status, the extra boost of being Eliezer Feldner's daughter sounds like a little insurance policy, a leg up in a world not so impressed with me."

Tovah was winking real tears from her eyes. She turned back to purely practical matters. "So, Dad, you'll send me the list of jobs?"

"Of course I will. Fast, like we do everything now; one, two, three, by fax no less."

"Thank you, Rabbi," she said, all formality.

"You're welcome, Rabbi," he said, mirroring her tone.

She thought their conversation had ended, but her father continued.

"When you have the list in your hand, call me. We'll go over what's available. There's a job in Chicago. It's convenient of course, so close to Madison. You'd have Ben and Hillel there, which would be good. Still, I wouldn't recommend it. There are problems.

"Also, you might be tempted by the job in the South. I've forgotten which state. A lot of the South takes a special touch. It's not for you."

He spoke quickly, as though he was afraid she'd stop him before he could finish. "There's one in California. It would probably be best, if they'll take you. It's a fairly new place, but they have some resources, even some kind of a building. Apparently, there's a particularly eager group of congregants."

Sitting in her desk chair, Tovah swiveled until she faced the window behind her. She didn't know whether to feel grateful or insulted. Had her father been maneuvering her into this?

"Suddenly you know all about this year's left-over jobs. How come? You haven't changed jobs in over thirty years. You've been researching this, just in case I asked."

Her tone had become accusatory, but her father kept his voice very level and said, "I'm not prescient. What if you needed to know these things and I had no information whatsoever? So, I prepared a little. If you had never asked, what would have been the harm?"

"You're right," Tovah said.

"Don't make me right so easily. Easy victory with you makes me nervous." He hung up.

As she replaced the phone, Tovah was already planning what she'd say in her letter of application. She'd send it out tomorrow, her day off. No more sleeping in for her. She was up with the children every morning. As a result she'd given up working late into the night.

Why had she put in all those extra hours? Had she really believed she could make the wrong job right? She had only exhausted herself and destroyed her relationship with Dan. How had he felt when her study door closed in his face evening after evening?

Never again would she focus so exclusively on her work. Not even in a new position. If success had to come at the expense of home and family, the price was too high. She had all but ignored Dan when he'd gone out that last night.

Finally Tovah turned to the untidy piles of paper on her desk. No matter what problems she found there, she'd be at Robin's to pick up the children by five or five-thirty. It wasn't fair to take advantage of Robin, or any one else caring for them, including Dan. The children deserved better. Dan had deserved better.

When her father's list arrived she'd have to tell Rabbi Greenlough she was job hunting. Hopefully he'd approve as easily as she'd suggested he would.

This time her job hunt would be solitary. She'd had Dan's support for so long, she forgotten what it felt like, working without a cheering section.

During her job-hunting after ordination, she'd responded to the built-in competition in the placement system. The complex rules and the time limits the seminary put on job searches made it all seem like a game. You couldn't troll the job market. You were only allowed to consider one job at a time. Back then her father had once asked her if she thought she was right for Temple Isaiah. Had she considered his question at all?

Long before she'd applied for the job she now held, she'd heard about some of Temple Isaiah's High Holy Day customs. Right after the *shofar* sounded, there followed a volley of French horns. She'd joked about it the first time she heard about it, wondering if the Temple leadership thought God enjoyed complex orchestration and the superior, mellow tones of the French horn more than the primitive raw blasts of a ram's horn.

How could she have paid so little attention? She knew perfectly well it was no easy thing to banish traditions, even if they were outdated, even if she disapproved of them. To longtime members of Temple Isaiah – and there were families who had been affiliated with the Temple since it had been built in the 1890's – those damn French horns were a much–loved modern Jewish practice.

Somehow, once she'd decided the job should be hers, practices she'd abhorred, or she had laughed at, went from being important markers of philosophy and intent to harmless quirks she would simply sweep out of her way.

She'd even played to some of the Temple's known prejudices. At a talk she'd given to one of the Temple's women's groups during her try-out, her subject had been the styles of *tallitot* and *kippot,* how prayer shawls and head coverings differed from place to place, and how they had changed over time. It was a legitimate subject, but she'd turned it into an amusing talk about fashion. The ladies loved it.

In those days, Tovah had referred to the two-and-three days-long final interview for jobs as 'auditions.' While her label might be an accurate reflection of how the lengthy try-outs were conducted, it was also true she'd thought of herself as giving a performance. Recognizing her old attitude now embarrassed her profoundly.

How would she go about an interview this time, if she was lucky enough to get one?

Later, as she sat in her office, her father's list of jobs in hand, the mere thought of an interview made her stomach churn. The paperwork on her desk actually looked good, at least compared to facing people who might not want to hire her.

Well, better stage fright than another exhibition of the glib confidence she'd shown when she'd plotted her first appearance in Minneapolis. At one time she'd been willing to be some part performer, some part charlatan. It all had to be different this time.

# CHAPTER TEN

Several days after Dan first came to St. John the Divine he met Jo.

In the few days he'd been visiting the church regularly he'd managed to make a place for himself, in front of the Holocaust Memorial in one of the many bays along a side aisle of the main sanctuary.

He had finally admitted he was stuck. The plan he'd created in Minneapolis – it had seemed so reasonable there – now seemed foolish. Had he really expected to find people who'd known Adele, just by showing around an old sketch of her? He hadn't even tried it yet; but he knew it would never work.

He had no other ideas. He couldn't just go home. Inaction seemed to be the only course left to him. He spent many hours in the church, especially in the late afternoon. He would sit quietly holding the drawing of his mother in his hand. He couldn't spend much time there in the earlier part of the day, because there were too many children from the Cathedral's Choir School around.

Then, one afternoon, a woman's voice cut through the fog surrounding him. "Young man, are you praying to her or for her?"

He looked up. An older gray-haired woman, small, sturdy, wearing a tailored suit and a clerical collar was looking down at him. "I'm not ... I ... Can't I sit here?" Dan stuttered.

He had pulled his folding chair from a row of seats set up in front of the nearby war memorial, carefully replacing it every evening before he went home.

"Of course you can sit here. You've been sitting here by the hour for several days. I've seen you. I didn't mean to frighten you away, only to express concern. I'm Jo Waggoneer," she said, offering her hand. "Jo. J. O. Just like in Little Women. It was my mother's favorite book."

She must have seen confusion or questions in his eyes. "Does it sound like I'm picking on you?" she asked. "I'm not. I always say exactly what I mean."

Dan didn't doubt for one moment this woman would often need to label her intentions. Everything she said, even when expressing concern, sounded so stern.

"Did she die in the Holocaust?" Jo asked, her gesture indicating his drawing.

"The Holocaust?"

"This is our Holocaust Memorial. Some people make prayers here for the victims. Perhaps, if what you really want is to sit quietly, one of the small chapels behind the altar might be more comfortable."

"Well, thanks. This memorial is for Jews."

"Of course it is; because so many of them died."

"I mean this feels like the Jewish place in here."

Around them the huge cathedral had become curiously quiet. The setting sun had slipped below the level of the windows. He liked the Cathedral best then, at the end of the day. It was the quietest time, before the evening programs began. He'd noticed there was a moment when all the shadows within the church turned blue. And, as it gradually grew darker outside, the Cathedral's many stone carvings could actually be seen more clearly. As the areas around the windows and down the side aisles darkened, the shadows heightened the detailed patterns worked in stone, all the little faces of the gargoyles.

This woman had a gargoyle quality herself: odd, intense, watchful.

She answered several of his unspoken questions then, before she asked him anything more. "I'm one of the priests who work here. I always wear my collar as a kind of shorthand. It lets people know I belong here."

"Women are priests? I thought they were nuns. I see nuns here all the time."

"The nuns you see are usually Catholic. Any woman priest is Anglican. I'm Anglican."

"I'm Jewish," Dan said. "I'm sorry ..."

"Don't apologize for being Jewish. Unless you think it's some kind of a mistake. I mean, don't apologize anyway. Is that why you're here all the time? Do you think being Jewish is a mistake?"

Dan thought a minute. "Actually, I'm not sure right now. If it is a mistake, it's because of her." He looked down at his drawing as though again trying to assess what it meant and still failing.

"When I was younger, I thought it must be a problem. Then, for a long time it was fine. Now it's an open question. Everything in my life is an open question right now."

He held the picture out to this woman who seemed to take such an interest.

"She's my birth mother," he said. "She wasn't Jewish. She was Catholic. I'm looking for her."

The priest waited to see if he as going to add anything. When he'd been silent several seconds she walked over to the rows of chairs a few feet away and selected one. She brought it over, setting it beside him.

He had been sitting there, somewhat stoop-shouldered.

The woman actually rested one hand lightly on his shoulder before she sat down, a clear gesture of support. The touch caused him to square his shoulders. When she sat down she leaned close for a moment, handing back the drawing of Adele. "Tell me what you know about your mother. Tell me about this search of yours."

In the days immediately following, Dan and Jo usually met late in the afternoon, always near the Holocaust Memorial. Once or twice he wondered why she'd adopted him, although he didn't question her. Knowing he had Jo as a friend, an ally, seemed to make things possible again. It was at her urging he finally called Tovah.

He'd been thinking about calling home ever since he'd arrived in New York. After she'd heard his story, Jo said most emphatically that whatever else happened, he must call immediately.

"Hey, I thought you were on my side," he said. He agreed with her, but felt he ought to defend himself.

"There are no sides here. I don't like thinking that way when it comes to a marriage, even one clearly in trouble. I'm on the side of the angels."

Dan had tipped his chair back on its two rear legs, as if it gave him extra space from Jo, and what she thought he ought to do. Dan already knew this small woman, this priest, did not give up.

"I know I should call, but somehow I haven't been able to. I left a note, you know, and sent a letter right away."

She looked severe. "Sounds pretty thin. You've already waited far too long. You also said your letters didn't really tell her much." She glanced at her wristwatch. "It's already past nine here, past eight in the Midwest. I would imagine your children are in bed already."

"Well, yes, they are. I don't have a good spot to call from. I don't have a phone in my apartment. I didn't bring a cell phone to New York. There's a pay phone in the hall where I live, but it's so public. I'd need a lot of change…"

It all sounded pretty feeble to him too.

"If you have a five-dollar bill, there's a dispenser for calling cards right by the pay phone in the far corner of the main entrance. You've probably just never noticed it. We deliberately tucked it into a corner so people could have some privacy."

She stood up, gesturing for him to precede her; as though she were responding to his idea to call.

He'd wanted to phone. He even knew where the pay phone was located. He'd thought about talking to Tovah every moment since he'd left. Despite his fixation over finding his mother, despite the fact he believed his quest was crucial, even believing Tovah would never have allowed his project, he wanted to phone. Leaving Tovah and the children felt like a self-inflicted amputation.

He was hardly aware he'd walked up to the front entrance with Jo. After they stood there for a moment it was as though she melted away, saying, "I'll just go check on one or two things in my office."

The calling card was in his hand, although he couldn't remember how it got there. Punching in his phone number seemed like one of the riskiest things he'd ever undertaken. As the phone rang in Minneapolis, he leaned against the rough, sheltering stone.

Then he heard her. "Hello."

He couldn't say a word.

He heard Tovah's exasperated intake of breath. He had two seconds to speak, or she would hang up.

He opened his mouth, "Tovah." She barely heard, but at least her name caught her attention. She had not recognized his voice.

"This is Tovah Feldner. Who is this?"

"Tovah, it's me, Dan."

Silence again. Not silence preliminary to her hanging up, but silence thickening into a barrier. He waited for her to speak again.

"Dan?"

Could she only manage a single syllable?

"Tovah, please say something."

She'd hardly been able to utter his name. He heard her crying.

He started to say, "Please don't cry," then stopped. Tovah hated to cry; hated any admission of weakness. He didn't want to call attention to her tears. It would not be a good beginning. He stayed silent, holding the receiver, until her heard her voice, unnaturally tiny, "Are you all right? Where are you? What do you want? "

"I'm all right. I'm in New York. Are you and the kids okay?"

"We're fine." she said. He waited for her to say more, but there didn't seem to be anything she wanted to add. There was just a faint electronic hum to carry words between them, if he could find the words.

Finally Tovah said, "Dan . . " Then she stopped again. He had to say something.

"I've wanted to call …" he blurted. "I know I should have… I guess I should have. You found my note, right?"

"Not for a long time," Tovah said, voice clipped. "Maybe I should have known where you'd leave it, but no one found it for days. Some place obvious, like the kitchen table, would have saved us some very bad days." Tovah had regained sufficient composure. Her voice was crisp, brittle sounding.

"Tovah. I didn't mean to … I had to …"

"Never mind," Tovah said. She wouldn't cry again, not while they were on the phone. "You don't think I'll buy your answers, do you? I don't even know why I asked. My God. I thought you were dead!"

"I'm sorry you didn't find my note right away. I thought …" He didn't want to blame her. "I didn't think. I couldn't go back inside to change it. I'm sorry if it gave you … I didn't think you'd worry so long … not so much." How had he managed to convince himself?

"You didn't think I'd worry? What did you think I'd do?" she said.

"I couldn't explain. I mean even now, it doesn't make a lot of sense. Not even to me." He wasn't making much of a case for himself.

"What am I supposed to say?" Tovah had tapped into her anger, so she'd feel stronger. She wouldn't lean against a wall for support. Tovah would be up and walking. If he'd caught her in her study she'd pace back and forth, using every inch the telephone cord allowed. If she happened to be in the kitchen, she'd take advantage of the portable phone and circle around the first floor, going from the kitchen to the dining room and then through the living room. From the living room she'd stride back into the foyer and turn sharply; past the stairway leading to the second floor, and the short hall to her study.

She'd re-enter the kitchen through the swinging door. He'd have given a great deal to be at home, watching her.

Whoosh. He heard the swinging door slap shut behind her. She was back in the kitchen. If he didn't want to get run over by her hostility, he'd have to interrupt.

"Tovah, I want you to know why I left. I went, partly, because of what the doctor said. By now you must know what the doctor said."

"Leah's next appointment isn't for some time yet. Is this call a reminder? If it is, you're early. Are you checking up on me? I'll make sure she's at the appointment. I make sure her exercises get done, too. Maybe not like you, but they get done."

She was fighting to stay calm. Damn Jo. He should have waited to call. He wasn't prepared. How would he have prepared?

For the moment he only had to listen. "You said the doctor couldn't have been more pleased. You said there would be no surgery on her legs. He said she'd need glasses. Even you can't fix everything. I mean; you wear glasses. I wear them to read. Did he say something else? What could he possibly have said to make you leave? Did you think your job was over? Did you think there was nothing more for you to do? Was Leah's care the only reason for you to …?"

He broke in. "No. No. I guess I thought you'd phone the doctor. I didn't finish exactly, not all of what he said. I couldn't find a way to tell you. He said whatever the problem – they still don't really know of course – it might not be C.P. It could be something genetic. Something called Dystonia – one of many kinds of Dystonia. It would be something in the family. You'd have said if it was in your family. Your parents would have known.

You'd have said. So I had to try to find my mother, to find out if she had a similar condition."

Never before had he silenced Tovah so effectively. Long seconds ticked by. When she did speak again her tone of voice barely expressed her disbelief. "You went to New York because of Leah without telling me? Is something else wrong with her? She seems much better, not worse. Are you sure about this? Exactly what did the doctor say? And, what the hell is Dystonia? Is it a kind of C.P.?"

During his time in New York Dan had already realized he knew nothing about this possible new medical enemy, while he could have written a book about Cerebral Palsy symptoms in premature babies. He hadn't really left because of what the doctor had said.

"I don't know what it is, not exactly," he admitted. "Apparently it can look a lot like C.P.. But, it's not from a birth accident or from lack of oxygen. It's not from being premature."

Only silence again. This wasn't like Tovah. Dan knew perfectly well, even for this call, she would have rehearsed somewhat. She would have thought through what she would say if and when he called. Obviously, she had not anticipated this.

Finally she said, "Okay, Dan. We'll talk about the children. Leah is fine. I mean, her walking is better, even with her distress over your leaving. I don't think her hands give her as much trouble. I think when the doctor sees her he'll say she's had a leap to a new plateau, just like he did when she started walking.

"I suppose you want to hear about Ari too. It's not so easy to measure what's bothering him these days, since the main hero in his life left."

Dan winced. He had seen the beginning of Leah's new spurt in skills and mobility and assumed her C.P. symptoms were receding. He'd expected an excellent check up for Leah, until the doctor had mentioned possible Dystonia and made it necessary for him to leave.

Surely Leah was too little to be upset. And Ari always seems so resilient, just like Tovah.

"I know you are upset," he said, something of a revelation to him.

"Dan, what did you expect? You ... deserted us. Are you calling now because you want to come home?"

"Suppose I said, yes."

"I'd tell you 'no,' certainly not right now. I won't be here." Tovah said. "I've got a job interview."

"You've got what?" Dan said.

"I've got a job interview. In California. I should have talked about it before, but I never could quite figure out ..."

"Well, I don't see what changing Temples will accomplish. Even, if it's way out in California. Maybe, if it's a much smaller place. Even then it might not be different enough."

"It'll be different if it's Conservative," Tovah said.

"You're switching to Conservative? No discussion?"

"Who exactly was I supposed to discuss it with? You left. I talked to my father. He seemed to know I wanted to do it."

"Well, I knew too, and you never talked about it with me. Believe me, I tried."

There was another long silence from Tovah. Finally she said. 'You're right. I should have. I thought you'd hate the idea. I thought you might say leaving all Leah's doctors was irresponsible. I didn't want to force you ..."

Apparently, Tovah didn't know actually what to say. He didn't either; not as much a surprise. Had it taken his leaving to get Tovah to act on her career? Had he been an impediment?

"Dan." Now Tovah spoke quietly, clearly forcing herself to be calm. "It seems everyone in my life: you, Robin, Ilana, my parents, knew what I ought to do. I didn't know. Okay. I should have said something. But, you shouldn't have left. Not without telling me what Leah's doctor said. Not without telling me that you believed you had to find your mother. How could you? You shouldn't have left at all."

Dan didn't interrupt, even though Tovah paused. He waited.

"I'm going to California in a couple of days," Tovah said. She sounded embarrassed. Clearly she knew she should have said something to him months before.

Tovah actually gulped before she went on. "I'll be back late Thursday night. I didn't have any idea when you would call; if you'd ever call. If you want to talk after I've been in California, it would be good. Better than our not talking, certainly. If you don't want to, you're safe. I don't know how to reach you. I just want to say you ought to call your parents. They're frantic too. Although, they said you'd done this once or twice before. Michael said so, too. That you've just walked away before. I didn't know, and certainly never thought that you'd do it to us." Tovah finished up in a rush. She'd sounded most secure when sending a message about his parents.

What could Dan say? He hadn't even started his search. He certainly wasn't going to shut the last door between him and his wife and children.

"Okay," he said. "I'll call next Friday, early. I will phone my folks. I'll have a phone number next time we talk. I'll get a cell phone. I want to talk to the kids too."

Something more was needed, he thought. Some recognition of what Tovah was going through.

"I guess I don't really have to say 'good luck,' on the interview. You'll get it if you want it. You always get what you want, if you want it enough."

"I wanted all this to be a bad dream, but it's real," Tovah said. "So, you're wrong." She was crying again, but she hung up before he could say anything else.

Dan hung up too, than went back inside the church. The two chairs he and Jo were using had been put away. Dan walked past his usual spot and sat down heavily in one of the pews near the front.

He must have been quite noisy, or, he'd wandered into some meeting or worship service. It felt as though it ought to be too late for anyone else to be in the building. In fact he'd only been on the phone with Tovah for a few minutes.

A woman up in the High Pulpit was speaking to a group sitting under her gaze. Except right now her whole audience had turned to look at him, the interloper.

An entire congregation of female eyes looked reproachful. Not only were all those staring at him female, but, whether dressed in habits or secular clothing, it was obvious they were all nuns. All the women were middle aged or older.

Dan felt someone – it had to be Jo – come up behind him. Why hadn't she been around a few seconds before, to stop him from blundering into this conclave?

He felt her hand on his shoulder. Quietly he got up and left, following her up the center aisle until they were far enough away not to be intruding.

Jo turned. For a moment he thought he'd have to apologize to another woman. He was wrong. Jo was laughing so hard her eyes were tearing.

"That'll teach you to watch where you go in the Cathedral," she said. "Not only are all those women nuns. They're all seniors. Most of them have been friends of the Cathedral for more than forty years. Most of them are old enough to … "

"They're old enough to have known my mother," Dan said.

Jo stopped laughing so suddenly it might have seemed she'd strangled. She put her hand on Dan's arm and in a voice filled with genuine excitement, and without missing a beat, she agreed, "They could have known your mother. Of course! Why didn't I think of nuns? We'll start with nuns. I know just the community to get you started."

# CHAPTER ELEVEN

During her flight from Minneapolis to California, Tovah replayed her phone call with Dan over and over in her mind. There might be a shred of hope. He had promised to call again.

*Damn the man. First he leaves; then he wants to know why I didn't discuss this job opportunity with him.*

At the same time, Tovah knew she should have brought up the subject of changing from Reform to the more traditional Conservative wing of Judaism months earlier. But what if she'd felt commanded by that tradition, but Dan had not?

She tried to tell herself there hadn't been time. She'd been so late starting work. At first she'd thought being late was poisoning her job. Then, even as they were getting used to the fact that Leah needed so much care, came a creeping realization: she'd made a huge error in going after her job in the first place. That recognition had reeled her back to what kind of a rabbi she wanted to be, and the mistake she'd made in picking a seminary. Her error was fundamental.

Admitting to a huge error was so awful to contemplate it had taken her three years of effort and the shock of Dan's departure to admit it. How long had she been telling herself that if she did the job perfectly she'd come to love it?

At the same time, Dan was wrong too. How could he not immediately report what the doctor had said about Leah? Now she didn't even know if she could consider leaving Minneapolis. This time Dan didn't have any information.

She should have been at Leah's appointment. Ideally, she should have known as much about Leah's condition as Dan. Once the hospital in Indiana had been willing to discharge Leah, and they'd finally been able to get to Minneapolis, Tovah felt she had to concentrate on her job. If only she could have started work just before Labor Day; when she'd agreed to start. Instead, it had been November. She'd had no idea how to make up for those missing months.

Should she have told the Temple's selection committee she was pregnant at her first interview? None of the young women rabbis admitted it, especially if their baby was due during the summer. Leah was due in July, two months before her job's start date. But, Leah had arrived in May. That certainly wasn't Leah's fault. Not her own fault either, although for some time she thought so.

The final year placement game had required she try for what was considered the best job. How had such competitive thinking infected her? Rabbinical jobs should never be seen as the spoils of some kind of game.

Below her the Rockies marched along, mile after mile. She had never been so far west. The distance she'd have to travel to make her new start was sobering. Perhaps if she could get through this weekend without obsessing over things, it would be a sign she'd made the right choice this time.

She felt so confined at the moment. She was so anxious to get the interview over and done. They'd never hire her. She told herself: *Stop it, stop it. You're not going to obsess, right?*

*Right. Will yourself to relax. That's a good one.*

She did know what she was doing this time. This was right! She was going to prove it by behaving in a totally different manner from any other job search. If she got the job she would not work blindly, longer and longer hours. If the new position also proved wrong it wouldn't help. If she found the right place this time, she wouldn't need to keep trying to correct a fundamental error.

Of course one thing had never been true before. Dan's leaving had changed things forever; whether she ever saw him again or not.

So, she chose not to review yet again the profiles she'd gathered on the leadership of the synagogue. She put on the earphones the flight attendant handed her and dialed a pleasant music channel. Maybe she could even manage a little nap, although she really ought to be concerning herself with whether she wanted Dan to be a part of this next move or not.

Ilana and Robin, both women she respected and loved, seemed to think she and Dan could patch things up, even if he'd deserted her. How do you forgive someone for desertion? How could she ever be anything but angry? How could he have thought she'd scarcely notice he'd left? How had he convinced himself that leaving a note in an obscure location and being in touch later was sufficient? Why had Dan believed he suddenly had to find his mother? And, why he couldn't tell her?

Ilana was always a believer in *Shalom Bayit*, peace in the house. No one could fight with Ilana for very long. Tovah knew perfectly well her nature was totally different.

She didn't like where her thoughts were taking her. She ought to try to nap. She could use a nap. She had to be up so early with the children. She couldn't just get up and go anymore. And, ever since she'd spoken to Dan, she'd spent extra time watching Leah.

She couldn't tell very much as she helped Leah climb out of her crib, observed her using the bathroom, washing her hands, eating her cereal by herself. Even though the doctors had said she'd never be able to do those things, she'd been doing all of them, and more, for months. But she had seen the change in Leah that Dan must have noticed earlier, much more ease in doing all these everyday things.

The doctor would tell her more during their next round of appointments. She shouldn't have missed the earlier ones. Obviously, Dan had wanted her there, even if he hadn't said so. She should have known without being told. With Dan in command of Leah's therapy, it felt as though there was no reason for her to attend doctor appointments. Dan and the doctors spoke to each other like colleagues. She didn't always understand them. Right from the beginning Dan had been the one to question every diagnosis, to investigate every treatment. He'd never assumed the doctors knew better. He always said, "Leah and I know best. No one else can know as much."

How could he have left without investigating every nuance of a possible new diagnosis? Dan had always assumed any new diagnosis would be something less serious than C.P. He'd already proved Leah's problems less serious than the doctors' original predictions. What if some new diagnosis proved to be potentially more serious then C.P.? Dan would be devastated. Was that what forced him out the door without telling her? If he believed he might carry the gene causing Leah's condition, it could well have shattered him. Never mind he had no control over such things; never mind the condition would have been totally unknown to him.

When it came to the children, Dan had always seemed more vulnerable. He'd had nightmares after Ari was born. She'd wake him and ask about his dreams. He always claimed he could not remember. The two of them had assumed the nightmares were connected to his new responsibilities as a parent. She'd wondered if his nightmares had been something deeper, perhaps rooted in some early, even permanent, insecurity, part of being adopted. Dan hated to talk about his adoption. And, except for his nightmares, they'd been so happy. Even though there had been a period when Dan seemed depressed, beginning when Ari was about three months old. That had only lasted a few months, Tovah told herself.

Her father had suggested counseling for Dan. He'd never really had a reason that he'd explained. Once – she'd thought it was a joke – her father had said post-partum depression could be egalitarian. Anyway, at some point well before Ari's first birthday Dan's nightmares stopped, his depression lifted.

If there'd been a warning in those symptoms she'd missed it. She couldn't force Dan to talk about being adopted. He didn't like conversations centering on him. He hated when people talked about his looks. She'd thought of it as a guy thing; but maybe it related to his adoption. Once, early in their relationship, he'd actually asked her if he looked particularly Asian.

She would never have said 'yes' or 'no' to such a question, as if looking Asian was somehow especially good or bad. She only knew he was one of the most beautiful human beings she'd ever seen. To Tovah, Dan's exotic looks were an extra gift he'd brought to their marriage. His birth parents, whoever they were, had given him the intangible things that had helped him be a wonderful husband and father. Maybe she had not said it enough, or with enough emphasis.

Leah's birth had brought no depression, no nightmares. If there were any emotional issues, Dan didn't admit it. He hadn't seemed to suffer guilt at all. Not the way she did. Dan had been all action. She had to stay in Indiana with Leah. Dan had raced between where she and Leah had to be, near Stratton, to their newly rented house in Minneapolis, and to Madison, where Ari spent part of the time with her parents. Right from the first Dan had been positive he could correct whatever was wrong. He'd insisted Leah's condition was not Tovah's fault. His insistence had been one reason she'd finally been able to let go of a good part of her guilt.

He had exorcised her anxiety. Had he done it by taking it on himself? Tovah had never known real worry until Leah was born. Before, problems were small and existed to be solved. After her daughter's birth, she was often suffused with dread. She had never realized anxiety stuck in your throat, made it impossible to eat because it filled your belly.

Even after they knew Leah would survive, when they were living in Minneapolis, after Tovah had started her job, so many worries remained.

For months whenever she and Dan put Leah to bed they hooked up a machine monitoring her breathing. Dan insisted he felt reassured by helpful temporary equipment. This time Tovah had been the one plagued by nightmares. She remembered every one of those dark dreams. They were full of wires and tubes, all leading to a dead baby. Sometimes she was the one connected to the paraphernalia. In every dream she was helpless, tied down, kept away from Leah. Sometime during those early months, the idea that Dan's only job would be to look after Leah, Ari and the household had evolved.

Maybe he'd let his own interests go because she'd continued to wake with a start, time after time, even when the house was totally quiet. She'd wake, positive she could hear Leah cry, or the alarm blare. She'd only learned to sleep when she realized Dan heard every sound coming from Leah and responded instantaneously.

"You shouldn't have to do it all," she would say, struggling to get out of bed in the middle of the night.

"I'll rest when the kids nap," he'd say, sounding so confident. Eventually she must have believed him, because she'd learned to sleep again.

Occasionally, they'd had to go back to Southern Indiana to see the doctors who had treated Leah from the first moment of life.

Every trip was an ordeal. For months Leah remained a very fragile baby. It was a long time before they could have her in the car without also having Tovah's crushing anxiety along as a passenger. As it turned out, their first worry-free car trip came when Leah was sixteen months old. Dan had wanted the four of them to go to Madison for a long-planned Feldner-Goldin family reunion. Tovah couldn't imagine agreeing to a voluntary car trip, no matter how brief. But, she wanted to see her friends and family so badly, and maybe even show off her children a little. She'd let Dan persuade her. It had turned out well. It was as though Leah had passed over some barrier, taking her whole family along.

Dan had become so proficient with Leah's exercise regimen Tovah had wondered if he might make physical therapy a career. He said no. His efforts were reserved for his daughter.

Dan's most passionate efforts always seemed to be for reasons other than a career. When he'd set up his projects for children in Cincinnati, she'd asked if he wanted to be a teacher or a social worker. He'd said no. More than once, watching him sketching a building he liked, or making an elaborated detailed model of a building façade, she'd suggested he might like to study architecture. Dan said architects had to wait too long for their ideas to become real buildings.

Here she was, altering the course of her career, while Dan had still not had his chance to even choose one. Should she have insisted? Did he know what he wanted to do? She hadn't asked him recently, so how could he have told her?

It was embarrassing to have to admit, even to her self, but there was a good reason she's stopped asking. Leaving things as they were had made her life so much easier.

She knew Dan deserved all the credit for Leah's progress. He hadn't neglected their daughter's spirit, either. Every doctor commented that Leah not only allowed them to do what was necessary, she actually cooperated.

When Leah had an appointment each doctor wore the personalized hard hats Dan had given them.

One of their consulting surgeons kept his hat on display in his office. He said his business was reconstruction, too.

Now she was out looking for a new job, and she hadn't known until their phone call, but Leah might be facing a new diagnosis.

She picked at the kosher lunch she'd ordered. If she would be the one looking after Leah and Ari without Dan, she would need a good job. She told herself no matter what happened between herself and her husband, for the next forty-eight hours she had to concentrate on being the best possible rabbinical candidate.

In its six years of existence, The South Orange County Jewish Family Congregation had gained a fine reputation. All the student rabbis who had served the congregation said Tovah would love the place, the people, and the climate. They'd all assumed the congregation would be thrilled to have her as their full-time rabbi.

As for her nerves, she simply had to understand this was how most people felt during job interviews. She found it hard to believe, but before this, even try-outs – like the forty-eight hour marathon she now faced – seemed like fun.

Jeff Greenlough, the senior rabbi at Temple Isaiah, had tried to dissuade her from job hunting. He'd insisted she only felt she had to leave because of Dan's disappearance. She'd finally convinced him she was serious, telling him she'd been thinking about a move long before Dan left. She'd been as forceful as she dared, saying she'd prefer to job hunt immediately. She would wait if he insisted, but only until her contract ended. She'd made every effort at diplomacy, especially when he'd argued that good jobs were thin on the ground in mid-winter.

"It happens there's a job in California I'm very interested in." She didn't want to say one of her goals was to get far away from the kind of job she had now. "I like the idea of working with a new synagogue."

He must have finally realized he wasn't going to change her mind, because he stopped arguing.

"I can't say I wish you luck, exactly. We'll miss your special abilities," he'd said. "Of course any congregation will benefit from your energy. I'll admit you might do worse than a new congregation, one that's never had a full-time rabbi before. So many rabbis don't want to take jobs in places like Orange County. They feel they're too far from large Jewish centers. They lack the vision, or they feel there are few established day schools and not enough colleagues. You go ahead. I'll make it right with the board. Don't worry about a thing."

It was nice of him to talk about her 'special abilities.' She hoped he didn't think she was too fragile to hear what he really thought. Maybe her work had been better than she'd known. Certainly, she'd put in enough effort. As for not worrying, that was impossible. She'd worried through the conference call making up the first part of her interview. She'd worried every second since this on-site visit had been arranged.

As the airplane began its descent, Tovah could see palm trees and swimming pools. It looked unreal, as though she was being cast in the role of a rabbi in a Disneyland special. No! No negative attitudes allowed on this trip.

There was of course one big negative. No Dan. Before this he'd always been right there beside her.

# CHAPTER TWELVE

All of Southern California connived to seduce Tovah. She stepped out of the John Wayne Airport terminal following her hostess, Janice Stein, to her car. Warm sun shone down on her. It was February, but the slight breeze was gentle on her skin in a way she had never experienced in the Midwest. It seemed all the air, not just the sky, must be soft blue. There were palm trees, looking just as improbable as they did in the movies.

As Janice's drove her Mercedes out of the airport, an entire boulevard planted with Birds of Paradise, flamboyant orange and blue blossoms, welcomed them, pointing the way to the freeway.

It was just past five p.m., still full daylight. The license plate on the car ahead welcomed Tovah personally: HIBRNIS. Delighted, she read it out loud, "Hi, Brown Eyes?"

Another vanity plate – there must be many more in California than in the Midwest – appeared almost immediately, on a sleek sports car cutting in front of them in what seemed a perilously small space. It said SINXTY.

Deciphering it took her a second, "Sin City?"

"Oh, you're good at figuring them out. I can never manage it," Janice said as she effortlessly cut across three lanes of traffic, away from SINXTY, to enter the diamond carpool lane.

"It's almost like reading Hebrew; part consonants, part imagination."

"What a great way to put it. In my case, I need a lot more imagination. You shouldn't worry about Sin City stuff," Janice continued. "People here like to advertise and brag. Orange County is very conservative, actually. Those attitudes are much more of a problem. We've got schoolteachers, especially around us in South County, who think being a Christian is the same as being normal. We've got stealth school board candidates and actual board members who want to teach the kids Creationism, outlaw sex education and institute school prayer. If you become a rabbi here, that's what you'll have to contend with."

Tovah tried to assess her hostess without being too obvious. Janice certainly seemed friendly. She wore tight black jeans and a printed black, taupe and brown leopard-patterned sweatshirt. Her hair, a beautiful mixture of blonde shades, had been bundled into a black baseball cap with a gold brim. She had strong, capable looking hands. There were flecks of blue paint on her fingers and one smear of gold on the off-white polish of her otherwise perfectly manicured nails. Janice, and her husband Teddy, were part of the key leadership of the synagogue.

Tovah knew enough not to let personal friendliness confuse her goals during her interview. During the next few days there could be no such thing as a casual conversation. You had to watch your tongue every minute, because whatever you said would be repeated. The best you could hope for was the inevitable repetitions staying accurate.

The landscape flashing by was less interesting then the woman driving. They had passed several handsome but fairly conventional office buildings on either side of the wide, wide freeway. Now, on the driver's side, rows of tightly packed houses and apartments lined up behind high walls. Despite being cramped together they appeared to be large, expensive homes.

Tovah knew enough not to comment on the density. She wouldn't say anything until her hostess voiced an opinion, or until she saw the home where she would be staying. For all she knew the Steins might live in one of those houses. It made no sense to offend through casual remarks during an interview.

On the other side of the Freeway she saw open fields where farmhands worked. It seemed to be a safe area of inquiry.

"They're harvesting the early crops, probably broccoli, maybe even strawberries," Janice explained.

"Fresh produce this early in the year; in February?"

"Absolutely, you can't believe the produce here. You'll love it. We all do. We've got oranges and lemons on the trees all year round, strawberries from February to September."

California seemed a personal cause to Janice, as though she had helped produce its largesse.

Traffic slowed and darkness descended at the same time. Southern California was like Israel, with very little twilight. Cars ahead of them slowed and stopped; red taillights seeming to roll toward them. On the other side of the freeway the traffic remained a moving sea, with waves of headlights.

"Of course we're also blessed with some of the worst traffic in the world," Janice admitted, turning on the radio. "Fortunately if you come here you'd be living and working in South County, so you wouldn't have a daily commute."

Janice punched buttons until the dial settled at 1070. Within seconds the broadcaster was describing traffic conditions in what seemed to Tovah an unknowable salad of freeway names and numbers.

"There's an accident on the 5, just past the El Toro Y," Janice said. She had no more trouble decoding traffic information than Tovah had reading license plates. "We'll be here a while. I should have taken the new toll road, not the 405. But, I think a toll road is unethical. They charge almost $3.50 for just a few miles. It's highway robbery."

She laughed at her own familiar joke, or maybe at Tovah's enjoyment of it. "So, tell me about yourself," she said.

Tovah's days-long job interview had begun.

The Steins lived in a spectacular home, definitely not one crowded onto a tiny lot.

Before Tovah and Janice reached the house they left the highway and drove a few miles through sharply rising country. They finally came to a gatehouse with a flood-lit sign announcing they were at a development called Huntsmen Farms. They had been on the road for more than an hour.

"We have a fair amount of acreage here," Janice said, expertly directing her gleaming white Mercedes into the bay of a four-car garage as one of the doors opened before them.

Janice gestured toward two barn-like structures on the property, one fairly close to the house, the other several hundred yards away. "The kids love that we can keep their horses here. And, I have a studio."

"I thought you might be an artist," Tovah said.

Janice looked pleased. "Not really. I'm an interior designer. But I'm hands-on, more than most."

She glanced down at her hands as she easily lifted Tovah's suitcase out of the trunk of the car. "I see. The paint gave me away. It was clever of you to notice. I'm doing a small table for a client right now, fake lapis lazuli. Only I have to say faux, of course."

While they'd been stuck in traffic, Janice's first questions had been about the children, Dan, and her parents.

Those questions had only been the warm-up. Janice had also wanted to know why, having originally been ordained a Reform rabbi from Hebrew Union College in Cincinnati, Tovah now wanted to undertake the change to a Conservative congregation.

Tovah had paused deliberately before replying. It might have been a little theatrical, but it would give her words weight. Whatever she said on this all-important subject would be repeated over and over again. She wanted to keep it simple so it wouldn't get muddled, even after a series of repetitions.

"I was raised Conservative. I've discovered I need to return to my spiritual roots. My father is a rabbi. I wanted to be a rabbi. Of course when I was younger I think I had to tell myself I was totally different from him.

So I became a Reform rabbi. Now, I've had to radically re-think that."

She deliberately kept her voice casual, "You know how it is when you're young. You can't imagine you're just like your parents, even if it's obvious. Certainly, I have far more in common with them than I would have admitted to when I was younger."

"And your father is a well-known Conservative rabbi." Janice seemed happy to make that observation.

"True enough, although he started out Orthodox. Maybe making a change is a family trend, I don't know. As for being well known, he's been at it forty years. When I was a child I thought all established rabbis had his kind of reputation. I also thought they stayed in one place forever. Not true, of course."

Perhaps seeming just a tiny bit naïve was more disingenuous than necessary. Janice just nodded, saying, "Sure. It's like when your parent is a movie star. It doesn't occur to a child it's unusual in any way."

The analogy was very California and very accurate. Tovah didn't want to belabor any one point in an unofficial conversation, so she just said, "The listing for this job spoke to me. It offered an opportunity to return to Conservative Judaism. It would allow me to be a part of a beginning, a *shul* still starting out. It's hard to beat the combination, especially combined with such a beautiful place."

Even as they'd sat together in traffic, waiting, and now as they stood, having taken Tovah's suitcase out of the trunk of the car, her strategies felt uncomfortable, cynical. She followed her hostess across a beautifully landscaped area leading to the front of the Stein's huge home. She told herself she just needed to know she was quoted correctly.

Still, Tovah sensed something else was happening to her, something she couldn't yet identify.

Janice was speaking as she opened the front door, so Tovah tried to focus on what her hostess was saying. "Teddy and I tried Reform too. It never felt right. I suppose it wasn't familiar. Of course, I'm remembering Conservative synagogues in Chicago more than thirty years ago. And, I've forgotten so much. When you come, you'll have to hold Hebrew classes."

Tovah didn't want Janice to see her gape at the size and the affluence of the home they'd just entered. Fortunately, her hostess was trying to complete her thought, so she wasn't paying too much attention to Tovah's reaction.

And, even though Tovah was momentarily overwhelmed by her surroundings, she had noticed the little shift in what Janice had said: *When you come.* It was only a slip at this stage, but a very good omen.

In the Stein's home the foyer seemed as large as the rotunda of an office building, the walls elaborately painted. The room held a large center table with a floral arrangement more than three feet high. Centered over the table a chandelier apparently crafted from spun glass and ropes of light hung dramatically low.

"You have a magnificent home," Tovah said. She would have slid into hyperbole if she'd said anything more. Janice smiled in response, then led Tovah down one of the halls radiating off the foyer, and ushered her into a guest bedroom done in green and cream toile. "This is like a garden, it's glorious." Tovah said, pausing to take in all the details.

"Well, you know, it's advertising for my work," Janice said. "You rest now, and after we've had something to eat we'll take you over to the synagogue. If you go into shock the first time you see our building it shouldn't be in front of the whole board." Janice smiled at Tovah. She seemed delighted Tovah had noticed and commented on her surroundings. She also looked relieved, as though she'd managed to introduce the subject of the synagogue building in a sufficiently casual manner.

When Tovah awoke the next morning her first thoughts were about the building she'd seen the day before, just hours after she'd arrived. Janice had been right. It had been a surprise.

Teddy Stein, Janice's husband and the president of the synagogue, had driven them over the South Orange County Jewish Family Congregation building once Tovah unpacked and they'd had what Janice termed a snack, although the generous assortment of Japanese sushi rolls and salads felt like a full dinner to Tovah.

The South Orange County Jewish Family Congregation had a building as bland as its name. Since the setting and the building exterior was well lit, Tovah had seen it clearly, even though it was evening.

"Was it a factory?" Tovah had asked, surveying the long building. The exterior walls were made up of pale yellow metal panels and the roof was unpainted sheet metal.

"I suppose it could have been," Teddy said. He sounded defensive. "It's an industrial building, Rabbi. It's meant to be temporary."

Janice had insisted Tovah sit in the front seat with Teddy. From where she sat behind Tovah she jumped in. "It's the cheapest kind of building available. And, it really is temporary. When we're done with it they just take it away. It can even be resold," she explained.

"Admittedly temporary has been five years already," Teddy said as they got out of the SUV. "We had hoped to replace it in three. That was probably unrealistic. Plus, we decided we need a full time rabbi more than we need a new building."

"Absolutely," Tovah agreed. She trailed behind Teddy as they entered the building, trying to take in all the surroundings.

"We've learned temporary often lasts longer than you think it will," Janice said. They were walking up the long ramp, the main access to the synagogue. There was a flimsy looking set of stairs, but the ramp seemed much more substantial.

Tovah knew the Steins were waiting for her full reaction. "I think it shows great initiative to create a building for use now, without wasting resources." She said. "Eventually, you can build. There's …"

"Don't say there's so much land, Rabbi. We don't own all of this." Teddy Stein had waved his hand, encompassing the large parcel of scrub where the building was located. The Pacific Coast Highway split into two one-way streets not far from where the synagogue building stood. Hundreds of yards away, the length of at least two city blocks, Tovah could see the two roads merged back together.

"This parcel of land is called The Big Divide," Teddy went on. "As I said, we don't own all of it, only up to there." Teddy had pointed to a very inadequate row of bushes trying to hide a scrubby area of creosote spangled with a few dusty wildflowers and a bizarre building about twenty-five feet away. "We call this area next to our building, no man's land. We don't cross over the line."

"If we owned all the land, we certainly wouldn't have left those buildings standing, whether we could afford to build or not," Janice said as they'd entered the synagogue. The synagogue's sanctuary was furnished very simply. The floor was covered with gray industrial carpet. There were bookcases holding prayer books and Bibles, and nested stacks of metal chairs against one wall.

It wasn't much to look at but the essentials were there. The *bimah*, the raised area from which the cantor or rabbi led services, held a lovely simple, white painted, modern looking ark housing the Torah scrolls. On either side of the ark there were comfortable, ordinary looking armchairs upholstered in a soft purple/gray shade. The rabbi, the cantor, the president of the congregation and any pulpit guests would sit there. The Torah reader's lectern and the rabbi's pulpit were unadorned.

Tovah walked over to the ark and opened the sliding doors inset with frosted glass panels. Inside, three Torah scrolls dressed in traditional embroidered velvet covers, rested in stands of a design she'd never seen before.

"Earthquake proof," Teddy explained, when she'd asked about them.

"Well, I don't see anything to worry about in this building," Tovah had said. "It's perfectly adequate, and, replacing it gives us a good solid nuts and bolts goal. A lot of people like a measurable goal to shoot for."

It was almost a relief to know if she got the job, she'd be starting somewhere as different as possible from staid Temple Isaiah with its grand, classically beautiful, hundred year old building.

In contrast, this pale yellow bus of a building, of no architectural merit at all, meant any change they managed to make would be an improvement, and she'd be a part of it. After all, they weren't holding services in a tent.

As they'd left the synagogue building Tovah knew she'd be spending most of the next two days there. She had to ask about the other two buildings, the synagogue's near neighbors. At a distance of several hundred feet there was a huge semicircular structure of corrugated metal with a sign proclaiming, "U Wash It." Could it be a laundry?

"I've never seen anything like that," she admitted as they got back in Teddy's SUV.

"The far one is a coin operated car wash," Janice said. "You know – you put in quarters to turn on the water for a few minutes. They give you a packet of car wash detergent or something. You wet the car down, scrub it, then put more quarters in and spray the gunk off. It's all recycled water of course. God knows what's in it. I wouldn't go near the place."

"I wouldn't go near the restaurant either," Teddy said, making a face. They had just started to drive away but Teddy stopped his car when they had a clear view of their closest neighbor.

"I'm sure they're still using the original oil to cook their chickens. One guy owns all the land and both the buildings. He will never sell to us. He thinks I'm irresponsible, because I build commercial shopping centers and big houses. I think he ought to be arrested for littering. Just look at that place."

"It's hard to believe anyone would eat at a restaurant called Chicken Feathers," Tovah said.

"I think it was considered clever in the sixties or seventies when it was built, some kind of anti-commercial statement," Janice said.

The restaurant was made up of white, turquoise blue and aluminum finished triangles, tethered together in a metal frame to make a roughly teepee-shaped structure.

"What worries me is the time will come when someone will decide that thing is an historic landmark and they'll make us preserve it," Teddy said.

"They wouldn't," Tovah said.

"This is California, Rabbi," Teddy said. "You can't know what they'll do. We can only hope it doesn't happen. I can't do anything about it. I can't even get the owner – his name is Berg – to meet with me. He will not sell."

When they returned to the Stein's home Tovah could tell she'd passed some sort of a test. Her calm acceptance of the synagogue's building had clearly been a relief to Janice and Teddy.

Thinking back on it, not only did Tovah feel she'd done well in her response to the building, she also felt extremely well rested. It was only seven a.m. Of course it would be nine a.m. in Minneapolis. Not only had she caught up on sleep, she had a couple of hours before her round of meetings and interviews began.

This morning Tovah's surroundings couldn't have been more different from the building housing the congregation. French doors in her room led out to a private patio. She stepped outside into sparkling sunshine and picture-perfect surroundings. Her little patio was framed by an exotic garden. The distant view was of unending blue, the sky blending seamlessly into the Pacific Ocean.

Her response to these surroundings was nothing she would have expected. Two prayers came to her mind, and then to her lips. One was the blessing said on seeing great natural beauty, the other when seeing the ocean after a long interval.

*"Blessed are You, our God, Sovereign, who has such as these in the world. Blessed are you, our God, Ruler of the Universe, who has created the great sea."*

She'd said those words without forethought, a response to her childhood training. She was amazed and somewhat scornful of herself. Easy enough to be shocked into praise once in a while, when surrounded by such beauty. To be able to praise regularly, took conscious effort and hard work.

Then, without belaboring her own responses any further, and following the same instinct that had let her to say those prayers so spontaneously, she went inside, opened her suitcase and took out her prayer book, prayer shawl and phylacteries.

Start right now. This is what you wanted.

She hadn't thought of personal prayer when she'd packed her prayer paraphernalia. She needed some of it for the lesson she would present to the preteens who made up the synagogue's Bar and Bat Mitzvah class.

The last time Tovah had prayed regularly, at the fixed hours, had been in those terrible months right after Leah's birth.

Praying when your child was in trouble was obvious. The response of awe in such overwhelming new surroundings was also obvious. Both reactions were momentary. To really make prayer mean something, to connect, to have prayer serve, there had to be discipline. Prayers said at the time prescribed for them. Prayer as a regular practice got you somewhere. If you were going to grow spiritually, if you were ever going to have some sense of the Divine, you had to embrace a powerful *kavannah*, intention. Praying was just like exercise. The ritual of praying regularly helped you develop the ability to pray.

Well, if this synagogue wanted her as a spiritual leader, this was part of what she should be doing.

She went back out to the little patio and faced east toward Jerusalem, away from the ocean, she prayed the morning service.

When she finished twenty minutes later she noticed Janice standing in the doorway between her room and the patio.

"I knocked, honest. I've only been here a minute or two," her hostess said. She seemed embarrassed, as if one or the other of them had been caught doing something questionable or excruciatingly personal. "I thought you'd gone out for a walk or something, or maybe you were in the shower. I didn't think you'd mind." She lifted the tray she carried a little higher.

"You didn't need to bring me breakfast," Tovah said, speaking with calm she didn't actually feel. At the same time she quickly began un-wrapping the leather straps holding the phylacteries, one on her head and one on her left arm. Then she carefully folded her prayer shawl.

"I didn't," Janice said. "I mean I brought breakfast for both of us. Teddy and the girls have been up since five-thirty. They like to ride before school."

Tovah had to help Janice over the little hump of embarrassment she obviously felt. Just be ordinary, she told herself. This is all normal. "Breakfast for the two of us on this beautiful patio will be a treat," she said.

Together, the two women set out their breakfast on a small round mosaic table. Tovah kept up an easy chatter, even though she had some trouble thinking of what to say. The garden surrounding the patio, short, sturdy palm trees and several huge cacti, some of them topped with a large red or yellow blossom, provided one topic.

Janice had brought toasted bagels and a platter of cream cheese surrounded by fresh tomato slices, rounds of crisp cucumber, and purple onion slices. "This looks so delicious," Tovah said.

She knew enough to recognize the dishes her hostess used so casually were valuable collectibles, stoneware only made in California for a limited time early in the century. She would have liked to ask about them, but it wasn't the right moment. Clearly, Janice had something on her mind more important than her dishes.

By the time they sat down Tovah was more comfortable because Janice was more at ease. Tovah hadn't been doing anything wrong. In fact; quite the opposite. But she had to wait for Janice. Finally her hostess couldn't contain her questions.

"Do you do it every morning? Pray, I mean? I've never seen a woman use *t'fillen*. Are you really very, very religious?"

Those were not the questions Tovah had expected. She needed a few more seconds before she answered. She had to reach inside. Her arsenal, her tools, included the beauty of the place, the peace of the moment, and her prayers. She didn't want to sound lame, or sanctimonious, so she said, "What's the most important question to you?"

"You seem ... regular. Very normal," Janice said. "And you're a single mother. How will you manage here, if you're really religious? I guess I'm most curious about the *t'fillen*. I've never seen a woman pray with them."

In the few moments she'd had between Janice's eager questions, and her answer, Tovah made a choice. It was like taking off a jacket when it became too warm. Consciously, she tried to put aside as many of her old machinations as she could identify. She wouldn't try to make things happen here. If she really wanted to be a very different rabbi than she'd been in Minneapolis, everything had to be different. The difference had to be fundamental, including how she got the job.

It was almost as if she uttered another prayer: if this is going to happen, let it be because I'm as honest as possible. If it doesn't work, at the very least I want the people I meet this weekend to think of me as a *mensch*, not as a performer.

A *mensch* was a full human being. There could be no greater compliment.

Tovah had finished preparing her bagel and she'd stirred sweetener into her coffee. She said, "Tough questions though. All of them. Let me see."

She was happy Janice didn't seem to mind a delay.

Finally Tovah said, "I don't think I'm any more religious than other rabbis. I hope the m*itzvot* I observe would help me, not slow me down. *Mitzvot*, commandments, should do that. In strictly traditional terms, I'm probably less religious than many. I eat in restaurants, not meat. I don't eat shellfish or pork. I don't go driving aimlessly on the Sabbath, although I'll use the car to get to the synagogue or to a Sabbath activity.

"As to the *t'fillen*; any Jew can use them, they're traditional. So, any Jewish women can use them, once she knows how. It's not so difficult. Women have to think about them in a different way. They were exclusively male for so long."

She paused again then said, "Of course being a rabbi was a male thing too, for a very a long time. It isn't any more."

"No, it's not. It's certainly not," Janice agreed. She sat back, considering Tovah. "This is all going to be so fascinating," she said, with deep satisfaction.

Tovah knew she hadn't told Janice the whole truth. This wasn't about disclosure, and she really had no idea of what else she might have said. She had not said using *t'fillen* was still an experiment for her. She had not admitted she'd not said regular morning prayers in more than three years, and even when she had, it had only been for an isolated period of time, those months in Stratton staying with Leah. What was unusual was nothing she'd said had been planned. She hadn't intended to even mention being or becoming a rabbi might be different for a woman. It ought not to be any different, ideally. But, one thing she knew now; life was rarely ideal.

Since she'd agreed to this interview, she had experienced something profound and important. Clearly how she did things was changing. She would just have to live with the fact she wouldn't know if she was doing the right thing until this interview was over. It might take even longer.

# CHAPTER THIRTEEN

Tovah returned to Minneapolis late Thursday night, both exhilarated and exhausted. After California the cold February weather was a shock. Her successful trip wasn't the only reason for her flood of emotions. How was she going to tell Dan she was picking up and moving to California?

Robin was waiting for her. She'd put Leah and Ari to sleep in their own beds and established herself in the living room. It wasn't a very big room, and neither Dan nor Tovah had worried about making it look larger. They had painted the room a deep tan and then lined two of the walls with bookcases. The television, nestled in a corner, was hardly noticeable unless it was on. Robin had only one light on, the reading lamp beside the beige plush chair where she'd been sitting over one of her books.

The room probably looked more inviting than usual, because now Tovah knew they would be moving. For a second or two she tried to imagine how her furniture would look in California, in a vastly different home.

Robin went into the front hall to retrieve her ski jacket. Then she came back to pick up the pile of books she'd brought with her.

"Okay. I've got to run, but before I go, tell me: Do you have news?"

"I got the job. They told me just before I left. The husband in my host family is the president of the congregation. He loved being able to say 'yes.'"

"I hate he said yes." Robin finished putting on her jacket, holding up one hand to stop any comment from Tovah.

"I know, I know. You need to do this. But, I'll miss you. What am I going to do without you?"

"Just what I'm going to do without you: survive. But we're not going to lose touch, right?"

"Are you kidding? I still have all this stuff to get through." Robin gestured toward Tovah with the books now piled in her arms. "I've got to finish this Introduction to Judaism course and get converted."

"And get married," Tovah said.

"I'm not so sure about marriage right now," Robin said. She stood there a moment, her face impassive. Then she turned and walked out to the hall where she stepped into her boots. Tovah followed, waiting for Robin to say more. Something was going on, but it never paid to push Robin. She actually had her hand on the doorknob before Tovah was driven to ask, still trying to be as casual as possible.

"You're still not sure about marriage? Even with the baby coming? Is it Dave?"

Robin didn't meet Tovah's gaze, but she didn't turn the doorknob either.

"No, Dave's all for marriage, now," she said. Then, finally, she turned back to Tovah.

"I'm having trouble with Dave's level of commitment. It's like he wants me to be Jewish. I want to be Jewish. But, Dave doesn't want me to be too Jewish. I don't know how to do that. What if he thinks of marriage like that; not wanting to be too married?"

Robin tried to smile, but couldn't. Tovah rushed to her side.

"Dave would never feel that way. He's totally committed to you. You know it. He's committed to you, Sunny and to the baby. As for the Jewish part, it was something he avoided for so long. You'll have to give him time. Why didn't you say something before?"

Robin did smile this time. "You mean because you had nothing else on your mind."

"It doesn't matter what else is happening. Look at all the help you've been to me and you have a lot on your mind, too. Before I go we're going to set some dates."

"I'm not marrying Dave if I'm not sure," Robin said.

"I'm not leaving him either," she added. "We could just go on as we are, except I'll be Jewish."

"Of course you're not leaving him. But, Robin, your being Jewish will change things, maybe more than getting married. Before I go we'll get your date set for you conversion and then think about other dates, like for a wedding. Please, before I go, I've got to know you're moving forward." Tovah couldn't bear to leave Robin, her good friend, in limbo. Both of them so undecided about major aspects of their lives seemed unendurable.

Tovah watched as Robin ran across their two front yards and let herself in to her home. How long would it be before she had a friend like Robin again?

# CHAPTER FOURTEEN

Dan was grateful his first meeting with nuns was the same day Tovah landed in California for her job interview. Tovah would get the job if she wanted it. She always got the job. He was not going to think what her getting the job would mean. He would just focus on the task before him. He could concentrate too.

It was late afternoon when he and Jo walked over to the apartment where the Sisters of Sanctity lived in a complex of older, well-kept, three-story apartments not far from the Cathedral. Even though several of the sisters were obviously over seventy, their apartment was up two long flights of stairs

Every room in the apartment had one brightly painted wall—melon, yellow, or blue. The other three walls in each room were gleaming white. Each colored wall featured either a crucifix or a shrine of some sort while the white walls glowed with an amazing collection of art. Beside simple sketches, there were several large oils, watercolors and some complex computer art. Other than the art, the apartment was furnished very plainly. In the dining room there was a very long table with a dozen Windsor chairs around it. In the living room two long sofas faced each other, while several unmatched armchairs stood around in a random fashion, as though they were waiting for guests before they decided where they should be deployed.

Dan complimented Sister Delphine, who seemed to be the one in charge, on the art collection.

She said, "They've all been given to us as thank-yous, because some people think they ought to pay us somehow. I don't know why. But, one can't refuse a gift."

Sister Anne Marie, one of younger nuns, perhaps in her forties, smiled. "Sister Delphine would prefer all gifts were edible."

Sister Delphine seemed to be around fifty-five or sixty. She had arrived shortly after Dan and Jo, carrying a brief case as though she'd just come in from an office.

"We do need to eat, no matter what else happens. Beside guests, we have regulars like Marc and Jennifer. It gets very expensive."

"Marc and Jennifer are her son and daughter," Sister Anna Marie explained.

Dan didn't want to ask personal questions so he remained silent, but his face must have telegraphed his thoughts.

Sister Delphine didn't mind explaining. "I haven't always been a nun you know, just since some years after I was widowed. In religious life I'm just a beginner. Six years, isn't it? But, my comrades here made me the business manager. I handle the books, since I'm am accountant anyway. That's what I do for a living."

She reached down and patted her briefcase.

"Isn't being a nun for life?" Dan asked, confused.

"Of course it's for life," Sister Delphine said briskly. "But, from when I started to the end, not back to the beginning of time." They all laughed, including Dan.

These sisters didn't behave in the formal manner he'd expected from nuns. He knew very few nuns wore full habits any more, but even this group's clothing was a surprise. Delphine wore a fashionable royal-blue business suit, very much like something Tovah might have selected. Sister Anne Marie was wearing a "Save the Whales" t-shirt and creased chinos. The other members of the group wore either blue jeans and blouses, or simple cotton dresses.

Dan and Jo visited for more than an hour, sharing cake and coffee, passing the picture of Dan's mother from hand to hand.

No one knew Adele. Given the personal histories of the women in the group it wasn't surprising. The two oldest women had lived in a community in Brooklyn until their retirement. It turned out Sister Anna Marie taught physics at Columbia. She'd only been on staff there, and in this community, for five years. As Sister Delphine indicated, her day job as an accountant took her into Manhattan. Before becoming a nun she'd lived in the Midwest.

Sister Andrea taught at a private girls' school up near the very tip of Manhattan.

"My school is right next to The Cloisters," she explained to Dan. "Isn't a cloister an appropriate place for me to spend the day?" It took Dan a second or two to realize she was making a joke about nuns who lived in convents or cloisters.

The most valuable thing the nuns could offer Dan was contact with other religious communities.

"You need to contact these groups," Delphine said, handing him the list she'd tapped out on her computer, then printed. "When you're done – if you've not had any luck – call us and we'll prepare another list. These seem to us the most likely groups. They've been in the area the longest, and we think they have the highest percentage of sisters who've lived around here for a long time."

Dan couldn't figure out how he felt as he took the list – hopeful or overwhelmed.

Sister Delphine seemed to be able to read the ambiguity on his face.

"I know. This must seem hard. This project will keep you very busy, and there will be a lot of dead ends. But it's taken thirty-odd years – all of your life – not to find her. Now you look, and we'll pray."

When Dan and Jo parted company near her apartment she was complacent. "Well, you've got your work cut out for you in the next few days."

Dan didn't say anything, but somewhere deep inside panic welled up.

# CHAPTER FIFTEEN

Bzzzzzt. Bzzzzzt. Dan's eyes snapped open. He grabbed for the alarm clock. Eight-fifteen? He hadn't turned on the alarm last night. He hadn't turned it on for the last several days. How could something be ringing?

He didn't have a phone. Two more bursts of noise, briefer, but insistent: Bzzzt. Bzzzt. What was that?

Then he realized the ringing had to be the front door buzzer for his apartment. He'd never heard it before. He never had visitors. He closed his eyes. In another second the person at the front door would realize their error.

Bzzt, Bzzzt, Bzzzzzt. Whoever was perched on the doorstep was not leaving. He'd actually have to go downstairs and give them hell. People ought to be certain of an address before they ran around waking people out of a sound sleep so early in the morning.

Bzzzzt. Bzzzzt. The sound grated horribly on his tender nerves. He got out of bed. Could he see who was standing on the front stoop from the window? He climbed over the extended Murphy bed to get to the windows, but the once-elegant, decorative stonework around the building's front door blocked his view. He could see clearly across the street, but his own building's front door was out of sight.

Finally, exasperated, he climbed into a pair of dirty jeans, briefly considered adding the sweatshirt he been wearing ever since he'd come back from his first meeting with nuns. He rejected the shirt. He grabbed his keys and ran down the two flights of stairs to ground level, ready to break the finger resting on the bell. Bzzt. Bzzt. The sound grew somewhat fainter as it followed him down the stairs, but it persisted right up the moment he opened the door.

Jo stood on the top step of the stoop. She removed her finger from the bell when he opened the door.

Dan didn't know what to think, so he didn't even try to hide his surprise at finding her on his doorstep. "What's wrong? Where's the fire?"

"Well, not under you, that's for sure," she said. "Come on. We're going to breakfast. I'll wait right here while you get dressed."

Dan didn't argue. He trudged upstairs, jamming his key in the lock while trying to open the door. He scowled at his crowded, untidy room, but ignored the mess in favor of getting dressed. He'd been dreading this inevitable confrontation.

Without speaking a word Jo led him to a Broadway Avenue café just around the corner. There she ordered eggs over easy, toast and coffee for two without asking. She waited, still silent, until the food was on the table.

Dan sipped his coffee and looked down at his plate. "The condemned ate a hearty meal?"

"Eat. Then we'll talk."

"Look, Jo … I know you think I should have … at least started the calls. I couldn't quite … Anyway, I've decided to wait to go any further. What if Tovah asks me to come home? I thought I'd wait until I've talked to Tovah again, and that's sometime today."

"I think you should eat before we talk," she repeated.

Dan picked up his fork and poked at the eggs on his plate. He put the fork down again.

"I'm not sure what happened. But suddenly, it seemed to me that I wouldn't find her no matter what I did. No matter how many nuns prayed. Also, I've probably blown it with Tovah. I can tell. Maybe that was what I wanted, to be let off the hook."

"I don't believe you for one moment," Jo said. I know you didn't phone anyone, because I know people in many of the communities on your list. Someone would have called me. I think you've chickened out, because now you think you might actually find your mother"

"Now there's a logical theory," Dan said. Sarcasm made the breakfast in front of him look almost palatable.

"Being sarcastic isn't going to convince me you really believe that. You won't even convince yourself. You care too much about all this. If you find your mother you'll have to tell Tovah. If you find your mother, you'll have to deal with the question of why she left you. Maybe Tovah won't take you back. Maybe your mother doesn't want to be found. Yes, you might have two angry women to deal with. Counting me, there would be three, especially if you don't get going. At least you'll know why I'm angry. Maybe I'm partly a stand-in for the other two."

Surprisingly Jo put down her fork then, the expression on her face one of distaste. She must be very upset. Usually Jo could eat no matter what was going on.

"This is very risky stuff," she said. "If you're going to stop after you've come this far, put so much you value, so much you love, at risk, I think at least you ought to understand what you're doing to yourself."

Jo went silent, although, to have something to do with her hands she picked up her knife and toyed with it. Dan didn't respond. He couldn't think of a thing to say. All he did was watch as Jo spread grape jelly on a piece of toast. Mere silence wouldn't stop her anyway.

Jo drew in a deep breath; put her toast down on the edge of her plate. "Anyway, I'm not telling you anything you don't already know. You went to earth since our first meeting, like a bear with a bad paw. You know exactly what you're doing. But, you and I have a deal. I'm supposed to contact groups of nuns for you. That is exactly what I have done. Here are two more groups very willing to talk to you."

She reached into her pocket and pulled out a sheet of paper with two addresses and phone numbers in her careful script.

"I need to know what you are going to do with this," she said, carefully holding the sheet of paper between her thumb and two fingers, as though it was some highly volatile substance.

Dan wasn't quite ready to give in. "A friend wouldn't attack this way," he said.

"If you believe that, you know nothing about friendship. I don't believe it. I am your friend. That's why I had to speak up. I don't want to see this whole project, everything you value, put more at risk. Naturally you're frightened by the progress you've made. So, are you going to let anxiety stop you from getting started?" She waggled the sheet of paper she held in her fingers.

Without moving forward Dan reached out his arm and snapped the paper from between her fingers. "I'm going to make and keep these appointments," he said.

"Good," Jo said. "I thought you would if … if I pushed a little."

Then she did just what Dan expected her to do, once their important discussion was concluded.

Jo finished her breakfast.

Dan did the same.

For days now Dan had been trying to tell himself that a simple difference of distance between him and the rest of his family, Minneapolis or Orange County, wouldn't matter. But, it would be hard to deny the symbolism.

His family would move. Tovah would get the job. That had to increase his sense of isolation. Not only would they be much farther away; but Tovah, Ari and Leah would have started on a whole new life and he would have no part in it.

# CHAPTER SIXTEEN

During Tovah's last weeks in Minneapolis her anger with Dan, as much as anything else, allowed her to work harder than she ever had before. She went to work every day, and kept up Leah's exercise routine. She arranged for their move, held a garage sale, and packed up boxes of towels, sheets, children's toys and books. The synagogue in California paid for moving her household, but she didn't want them charged for packing that sort of thing.

There were only a few fragile objects she packed herself. Robin came over the last day of packing to find Tovah wrapping Dan's synagogue models in bubble wrap. She was well aware Robin was watching her do a job the movers would have undertaken.

"I know. I know," she finally said. "I wasn't sure I was even going to take them."

"What decided you?" Robin asked her voice carefully neutral. "Dave and I will keep them for you if you really don't want to take them."

Tovah turned from Robin abruptly and, moving very fast, she began jamming the carefully wrapped models into a half-filled china box.

"If you're going to break them, they'd be better off at our house," Robin said, wincing slightly at Tovah's unceremonious handling off Dan's work.

"Dave thinks they're real art pieces you know."

Tovah turned to face Robin, holding a bulbous packet in each hand.

"Don't look at me as though I'm out to break them. I'm not. I'm going to take them so the kids will continue to see them, so there's no point in them arriving broken. I could drop them from the second floor wrapped this way. They wouldn't break."

"You're probably right. But there's no reason to prove how carefully you wrapped them by treating them roughly," Robin said. "Let me finish this. Go work in the study. Once everything is boxed up we'll be finished." Robin took the wrapped synagogue models out of Tovah's hands then watched her friend retreat to her study to pack the last books.

A few minutes later, Robin joined Tovah in her study. Without asking what needed to be done, she sat down on one packed box of books, and, using a stack of two boxes as a desk, she began writing out sets of sequentially numbered labels, one for the each box, one for the mover's lists.

After several minutes Tovah said, "Nothing was going to break, you know."

"I know," Robin said. "But you'd talked about sending those models to Dan's parents. Then you decided you didn't want to be petty. You said you'd leave them with us. 'If Dan wants the damn things, he can arrange for them.' Dave would be happy to have them in the house. I'd bet he wouldn't even put them in the basement. He's put some of them on display. He really admires Dan's work."

"They're just models." Tovah. said, in the tone of voice an argumentative child might have used about another child's hobby.

"Tovah … "

"I know, I know. Believe me, every time I've walked past them in the last few weeks, and now, packing them up, I've wondered if my ignoring what you call 'Dan's work' drove him away, as much as anything else."

"You didn't drive him away. He had to go; a very different thing," Robin said.

Then she added hastily. "Or course he shouldn't have gone without saying something."

Tovah knew Robin half expected her to blow her top. Any defense of Dan tended to infuriate her. Today she just turned to look at her friend. Then, as though they'd orchestrated it, they looked away from each other.

There wasn't much for them to focus on in Tovah's study. She had sold her heavy old desk and the matching office chair. Now the room was only furnished with towers of packed book boxes and two rickety folding chairs not worth moving.

Tovah had no real idea of what her feelings were at the moment, besides being relieved they were almost finished all the packing, including Dan's damn models. To relieve her feelings, she kicked at the bottom of a stack of packed boxes piled five high.

"That would be one way to get them across the country; one good kick at a time." Robin teased, welcoming the opportunity to make a small joke.

"God, what a job this has been," Tovah said.

"We're almost done," Robin said. She handed the last batch of labels to Tovah, then stood up. With her hands on her hips and with her back arched, a typical position for a pregnant woman, she stretched.

"You're not doing too much, are you?"

"Are you kidding? All we're doing here is packing books, linens and toys. All I did tonight was write labels and count boxes. When Dave and I moved to Minneapolis from Fargo we did the whole thing. We hired a few men to load and unload, but we packed all the boxes, drove the truck, the works. That was on top of totally renovating the house. This is like a classy corporate move. A piece of cake."

"Well, you've done enough, more than enough. Sit down. It's only because I had your help that everything is finished. We even had a garage sale. I couldn't have done it alone. Dan couldn't have done it alone."

"I'm sure he could have managed, just as you have," Robin said. "Of course you're not required to admit anything, as long as your official position is that Dan has never done anything right"

"You can't really believe I'm being too hard on him?" Tovah knew her voice rose sharply when she talked about Dan. On the phone, talking to him, she could usually control it better. They had spoken several times. Some of their more heated conversations still reverberated.

"He's so ... so ..."

"I believe you've used stubborn, pig-headed and unreasonable in the last day or two," Robin said dryly. She perched on a stack of boxes three high. She gulped down a soft drink, watching as Tovah closed the very last box.

Tovah didn't respond directly. "He wanted to come here and stay with the kids until I got settled in California, then escort them out there. He almost had me convinced. He should have finished law school. He'd make quite a lawyer."

"Well, that wasn't the most practical idea. The place will be stripped. With hotels and everything...

"It was dumb. If he wants to see the kids he should say so."

Tovah was wielding a commercial packing-tape 'gun' like a professional. She pushed the last box into a corner, sat down heavily next to Robin. She picked up her own can of soda with one hand, using her other hand to finger-comb her black curls back into some kind of order even though she knew it just made her hair-do wilder.

"He hasn't upset the kids in some way, has he?" Robin asked.

"Only me. He's been the perfect long-distance dad. Last night he even read them a bedtime story over the phone. He's been absolutely positive with them about this move. He talks about Mommy's wonderful new job. He even ducks Ari's questions about visiting us."

"Visiting? Ari asked him when he's going to visit?"

"Well, no. Ari asked him when he was coming home to live with us forever."

"Dan didn't answer him directly? Didn't that upset Ari?"

"I think for the moment the kids are just happy to talk to him. It took Leah a little more time to warm up than Ari, but yesterday she was telling him all about our visit with her doctor."

"Tovah, everything the doctor told you was such good news. You were so excited. Shouldn't Dan know? After all, he did most of ..."

Tovah interrupted her. "He knows. He was just getting Leah's version. I spoke to him. I told him every word the doctor said. When we talk like that it's almost … it's okay. I know he did most of the work with Leah. I'm not quite sure why I let that happen. But, is the fact I didn't know every single thing any worse than Dan's reaction when the doctor suggested she might have Dystonia? Dan wouldn't normally have paid attention to an off-hand remark like that, unless everything was confirmed, checked and double-checked. Except this time he'd wanted to leave. He admitted as much. He didn't even do any research before he left, except for finding the Dystonia Foundation in Chicago. He ordered some material from them, but he didn't even wait for it to arrive. It came about a week ago."

"What did it say?"

"I didn't read it. I didn't even open it. I sent it on to him like a good wife. Before I saw the doctor I didn't want to know anything about it or I'd have seen the symptoms just watching Leah. She does not have Dystonia. The doctor assured me. He likes to float ideas past Dan, because Dan has such an incredible mind. The doctor thought Dan's response would be interesting. He thinks Dan should do more with the knowledge he has now."

"Well, what did Dan say when he heard it wasn't Dystonia?"

"He said clearly he'd jumped the gun. He badly needed to believe he had to find his mother. So, when the doctor mentioned the possibility of Dystonia he latched on to it. He said it gave him a reason to leave, an excuse."

"That was a big admission on his part," Robin said.

"Yes it was," Tovah agreed, clearly reluctant to make any kind of concession regarding Dan, but, equally, compelled to be fair.

Robin waited to hear more.

Tovah said, "I told him that. I used exactly the words you just used. I acknowledged he'd just made a major admission."

"And ..."

"He said, 'Thank you.'"

# CHAPTER SEVENTEEN

Janice Stein was directing Tovah and the children to her car.

"I brought the SUV for the baggage. It's over there."

Both women were steering luggage carts stacked high with suitcases. Janice grabbed at a duffel bag that kept slipping. The big white van was still a few cars further on.

Tovah grabbed for the duffel bag too, but she had to momentarily let go of her cart. It kept rolling. She didn't know if the duffle bag had fallen or not, because she heard something behind her and spun around to make sure the children were safe. They were fine, but a car was traveling toward them, moving too fast for her peace of mind. She hustled over to the children and took each one by the hand. As they walked back she could see her hostess holding on to both carts as she waited.

"Janice, I'm sorry you have to deal with all this. Someone else should have drawn airport duty. This is the second time for you."

"Are you kidding? This is my reward. I wanted to be the first to meet these two." Janice thumbed the SUV key ring and the rear hatch opened. She smiled at the children, and continued to corral both luggage carts, all without seeming stressed.

When Tovah had introduced the children to Janice in the luggage area at John Wayne Airport, both children had gravely offered to shake hands with her, just as Tovah had rehearsed them. Janice was much more the type to sweep a child into a hug, but she'd solemnly followed their lead.

She'd obviously given careful thought as to how to welcome children to California. "I brought some friends along," she said. "This is an Orca and her baby." She gave Ari two boldly patterned black and white plush toys linked together. "Did you know that Orcas aren't whales at all, they're dolphins?"

"This is a mother seal and her baby," she said to Leah. The seal mother was sleek and black and her pup was fuzzy gray. "Seal families come to California from far, far away, every single year. Just like you and your mom and your brother. You'll be able to see seals, and sometimes even whales, way out in the ocean, from a beach near your new house. You may have missed them this year, but they'll be back next winter."

The children looked sideways at Tovah, who smiled it was okay to accept the gifts, also mouthing they should say, "Thank You." Receiving a gift first thing hadn't occurred to her as a possibility, so she hadn't rehearsed that.

It was just past mid-day, so the traffic as they left the airport wasn't too bad. After a little more than half an hour of assuring the children that yes, the palm trees were real, and yes, it was still winter in Minneapolis, they arrived at their new home.

When Janice stopped the car in front of the house, the children stared even more than they had at the exotic trees and flowers. Tovah had forgotten how large the house was, even though their apartment just occupied the first floor.

"Here we are, about to move into a mansion and the *shul* is in what's basically a trailer. It's too bad we can't reverse it."

She'd already noticed Teddy and Janice Stein already corrected her when she referred to the synagogue as anything other than an industrial building. She tried to remember, but it really did look just like a big trailer.

"It's an industrial building, Rabbi," Janice said now. "And you're right, we can't reverse it. You can't have a synagogue right in the middle of a residential block anyway. And, there's not enough parking."

As they were getting out of the SUV, Janice laughed at the expressions on her passengers' faces.

"It is kind of California King Size. When we first built it, the architectural critic of the L.A. Times happened to be writing an article on these big new houses. He said developers like Teddy had delusions of grandeur. Teddy wanted to name this house Delusion of Grandeur, but of course I wouldn't let him."

She led the way up to the wrought-iron front gate that opened into a courtyard. The iron-trimmed front door had black iron-strap hinges. Once inside the house, they all stood a little crowded together, as though for comfort. The newly created vestibule still seemed too large.

Janice and Teddy had decided to convert a large home Teddy had built five years ago into two apartments.

Even half the building made a far larger home than any-thing Tovah had ever lived in before. There were large rooms, and an enormous kitchen, even a work room at the back of the apartment that would be perfect for Dan, if only …

Tovah couldn't go there, even in her imagination. Instead she concentrated on showing the children their bedrooms and thanking Janice for creating a perfect spot for Leah's exercise equipment, right off the new family room, separated by a three-quarter-height wall painted an intense shade of terracotta.

Tovah revisited the kitchen. Teddy had mentioned the kitchen was one of Janice's more innovative designs; a round room, with a curving granite counter encircled the large work space.

"Janice, you must know how spectacular I think this place is," Tovah said. "But, are you certain you'll want us living here long term? What if a customer for the house comes along?"

"'From your lips,' as they say. No, this is the right thing to do. We built this place almost five years ago. It's never been lived in, except for a few isolated rentals. We've already rented the other half. They don't move in for a month. Anyway, it's all been worth-while, just to see your face.

"But, right now we ought to go. When your furniture arrives you'll be able to get settled. Until then you guys bunk in our pool house. All three of my girls, but especially Shannon, want to introduce Ari and Leah to our horses."

The day after Tovah's furniture arrived, Janice and Teddy showed up bearing pizza and offering assistance with the unpacking. The children were already asleep in their new bedrooms.

Tovah greeted them, "You two, I do not have enough furniture for this place. I ought to be living in one of the cottages around here. They're more my size."

"If you need more furniture, we'll go shopping. But, no cottages for anyone I know, no matter what. They're tiny and they're dangerous. They tend to collapse during an earthquake."

Teddy Stein came in from the dining room where he had started flattening the boxes already unpacked. "Don't worry about furniture right now. This is going to look great. Don't worry about needing to move again. I may leave this place a duplex forever. I think it was jinxed as a single-family house. You'd think Dana Point would catch up with the times. Up and down the coast people buy up cottages, especially close to the ocean. They tear them down and rebuild. All the new houses are big, built right to the lot line. Everyone will do it here too, eventually. My problem was that for some reason I had to be first. I'm telling you, Rabbi, the guy who said never build the biggest, most expensive house on the block was right. To which I would add, don't do it first."

"I can promise you I'll never do it. Just moving into one part of this house is daunting. I can't imagine living in the whole space."

Teddy said, "Even Janice's kitchen didn't save this place. I made the worst error of my career on this house." Then, seemingly satisfied by his declaration, Teddy returned to the dining room.

Tovah had already figured out that Teddy Stein's official view of any subject of importance was run-away pessimism. She wasn't sure if it was a complex form of whistling in the dark, or psychologically more complicated. After many phone calls and a few days in California, she'd learned just to listen.

Speaking in the general direction of the next room, Tovah said, "You know, besides being beautiful, any kitchen that has space for all my dishes: meat, milk, Passover, good stuff and everyday stuff, plus all my collections, is a wonderful kitchen."

Teddy didn't come back into the room, but he shouted, "Great. When I do something right for someone, it's totally by accident. Just remember, you don't have a basement for extra storage. What you see; that's it."

Tovah had never lived in a house without a basement. "Do I need one? Where do we go if there's a big storm ... or an earthquake?"

"We'll make sure you have all the earthquake instructions. Don't worry. There wouldn't be any time to get to the basement. That's Midwestern; only good for tornadoes. It wouldn't help in an earthquake. You wouldn't want a building to cave in on you."

He came back into the kitchen. "You can just roll off the bed if it's night time. You stay there on the floor, or find a spot under a table, until things stop rocking and rolling."

Teddy put his arm around his wife. "Janice's earthquake guy is coming in the next couple of days. He'll fasten things to the wall. Bookcases, china cabinets, all the very big, heavy things or tall things need to be attached to the wall with special cables.

"This lady," Teddy gave his wife a big hug, "she'll mark where your pictures and mirrors will go. The earthquake guy will hang them with special hardware, so they don't jump off the wall and hit you during a quake."

It was clear from the expression of Janice's face that earthquakes were not her favorite topic. "I want to see if we created enough space for Leah's exercise equipment," she said.

Tovah went ahead of Janice. "I'll show you all her exercise gadgets, but the table is the most important. There's plenty of room; more than we had before actually. We even got started on Leah's routine. Yesterday and today we got her exercises done before we did anything else."

"I know it's none of my business," Janice said, "But there's not much wrong with her that I can see. She doesn't seem to really limp. Her run is a little halting. I've seen her running after our new pony. My girls said she can sit astride, no problem. I've noticed sometimes she seems to sort of sit on her hand, or at least shove it under her thigh. Oh, and I guess one eye turns out, but just a little. Is it lazy eye? They just patch the good eye; it's no big thing, you know."

"I'll have to tell Dan you wanted to know what was wrong with her. He'll be thrilled you couldn't see much. I'm thrilled. What she does with her hand is her way of stopping a spasm. Those might go on for a long time, we don't know. We're not sure what she'll need for her eyes, beyond glasses. What you see – or rather what you don't see – is the result of my husband spending more than three years working with Leah."

Before this Dan had always been the one to explain Leah's condition to people. After all, he was the expert. Tovah had never realized leaving it to him had been a kind of cowardice.

Dan had always been so calm and matter of fact when he talked about Leah. Exactly how she wanted to appear. Had it cost Dan as much effort as she now had to put into a simple explanation?

She had to find something to do as she talked, so she started to roll up a bright blue exercise mat, adjusting the Velcro straps carefully so the mat would stay in a tight coil when she put it away. "I'm thrilled to see her run. That's new. For the moment, I'll take halting without complaint. They said she'd probably never walk unaided. Originally the doctors said that she had Cerebral Palsy or worse. They said she'd need surgery, probably multiple operations, especially on her legs."

"Did your husband get overwhelmed by her condition?" Janice asked. Plainly, she was curious, but at the same time she obviously didn't want to appear too nosey. She gave Tovah a graceful out. "It's not really any of my business."

But Tovah had been looking for an opportunity to bring up Dan's name and this was it. "No, he wasn't overwhelmed. He did most of the work with her. Actually, he kept me from being overwhelmed. And, I guess I should tell you right now. He may be joining us. We've – the two of us – have been talking about it a little."

Janice only nodded, thankfully not pursuing the subject.

Tovah wasn't sure why she'd told Janice and Teddy Dan might move to California. It wasn't really true. The idea Dan might join them had barely been mentioned between them. She also realized that having a husband show up when they were legally separated would be almost as embarrassing as having had one disappear.

Neither of the Steins questioned her more closely. Teddy, who had been hovering nearby, probably to hear Tovah's answer too, helped moved things past the awkward moment by clapping his hands together and announcing, "Okay, ladies, fun time is over, let's get back to work."

# CHAPTER EIGHTEEN

Dan ended his day by walking over to meet Jo in her office at St. John the Divine. It seemed to him the only accurate measure of what he'd accomplish in New York would be how many cups of tea he'd had with what number of gracious middle-aged women. How many cookies had how many communities of nuns fed him? How many prayers, all useless so far, had been offered up on his behalf?

"Much more of this and I'm going to have to quit. Three meetings today, no sign of Adele as usual," he said to Jo. He dropped into an old club chair Jo kept for visitors.

Working in an elegant Cathedral didn't ensure elegant surroundings. Jo's office was much like Tovah's office at Temple Isaiah in Minneapolis, long and narrow, with furniture that was functional but not much more.

Jo glanced at the clock on the wall. Five p.m. She was ready to leave. She flipped off her computer, tapped some file folders together, looked at the huge lateral file in her office, clearly decided against putting the files away properly. Instead she jammed them into a desk drawer. Jo grabbed her tailored camel-hair coat, wound a gray, black and brown scarf around her neck and said, "Never mind quitting at this moment. You can always quit. Right now we have a dinner date."

"Okay," Dan said. He'd have to tell his story to yet another person, but he welcomed companionship at any meal. He tried to think of it as singing for his supper.

"We're meeting with Father Art. I think I told you, he's the more elderly of the two. He'd never admit it, of course. He and Father Angelo don't much like each other. Not that either of them would ever say so. It's far too uncharitable. But, I always meet them separately, and they never suggest otherwise. They're two of my regular monthly dates. It only occurred to me today, when I confirmed dinner with Father Art; he'd be a good person to talk to. I told him I was bringing a one-time guest. We'll meet with Father Angelo later."

In a few minutes they were sitting in a little bistro just off Amsterdam Avenue. A second or two after they were settled, Jo pointed to the door. "There he is."

Dan stood up, bracing himself for another encounter where he had to talk about Adele. He introduced himself to The Reverend Father Art Toscan and took the elderly priest's coat and his walker, folding it up and storing it neatly. "No one will take it, will they?" Dan said as he sat down again.

"They wouldn't dare," the frail-looking old man said emphatically. Father Art had to be close to ninety. His complexion was what Tovah referred to as "cancer-treatment gray."

After they'd ordered and their salads were in front of them, the priest said, "Since we don't usually have company at dinner, you must be one of Jo's special cases." He peered at Dan, seemed to find him satisfactory. "She adopts people, you know. After they've passed a most rigorous screening."

Jo made a face. "He thinks I ought to take a leaf out of the book of St. Jude when I try to help someone. He thinks it would be good for me to be disappointed sometime."

"St. Jude?"

"He's the patron saint of lost causes. I don't like lost causes. I like solvable causes."

"She always knows which is which," the priest said. "So, I assume you are a 'solvable?'"

"Well, I hope so. But, so far, we haven't solved a thing."

The expression on Jo's face telegraphed a question to Dan: did he mind being categorized as one of her "causes?" Dan smiled back at her. He didn't mind at all. He'd needed every moment of her help just to get this far.

Since the subject of his 'cause' had already been introduced, Dan pulled out his all-important drawing and without explanation he put it on the table in front of Father Art.

However physically frail Father Art might be his intellect was untouched. When he saw the drawing he put his salad to one side. "I can see food is a secondary consideration tonight."

He picked up the drawing, and turned it slightly to eliminate any glare from the plastic cover. He examined the image minutely. Then he refocused on Dan, looking at him even more intently than before. "Your mother," he said, not a question.

Dan nodded.

"Of course, you'd like to find her."

Dan nodded again.

Father Art examined the picture again for several long seconds.

"I never thought I'd see her again," Father Art said to Dan, in the most matter-of-fact way.

This man had better say something more very quickly, Dan thought, or I'll die on the spot. The words he'd just heard seemed to have quashed the beating of his heart.

When the old priest finally did speak again, Dan could feel his heart thump loudly back into operation. "Her name is Adele, right? She lived over at Holy Family. It has to be forty years ago."

Speaking very calmly, Jo said, "Not quite forty, but close."

"Of course, you're the baby. She was going to have a baby. She was terribly afraid her husband would find her before her baby was born," Father Art said, as though such a precious piece of information was common knowledge.

Dan blinked and managed to say, "Husband? She didn't have a husband."

"She didn't? For a woman without a husband, she certainly was afraid of him. Now I realize it must have been a situation of domestic abuse. God help me – and her – I used to tell her we could help her make peace with him. I said it so easily: first peace, then she could go back home and have her baby and they'd live happily."

"She didn't listen to you?" Jo asked. She realized the double shock Dan had just received, first having his mother whereabouts around the time of his birth confirmed by someone who'd known her, plus being told she'd been married, had robbed him of the ability to speak.

"No, she didn't. She knew her own mind. She knew better than I did. Once or twice when we talked, she looked at me as though I must be a simpleton, or a child. She said, 'Father, just because you cannot fathom these kinds of things, doesn't mean they don't happen.'"

The old man seemed to still regret the errors he'd made so long ago. His sigh was large and gusty. "She was right of course."

"He hit her?" Outrage made Dan capable of spitting out those few words.

"I don't know exactly what he did. She did say there were worse things than hitting. She wouldn't talk about it. She seemed to know I was trying to help, but as I said, she thought I was impossibly naïve. She was right. I don't think she'd have left him over occasional abuse. Unfortunately, she might have accepted that as normal. She left because she knew he would take their baby away with him. Then she'd have to go, too. He felt it was their country; they had an obligation to help. He believed they'd be welcomed. She didn't believe that for one minute."

"Take the baby? Take it where?" Those questions tumbled from Dan, as though the baby they were discussing had nothing to do with him.

The priest was looking past Dan and Jo now, recalling long-ago memories.

"To Vietnam, of course. You do know she was from Vietnam?"

Dan parroted, "Vietnam," as though he'd never heard of the place.

"It's amazing how clear it all is to me," the old priest said. "As though it happened yesterday. In fact, yesterday isn't nearly as clear."

"Sure it is," Jo said, patting his hand companionably.

"Their families were in part Vietnamese. They had very different reactions to their personal histories. He apparently believed his background gave him rights to the whole world. She believed that because of her family she'd never fit in anywhere. She said she'd felt that way all her life."

An electric pain ran through Dan, a moment of intense kinship. It wasn't love. He loved his adoptive parents. He knew they loved him. Despite their love, all his life he'd felt like a stranger. Now he was being told his mother had felt the same.

He didn't say anything. Jo was silent too. They could not have stopped Father Art's cascade of memories anyway.

"They were both such handsome people. She showed me a few of the family pictures she'd taken with her when she left.

"She was very beautiful. She said her husband had married her, because she was beautiful and well educated. She certainly had no vanity about it; if anything it seemed to be a burden. Anyway, her husband had once admitted to her that no highborn Chinese family would consider him as a husband for their daughters. That had made him very angry."

"Chinese?" Dan's fragile moorings had been slashed again. "What does China have to do with this?"

"He was born in China. You don't know? He'd never been to Vietnam. His family was mostly French, and in some part Vietnamese and Chinese. Her family was essentially similar, although only Vietnamese I believe. She'd been born there, lived there until she was sent away to school."

Father Art handed the drawing back to Dan saying, "This doesn't really do her justice." He looked around, clearly ready to eat.

Dan took the picture. He still couldn't find the words for the myriad questions flooding through his brain.

"You're sure she was married?" Somehow, as Dan's surrogate, Jo knew just the right questions.

"She was. She didn't want to be, not any more. She didn't know what to do about it. We talked about a church annulment. A Catholic marriage, you know."

Jo spoke again, watching Dan. "And she didn't want to go to Vietnam?"

"She wouldn't go," the priest said emphatically. "She said they'd all be killed if they went. I think it might have been a very extreme reaction, but she believed it, absolutely."

"He didn't agree?"

Father Art put his fork down, resigning himself to not eating yet. "No. Her husband believed they would be treated as heroes returning to help their country. She said he'd never been there, he couldn't possibly understand. She said the authorities wouldn't listen long enough to welcome them. They were both from what were considered exploitive colonial families. The time when Vietnam was a French Colony had been very bad. She knew there would be a list with their names on it. They'd be killed as soon as they arrived. She said even if the government accepted them initially, because they needed their skills, they'd be killed later. Some fanatic would do it if the government did not. Either way, they would be going to their death."

"So he wanted to go to North Vietnam, to the Communists?" Jo kept the conversation going because clearly Dan could not.

"I don't think he made such a distinction. He felt the country would be united very soon. The Communist government would be in charge. Of course he proved to be correct in his prediction. Certainly he intended to go to the North. His timing was off, of course, but, in the long run he was correct. The country became one again."

"She ran away to be safe?" Dan managed to ask.

"Well, I suppose, in part. She really left him so her child -— you – would be safe. Not obeying her husband was very hard. So was hiding from him. She left while he was out of the country on a work-related assignment."

"What was his work?"

Retrieving the memory took Father Art a few moments. He picked up his fork, as though he might be able to work in a bite or two of salad. He even took a piece of French bread out of the basket on the table. If Father Art had actually started eating, Dan would have wrenched his fork out of his hand. But, just then the old priest said triumphantly. "He did some kind of analysis of natural resources for an arm of the U.N. He was a graduate of one of the major western military colleges, you know." He grinned at the two of them triumphantly, delighted at his powers of recollection.

Father Art didn't seem to understand Dan knew very little about his mother and nothing about his father. The possibility he would be able to identify his father had never occurred to him. Only Adele had any reality. His parents had met her. He had the drawing. He knew Adele had never mentioned his father to his parents, except to claim that of the two of them he was 'more white.' Dan had worried 'more white' had been her way of saying there had been many men – all of them 'more white.' He'd worried his mother might not have known which man had been his father.

"She had to leave her job at the U.N. Just walk out. She couldn't give notice or anything. It bothered her. She was a respected translator." Dan could nod agreement on that point of information at least.

"Then, once she came here, she stayed very close to the churches and her other places of refuge."

"She didn't think he'd come searching for her?"

"She hoped he'd think she'd gone to her family in France. He didn't know the strength of her belief. He wouldn't think of a church as her refuge."

Dan's shock had ebbed somewhat by now; at least he'd found his tongue.

"But my parents, my adoptive parents, are Jewish, not Catholic."

"She told me. She said our Lord was a Jew too."

"So she told you quite a lot. You just said she thought …"

"She thought I was naïve. Yes. Well. She was right, you know. Eventually I promised I would not look for her husband. I swore it. Most of what she told me came all at once, one day toward the end of her pregnancy. It all poured out. By then she understood I respected her choices. I knew I would not be able to change her mind."

"Change her mind about what?" Had Adele not wanted to give him up? Had this priest been the one who'd suggested adoption as a course of action to her?

"Change her mind about any or all of it. She knew I accepted, I honored, all her decisions, including giving up her child. She said her child would have a family, a stable family, if she gave him or her up for adoption. If she kept her baby – if she kept you – both of you would be on the run all your lives. Her husband would pursue her if he knew she'd kept their child. It would be worse if he ever found out she'd had a boy. She always thought you'd be a boy."

"She was determined her baby would be an American, with an American family, a white family. That was important to her. So he would belong someplace, she said."

The elderly priest seemed lost in his memories again. Then he added something Dan didn't understand, but something Jo understood immediately. "Of course once I knew it also involved a vocation, I couldn't stand in her way."

"She had a vocation?" Jo asked. Surprise made her voice high and thin.

"She certainly seemed to. Once I knew, I felt all I could do was support her. It isn't always for us to repair every problem. That can be a kind of mania too. She wasn't a congregant. She was one of our Catholic waifs."

This last was another aside to Jo, one religious professional to another. "I was finally able to let go of the idea I could fix everything for her. She didn't tell me about her vocation or her long-range plans until she saw that was true."

"What was her plan? What do you mean; a vocation?" Dan said. Although still shocked from his new discoveries, he could speak again. In fact his questions were aggressive, although he was afraid of the answers he might get, things he'd never anticipated.

"She was going to have her baby, and then she was going to join a very strict religious community somewhere, the Sisters of the Sacred Infant of Mary, some such name. I wonder if she did it. Is she still with them? I don't see why she wouldn't have done it. She was a most determined young woman, a real force."

Father Art looked Dan up and down as though searching for traces of the force of his mother's personality.

Dan doubted he exhibited anything like force. He couldn't even figure out how he was supposed to respond to all this news. No part of this would help him locate Adele. Did he still want to find her? Originally there had been the reason, or the excuse, of needing to find his mother's medical history.

But, if leaving his family was to have some meaning, there had to be more than what he'd just learned from this elderly priest.

Certainly Father Art would never have asked Adele about her medical background. As to the story of the conflict between his birth parents, he wasn't sure how he felt hearing about it. He had a loving family. Leah did not have Dystonia. Did he really need to know more? Would he be wrong to search further? Perhaps this new information would be enough to bring back to Tovah and the children. At least he'd be able to claim he'd resolved some of the question that had pulled him away from his family.

But now there were so many more dimensions to his mother. Adele wasn't just a face in a sketch anymore.

What resonated most, and terribly, was that for all her life Adele had felt an alien in the world around her. Nothing could have made her more real to Dan. How terrible, despite everything she'd tried to do for him, he felt the same way. Could you inherit such feelings? Common sense said no. But a mother and son might well have come to share similar feelings. Vastly differing circumstances could have produced the same sense of alienation.

He didn't especially welcome a creeping sense of identification with Adele. He'd come looking for information, not emotion.

Father Art had no idea what Dan was thinking, but unwittingly he addressed the issue. "I tried to argue that the major reason her husband felt so differently from her, was because as a male and an eldest son he had always been valued."

"Did she agree with you?" Dan said.

"She seemed to think it might be true, at least in part. She knew perfectly well to the Chinese a first born son is almost revered."

Dan flushed when he heard what the priest had said. He was a first-born son and his mother was able to give him up.

Dan leaned urgently toward Father Art, grasping his arm. "What else can you tell me?"

Apparently one simply did not clutch at the elderly priest. Jo scowled at Dan. Father Art looked like he'd been struck. Jo reached over and patted her old friend's hand.

Father Art shifted away from Dan. "I don't think I really understood how she felt. Pointing out to her that to anyone in this country most of her family appeared to be Caucasian didn't seem to help. Besides, "passing" for white isn't now and wasn't then a value I wanted to espouse."

Dan could feel his own cheeks burning. When he'd first met Tovah, he'd sometimes tried to get her to say he looked white. She never would. He might very well have hated her, not loved her, if she'd agreed looking white was preferable. Even though, at that time, he would have liked to hear her say it.

Father Art said, "She liked to hear they appeared Caucasian. She thought looking white – the term she used – would help her son." Had he somehow absorb Adele's attitude? He'd always heard the comments about how handsome or exotic looking he was as code for looking like an outsider.

When Dan was a child his father had developed a stock answer for people who commented on his son's looks, or who pointed out that he didn't resemble either of his parents. Alan Goldin always said, "Lucky, isn't he?"

Obviously his father had wanted to protect him, to deflect any further questions, but perhaps his careful response had helped make Dan ultra-sensitive about his appearance.

So far the three of them around the table had barely started on their salads. The waiter came over to see if anything was wrong. He hovered for a very long moment, but no one said a word to him. Jo and Dan were caught up in Father Art's memories.

"Apparently it was a Jewish man who helped her get away, who found Holy Family for her, who gave her enough cash to get through all those months. She stayed with his family for a while too, until things were arranged for her at Holy Family. He was a lawyer who worked at the U.N."

A lawyer? His father's late partner, Dan thought. Their firm had always done international work. His parents had said he'd been the partner who had 'helped' with Dan's adoption. Dan always assumed he'd helped with paperwork. Now he understood what they really meant, and why his wife had been able to sketch Adele. She'd known Adele even before his parents met her.

"She said he was very kind. He would have helped her get to France, if she'd insisted. But, he was the one who convinced her that her husband would look in France the very first thing. He made a very good argument; it wouldn't occur to her husband to look for her in uptown New York, close to Harlem, in this somewhat 'tough' neighborhood."

Dan looked around. Their surroundings didn't appear very tough. It was just a little neighborhood bistro. There were hundreds of them in New York. He'd never come back to this one though. It would be too painful. He'd probably never eat wild mushroom risotto again. Forever, this would be the place where he'd found it awkward to think of his mother as simply Adele, a character in a melodrama.

How he wished Tovah was at their table. Her presence would have made the evening perfect. He would have liked to be able to take her hand, to share this with her. He'd also have liked her to acknowledge his search had been a reasonable undertaking.

Dan wasn't paying strict attention to Father Art any longer. The elderly priest's recollections had meandered a little into a more general vein. "This neighborhood wasn't really so rough then, but people were moving much farther downtown, or out to the suburbs. It got much worse later. Now it's getting better again."

Jo knew Dan still didn't have the information he wanted. "How did she come to select Dan's family?" she asked.

"The lawyer said he knew a family who wanted a child very badly, a Jewish family.

"Adele thought it would be extra protection. Who would consider a Jewish child might be part Asian? Of course we know many such children now. We were much more parochial then. Multi-racial adoptions were just getting started."

During his childhood Dan had often wondered how he could be Jewish. He'd only heard of one or two Asian-Jewish people his age. Later, even when he knew many American Jewish families had adopted Asian and part-Asian children, it hadn't changed his feelings.

Father Art had picked up his fork again, toying with it. He must be hungry. By now he seemed to understand Dan needed any details he could recall. "There's one other important thing: your adoptive family was willing to meet with her. Such a meeting was a very unusual thing then. She liked them very much. She said they were good people; educated, cultured people. She said over and over; they were people who knew who they were. They would make sure her child felt the same, the most important thing to her."

Maybe he should stop looking for Adele, Dan thought. How could he ever tell her the most important part of her plan had failed? She would hate to hear it. He'd hate to have to tell her.

"She was impressed the woman lent her -– she actually said, gave her – the use of her name. She was registered under your adopted mother's name at the hospital, and with her doctor, too. It was quite a common practice then, in private adoptions."

Jo leaned back in her chair. "So! A much more amazing story than we thought. But, we found her."

Dan had enjoyed a fleeting moment of triumph initially, when he'd imagined sharing this news with Tovah. But, as they actually ate their dinner, he had to consider what all this new information meant to him. He had no real idea.

✡

When Dan returned from his dinner with Father Art and Jo he did the only thing he could think of. He called Tovah, who was still at her office. The phone in the ground floor vestibule of his apartment building no longer seemed too public.

"Tovah, I found her," he said. Then, to his horror, he started to cry.

"Dan, are you all right? Did you say you found her? You found your mother? Is she in New York?"

Bless her; she didn't mention his crying.

"No. I have no idea where she is. I mean I know exactly where she was while she was pregnant. And, she was married. So much is different from what I thought. A retired priest at St John knew her very well."

"Oh, Dan. She was married? My goodness! But, she wasn't sick was she? She didn't have any kind of condition, nothing like Leah's problems? I don't believe it. The doctor assured me he'd only floated the idea of Dystonia as a possibility; it wasn't …"

He would have liked to say much more about the two of them as a couple. But soon the call would be over. He would go up to bed, alone. As alone as Tovah would be.

He concentrated on reassuring her. "No she didn't. There's no indication of anything like Dystonia. But it's all so different … She didn't belong anywhere. She felt she didn't belong, even though she had a husband. She would have liked to be white. She felt … I've felt …"

He couldn't say it, but he didn't need to. Tovah knew immediately. There was a long silence on her end, a listening silence. Finally, slowly, she said, "She felt the way you've always felt. You've never admitted it to anyone before. Not even to me."

Tovah understood his silence as agreement; he couldn't manage another word

"Oh, Dan, I should have listened. I should have insisted we talk about her more. I'm sorry. I didn't know. Maybe I didn't want to know. I wanted you to be … I thought we were so happy." It sounded as though being wrong on such a crucial fact was her greatest defeat.

"We were happy. It wasn't you. I should have said it to someone, but, it seemed so ungrateful. Once we were married, I did belong. I really did. Only …"

"Only it got lost. So much got lost. It got lost when Leah got sick, when my job was wrong, and I couldn't admit it. We would have to find it all over again."

"We would have to," Dan agreed. Just then neither of them suggested they begin looking.

# CHAPTER NINETEEN

It's been a very long time since I've actually heard what Dan is saying, Tovah thought. She looked around her new home. How had they ended up so removed, so far from each other?

When had she stopped listening to what he meant rather than just the actual words? It might have been from the very first moments she began in Minneapolis. If true, could she expect to do the best for her family and as a rabbi? Dan said Jo, an Episcopal priest, never considered combining career and family. Surely it was possible? Tovah's father had done it. But, could he have done it without his wife to help?

No, and she probably couldn't do it without Dan. But, that didn't mean Dan had to be the one looking after the house. Such a person was a housekeeper, not a husband. If they were ever to be together again they'd have to find a new way.

Not really listening to Dan must have started when the din in her head began to say that she'd made a big mistake in her career. There had been a constant roar telling her she'd gone after the wrong job, building on the error of the wrong seminary.

There had even been days when she wondered if the choice to be a rabbi was wrong. Maybe she'd just wanted to do something for her father that none of her brothers had accomplished? Not one of them had ever considered being a rabbi.

No, she didn't believe it. It wasn't a psychological mystery. She couldn't imagine doing different work.

Right after Leah was born Tovah had feared her choices had caused her daughter's premature birth and subsequent problems. She'd shut the door hard on any such rumination. How many other important things she'd locked out at the same time?

She'd been the one supposedly saving Leah in those months in Indiana. She'd tried to feel ennobled by the effort. Now it seemed that brief period – it had seemed so long then – might have saved her too, given her time to confront what she was doing with her life. Even if she'd ignored the lessons, it had really started then.

She'd first realized she'd made an error in choosing the seminary where she'd just been ordained. And, she'd had no inkling of how to fix things.

While Leah was in neonatal intensive care, Tovah would get up every morning and put on her phylacteries to pray *shacharit*, the morning service. Until she came to California; in distress, but with great clarity about needing to change things, the interval following Leah's birth had been the last time she'd prayed at the set times. She'd realized there was no room for time-bound prayer once she was at Temple Isaiah. No one would have actually stopped her. But the atmosphere of a liberal Reform congregation made such observance impossible. Once she started work in Minneapolis, she never felt empowered to do things differently from the other rabbis. Nor had she realized what the loss of ritual observance had cost.

During the first months of Leah's life there had been times when a crisis had kept her at the hospital all night. She'd learned to keep her prayer paraphernalia with her. Often she'd find herself praying, standing beside Leah's incubator.

She'd wanted to scoop Leah up, to bind her baby to herself with the straps holding her phylacteries in place. She'd told herself: these bonds, these prayers, will save my daughter. It had been so strange, a little frightening, but exhilarating too. Traditionally, women had never used phylacteries. She'd been thinking of them in a totally new, radical manner. Her passionate musings had been a little embarrassing. But, who knew what had helped Leah? Maybe it had been both the passion and the prayers.

It turned out, Leah had saved her. Despite all the upset they were going through now, if she'd not had those enforced months of solitude and prayer in Indiana she'd probably have put off her decision to change from Reform to Conservative Judaism. How much damage would have been done if she'd waited even longer?

Tovah had always believed bravery meant facing up to things, sticking it out, making difficult circumstances work. How disconcerting to discover that a good habit used in the wrong way could trap you. If you used all our energy and ingenuity to prop up something fundamentally wrong, you could destroy yourself, and the people you loved. Being gutsy might mean looking at a bad situation, an error, in the most clear-eyed way, admitting you'd done something wrong, and then changing it.

She'd started with the wrong premise and she might very well have lost everything. Her frenzy to patch, correct, and—above all else, to deny her fundamental error, might easily have destroyed her family. In the end she'd hidden herself away so effectively, not even Dan could find her.

# CHAPTER TWENTY

Almost as bad as not hearing what Dan was really saying, Tovah was realizing after a few short weeks in Orange County she was falling back into her bad old habits. Would anxiety and distress always turn her into a mindless workaholic?

After several conversations with Dan, Ari and Leah began to ask when Daddy was coming home. She'd been able to answer them somehow, without committing to anything concrete. But, she saw changes in their behavior. Instead of going along with the exercise routine in her usual obliging manner, Leah had several full-blown temper tantrums. More and more, Ari was unwilling to settle down at bedtime, inventing excuse after excuse.

"I've got one more question," he kept saying. His last question on Thursday night had been, "Do Leah and me still love Daddy?"

Tovah finally snapped, "Ari, how would I know? Do you?" Ari had retreated to his bedroom for the night.

Tovah's response to her son had left her feeling foolish and inadequate. And it wasn't just what she'd said to Ari.

Once again she'd brought home her sermon for the next night and kept trying to perfect it. She'd been struggling with her sermon all week, without improving it at all. Endlessly rewriting sermons was something she'd thought she'd left behind in Minneapolis.

Friday afternoon Tovah was rushing wildly to get to the daycare center to pick up the children. On the way home she was driving too fast. She parked the car at home realizing she hadn't heard a single word of Ari or Leah's chatter.

She'd think about slowing down later she told herself as she raced toward the house to 'make *Shabbes*.' After all she had to get some kind of a meal on the table before rushing back to the *shul* for Friday night services.

As they all spilled into the house from day care, her baby sitter arrived.

Tovah took a deep breath and was about to start snapping out orders, when she realized that preparations for the Sabbath were going forward smoothly without her saying a word.

Angie, her sitter, had come three Sabbaths in a row by now. She was the fifteen-year-old daughter of a congregant who'd said her daughter wasn't "much interested in Jewish stuff." Tovah had no idea how much formal Jewish education the teenager had received. No matter her formal education, she'd obviously caught the essence of what had to happen. She grabbed a container of frozen soup out of the freezer, put it in the microwave and pulled out a bag of precut salad greens and some vegetables to add to it.

"You said even pizza's fine, if it's in the right spirit? So, it'll be pizza, okay? I'll get a big frozen ones going in a minute. But, no chicken soup, not with cheese on the pizza. So I picked your yummy squash soup instead. Okay?"

With a glance at the clock, Angie said, "You've got just enough time for a shower, if the kids will set the table."

"Soup, salad and pizza will be terrific," was all Tovah could manage in response.

In the shower she found herself crying; the water, her tears, all part of a cleansing. If Angie had learned so much about the spirit of *Shabbat* in three weeks, how dare she complain?

When she returned to the scene of the action, Ari was setting the table. Leah had dragged the step stool over to the sideboard in the dining room and was plugging Sabbath candles into five candlesticks that she'd selected from Tovah's collection.

The little girl seemed to be reciting her understanding of what she was doing as though it was some familiar nursery rhyme, quite content not to have an attentive audience.

"So, this one is for me and this one is for Ari," she was saying, sing-song fashion. "This is one for Angie." "And these two," here Leah gestured to someone, somewhere, with the last two candles in her hand. "These two are for Mommy and Daddy." Her tone of voice suggested those two candles had very special powers.

Tovah picked Leah up and said, "May I do those two, sweetheart?"

Leah was willing. "Sure mommy."

Some instinct Tovah didn't understand, but one she didn't fight either, caused her to reach to the back of the sideboard and pull forward the candlesticks that had been Dan's engagement gift. Tovah had always included a candle for Dan on Friday night. The children would have been shocked if she had not. But, she hadn't used these special candlesticks since Dan deserted them.

A few minutes later, having blessed the candles, the wine, the bread, and her children, they began their somewhat unconventional Sabbath meal. There was no doubt the Sabbath had arrived in her new home. She felt magnified with a *neshamah yetira*, that extra Sabbath soul. It had descended on her the Sabbath after Dan left, when awareness had been so unwelcome. Now, once again, it felt like a gift.

With the children and the sitter in tow – she never attempted being Mommy and the Rabbi at the same time, without help – they were back at the synagogue in good time, feeling rejuvenated, not rushed.

# CHAPTER TWENTY-ONE

Tovah watched as her congregation filed in. Not a big crowd, but a few more than Teddy's estimated twenty-five or thirty. She had to remember Teddy's way of dealing with important issues was pessimism. It didn't have to become her way.

By the time services began, she knew there was no point worrying about the people who weren't there. It was too late.

She would lead the best possible service for those who'd come. She wouldn't give another thought to attendance. She didn't wait for the stragglers either. She began the service right on the minute.

As the evening moved along she had to admit to some relief as she heard and saw more people arriving. She even allowed herself an extra five seconds to count the house as she was beginning her sermon. There had to be at least sixty-five people in the sanctuary.

A few souls seemed to be in the wrong place, especially three newcomers in the last row.

Only in California, Tovah thought. Despite the congregation's flimsy folding chairs, these visitors had managed to achieve the folded leg posture of Zen disciples. Their posture was a natural adjunct to their all-white clothing; thick cotton pants and tops apparently hand-woven. All of them were able to stand and sit at the given times during the services without a problem. She hadn't heard anyone crashing to the floor.

There was a fourth person with the group – at least judging by his appearance he belonged to the Zen-inspired. He didn't bother with a chair. He sat on the floor next to his friends, in the full lotus position, with Buddhist prayer beads woven through his fingers. Tovah wouldn't have been surprised to find someone in the congregation telling rosary beads.

Anyone here tonight for the first time is committed to a spiritual search, Tovah told herself. Anyone who had been practicing another religion, or studying one, but who showed up at her Sabbath service, was a seeker. *I have to be able to tap into this. I have to be able to reach them. They've come here, to me. I'm the new element.*

Then Tovah did something she'd never even imagined before. It was as alien as living without Dan, as new as being in California. She picked up the sermon she'd worked on so hard, too hard, and stowed it on the shelf under the lectern. It wouldn't do. It wasn't what she wanted to say. Never before had she considered delivering an extemporaneous sermon. Never before had she trusted herself to ad lib. She might never do it again. But, what she really wanted to say had just wafted down on her.

*"I'm particularly envious of those of you either seated on the floor, or on folding chairs, who can*

manage to get up from a crossed leg position, without flinching. But, I shouldn't be surprised. I know many of you are ardent physical fitness practitioners: swimming, biking, running in the surf and on the beach. And, of course it's all made somewhat easier because we live in this beautiful place with wonderful weather year 'round. But, without your commitment to achieving physical fitness, those things would never happen.

"All of you know no program of exercise, or anything else, works unless you are committed to it, unless you put in the time. So, it's surprising to realize disciplined people, who practice their profession, care for their family, are able to work out every day, run on the beach, in sand or through water, to make their exercise routine more effective, have no idea they need the same practice, the same efficient work-out in their religious life, for it to be effective.

We are approaching the time of Passover. Now, there was a workout! They walked all the way to the Holy Land, though sand. They did it twice. Check Exodus. The first time they moved really fast. They were all the way there, then the spies who went into the land – except for two of them – came back with wild, frightening stories.

So, God took them back out into the wilderness. Then it was forty years of wandering. They became long distance trekkers, not sprinters who'd initially crossed the desert quickly. They had to keep moving. And they carried everything with them, including a specially built portable tent, The Mishkan or Sanctuary, which housed the Ark of the Covenant, the original stone tablets.

*That was a lot of weight, actual and metaphorical. They didn't like it particularly. They kvetched all the time. Kvetching, for those who don't speak the lingo, is complaining, Olympic-caliber complaining. After they'd crossed the desert the first time, God told Moses the kvetching, the complaining, the lack of faith, the unwillingness to face something new – there are a lot of ways to characterize it – meant they had to go and work out – they had to wander – for forty years. Until the generation born slaves in Egypt died out.*

*Talk about discouraging. You leave Egypt. You work out – you quick-march to the Holy Land. All that and then you find out you're going to die without getting there.*

*Well, we are the generation, largely, that relocated to California. We will not wait forty years for anything. We are not isolated in the dessert. We're not at all sure there will be a sufficiently large, or sufficiently motivated, next generation if we wait. Yet, we know we carry something worthwhile. If we doubted our message, we wouldn't worry about passing it along.*

*Right now some of you are saying to yourselves, 'why is she talking to me. I'm here. I'm committed.'*

*I know. But, those who are not here are going to get this sermon anyway. Attached to our website, and reprinted in the newsletter. So, they won't escape. But, if you agree with me on any of this you can give me a hand, help spread the word. I need as much help as possible. Think of the help those on the first trek could have used.*

*The Exodus group did it on* manna *alone. Well, they had water too, but nothing very grand. No Evian.*

*Would you be willing to rely on a well following
you around? And, only because of Miriam, because
of her merit? I mean, suppose she got a better offer?
Suppose she had an off day, didn't behave, and the
well went dry? Suppose you wanted a different flavor?
Or, one night you wanted sparkling, not still, with your
manna? I suppose having a well at your service made
up a little for it being* l'eau ordinaire *all the time. But,
somehow, I'm sure people* kvetched *about that too."*

Tovah wasn't trying to read faces before her now.
She was committed to her theme and she didn't want
to know – not yet anyway – if they hated what she was
saying. At least there was none of the tell-tale restless-
ness that so quickly lets a speaker know an audience
is not engaged.

She'd have known if someone even twitched. Every
chair in the sanctuary squeaked or squealed if the person
seated on it shifted at all.

Tovah knew a speaker can pause for several seconds,
even in the middle of sermon. She paused, right there.
Let them absorb what she was saying. She needed a
minute to organize the rest of her thoughts.

*Forty years of walking through sand. Can you imag-
ine? We don't have to plan for so many years. Right now
we only have to concern ourselves with the weeks until
Passover. And, we are not all of Israel, not an entire
generation.*

A nightmare thought, one of the old ones, flashed
through her mind, threatened to derail her: what if
delivering this sermon ended her career in California?

No, she wouldn't allow the thought. She wouldn't sec-
ond-guess herself. You've decided to do things differently,

she told herself. This is different. Be realistic: how can one early sermon do much damage?

She took another fraction of a second to actually issue a mental command to the critic who lived within her: Go away; you'll get your chance later.

She took a sip of water: Finish your sermon. If they hate it, it's not the end of the world, even if you think so for a while. You'll know something about this congregation. You'll know something about yourself.

Consciously releasing the tight grip she'd taken on each side of the lectern, she smiled at the group in front of her, and went on.

*"I'm going to propose a work-out schedule, otherwise called our spring program. Do we have a real spring here, other than things becoming even more gorgeous? This workout is going to consist of an adult class one night a week, or on Sunday morning. Those who are interested can tell me which time they prefer. And we're going to modify our Sunday School program right now, at least for everyone over the age of twelve. All the adults will be studying what the kids are studying. Of course, it'll be a simpler version. It has to be easier for the adults.*

They actually laughed then, and the teenagers in the room whistled, clapped and hooted. Tovah heard one young voice, "That's for sure, Rabbi T."

"Rabbi T." A nickname had to be a good sign.

*We're going to institute a religious work out, with check ups at fixed intervals before Passover. If we were the Exodus generation at the first Passover, we would have taken our bread without waiting for it to rise, and left for the open dessert. We are not that generation. We only have to show up for classes, not for the whole desert trek. We also have to show up for two* Seders.

*I know some of you are going to roll your eyes. You're thinking: Who would think a rabbi this young could be so corny? You're thinking this is* kitsch *beyond belief. But I've been shopping with our favorite designer. You know her.*

There was some clapping and Tovah saw Janice half rise in her seat and take a very small bow. Janice was smiling hugely. That had to be a good sign.

*She tells me retro is in. It must be. I just bought some furniture looking suspiciously like what my parents dumped years ago because it was too old-fashioned.*

*Well, if you want retro, you can't do much better then the Bible. Experts tell us the Exodus is dated to something like twelve hundred years before the Common Era, some three thousand years ago. Some of those experts have got a lot more to say, some of it very controversial, as to what did or did not happen in Egypt and Sinai. If you want to find out about it, you have to show up for the classes. And, for those of you fortunate enough to have a solid Jewish educational background, I need you. You'll be like the two good scouts, bringing in accurate information. Only now you're not called scouts, you're called peer tutors.*

*I know there are some of you here I've barely met. Well, what better way is there for us to get to know each other? Take a trip with a person and you really find out what they are like. So, sign up for this one, limited Exodus round, and see what it's like. See what I'm like.*

*You haven't found whatever it is you are seeking in any other place. I think it's here. If all this embarrasses you somehow, just don't tell anyone for a while.*

*But, all this will be in the local papers. You might want to warn your friends in advance. Tell them you have to be nice to the new rabbi. She's a woman with children. For all you know she might cry if someone heckles, or doesn't cooperate. You never know.*

*If you're the one who gets heckled, refer them to me, either by phone even by e-mail. Tell the heckler – we seemed to have traded in the* kvetchers *for hecklers these days – to drop by if they want to talk about it.*

*We're in the yellow industrial building located on The Big Divide at the far south end of Dana Point.*

Tovah started to wind up. Her sermon had been shorter than she'd planned, but she doubted anyone objected.

She let the faces in the congregation come into focus as she said:

*Here's what you can tell people: We start out on this limited trek with a lot more than our ancestors ever had. They left Egypt with very little, with* matzah, *and some strong leaders. Of course they had a very big, very new, idea. They had the word of God, saying that they would be his people. Soon after they left they also had the Ark of the Covenant, the Commandments, and a relationship with their God. That's very big stuff.*

*They had to carry it then. We have to carry it now. Maybe even then the physical part wasn't the hardest thing.*

*This building stands; we don't have to move it. We certainly don't have to carry it. Rather, it carries us. It cradles us against the wind. We can hear the wind now, a Santa Ana I'm told, throwing stinging sand up against the sides and roof.*

*They would have known a very similar wind. If you've been in Israel or Egypt you know it as a* hamsin. *Here it's the Santa Ana. But, we don't have sand in our eyes. Nor do we have the grit getting into our clothes and between our teeth. The wind and sand doesn't obscure every word we say. We have warmth, fellowship and tradition on our side. Soon, if there are enough of us, we may be able to work on having a more permanent home. Today we begin to learn and to work toward being worthy of a new home when it becomes possible.*

The man sitting on the floor now wrapped his prayer beads around one wrist, securing them in some way so that they became a tight-fitting bracelet. He opened one eye – bright blue – and a small smile played over his face. He flashed her a sign with his palm up, his thumb in, his remaining four fingers vee'd. It was the sign made by the *Cohanim*, the traditional heredity priesthood within Judaism, when they blessed a congregation. Or – and a lot more likely in this context – it was Spock's 'live long and prosper' sign from the original *Star Trek* of the sixties. Her blue-eyed new friend saw she understood. His eye closed. Feeling blessed, whichever sign he'd intended, Tovah asked the congregation to stand for the closing prayers, and for the memorial prayer, the *Kaddish*, following. Like his companions, her new friend managed to rise to his feet without opening either one of his eyes again, and without using his hands.

# CHAPTER TWENTY-TWO

The same weekend as her extemporaneous sermon, on Sunday night, Tovah realized that for the first time since she'd arrived in California she had no commitments and everything in the house was unpacked and put away.

She was contemplating choosing between a trashy novel and a mindless television program when the phone rang. Her parents' home number flashed on the caller I.D. It was far too late in the Midwest for them to be making casual phone calls.

"What's wrong?" she said as she picked up the phone, anxiety flooding through her.

"It's Michael," Her mother said, also without any preamble or word of greeting. "Your father just called. Michael Bregman had a fatal heart attack less than an hour ago."

It took Tovah several seconds to understand what she'd just heard. She looked at the phone in her hand as though it was defective. She glanced around her home for someone to share this horrible news. There was no one to tell except Dan, who was three thousand miles away.

Michael had been Dan's friend for years before Tovah met him. Tovah and Dan had introduced him to Ilana, a *'shidduch,'* a match, that had taken, much to everyone's delight.

As though her mother was reading her mind, she said, "You'll have to call Dan and tell him, of course. In the meantime what shall I tell Ilana? The funeral will likely be Tuesday, the day after tomorrow. Will you come?"

"Of course I'll come," Tovah said automatically. She knew the full impact of what had happened hadn't struck home yet. She didn't feel a thing. Her mind raced ahead, planning. What about the children?

Her mother anticipated her there, too. "You probably don't have anyone you want to leave the children with. Can you manage tickets for all three of you? Dad already spoke to Hillel. He can arrange a flight. He said if you're able to leave from L.A., not Orange County, flying standby tomorrow should be fine. You'll all stay here of course. The children can stay in the extra spare room or we'll put them in the boys' old dormitory on the third floor, depending on who else gets here."

Tovah had always said that her mother could arrange the Messiah's arrival, but she didn't tease her just then. Instead, her mind racing, she said, "Uh huh, yes, stand-by will help. I'll call Hillel first thing in the morning. We'll probably be in tomorrow night."

She wrote her brother's name, Hillel, on the scratch pad beside the phone, as though she'd forget it otherwise. Hillel was a pilot with a major airline, and invaluable in arranging emergency travel.

Trying hard to focus only on what her mother was saying, she sank down into a chair, the phone clutched tightly in her hand.

Ilana had mentioned Michael had experienced some troubling physical symptoms. That was why they'd made a trip to Minneapolis. They'd also been talking about going to the world famous clinic in Rochester, Minnesota. But, there'd certainly been no suggestion he might die. Michael was only a few years older than Dan. What if it had been Dan?

Her mother was saying, "He collapsed right into the arms of a cardiac specialist. Nothing helped."

"Where are Ilana and the children right now?" Tovah pushed thoughts of Dan, of herself, away.

She kept glancing around her kitchen, as though she'd find help somewhere. There was nothing. No Dan.

Desperately she said to her mother, "Give me a minute." She was totally alone. She put the phone down on the table, buried her head in her hands. When she picked up the phone again her hand was slick with her tears. "What happens now? Where's Ilana right now?"

"She's probably on her way home. Dad is with her."

Tovah's thoughts scrambled over each other. What to do? No, what to do first?. She had to get to Ilana. She had to let Dan know about Michael. Thank God they were in touch with each other. She had his new New York cell phone number.

Her mother's voice recalled her. "Dad said Ilana asked for you, first thing."

"Tell her I'll be there tomorrow. Tell her to hang on. Tell her I love her. The funeral won't be tomorrow, for sure? I need a day to get there."

"No. The earliest possible day is Tuesday. Michael's father lives in Florida. He's elderly, and someone needs to come with him. Ilana's parents are here of course. They'll be as devastated as she is. I don't know how she's going to manage. But, of course she will, somehow."

"Oh, my God, how will she tell the children? What will she say?"

"I can't imagine. I've never known how people live through these things, even though I've seen them do it. I don't know how your father does this, either. Rachel and Doron will understand. Amir is too young to understand fully. But he is certainly old enough to miss his Daddy. Can you get word to Dan?"

"Yes … I'll get word to him," Tovah said. She immediately felt guilty. She had not yet told her parents that she and Dan had spoken to each other, and they'd been so supportive.

But her mother didn't question her. She just said, "Good. He should know."

At that, Tovah started to cry again. It seemed to her crying had been her response to everything since Dan's departure. Was she crying for Michael, or for Ilana? Or, maybe her tears were for herself and for Dan. She could hardly believe that when she'd first realized Dan had walked out, she'd actually wished he'd died instead.

The next day, somewhat breathless, but sitting on the plane for the long leg of their flight, LAX to Minneapolis, where they would change planes for Madison, she said to the children, "So, can you two tell me why we're suddenly on this airplane?" If she was a child she'd hate the false, hearty, 'parent' voice.

Fortunately, Ari and Leah were less critical. As usual, Ari became the spokesman, while Leah nodded vigorously, agreeing with every word her brother said.

"We're going to see Zaida and Baba, but that's not the real reason for us to go. It's for a fun-eral," he said.

"That's right. We had to rush so much, so we could get to this airplane Uncle Hillel arranged for us."

Ari, sitting in the aisle seat, looked around. "I bet Daddy could fly this plane just like Uncle Hillel, if he was the pilot. Daddy could have done it, if he wanted to. Except now he can't ever do it."

Leah, sitting next to the window, leaned across Tovah and said, "He could so fly it right now."

"You both mean he could fly it if he was here, right? I don't know if he could fly it right now, because there's lots of learn to fly a plane. But, if Daddy wanted to learn, he could. He'd probably be good at flying a plane, if he wanted to do it."

"Not if there's a fun-eral, he couldn't," Ari said, somewhat grimly, but with great certainty.

It took Tovah a few minutes to follow his logic, then speaking very calmly, much more calmly then she actually felt, she said, "Ari, do you remember why we have to go to this funeral?"

"Cause Daddy died," Ari said, still sounding calm, although now he looked a little uncertain.

"Ari!" Tovah couldn't help the fact that her son's name came out in a yelp. How had he come up with such an idea?

Leah leaned across Tovah again and patted her brother's hand. "Not our Daddy. I told you."

"Ari, Daddy did not die. Not our Daddy. It's Michael. He's Rachel, Doron and Amir's daddy. You know. Remember, we looked at all those pictures of our two families together."

To prepare the children for this trip and for the funeral Tovah had rooted through boxes of pictures, looking for photos of a trip they'd made to Madison the previous winter. Over their very early breakfast, she'd gone through the pictures with Ari and Leah. Reliving the visit had made her cry, but the children just seemed to think it was funny to see their heavy snow suits of the year before, compared to the kind of clothing they now wore, living in Southern California.

Tovah couldn't quite imagine what she'd said to her son to make him think Dan had died, and, why, if he believed her, he was so calm. But, she couldn't contemplate the why of his confusion at that moment. She had to deal with it. She scrambled to find her bag under the seat in front of her. She dug for the pictures in their bright yellow folders. She'd never found the time to put them properly in an album.

When she pulled out one of the pictures she understood Ari's confusion a little better. The picture showed all of them together; Ilana's two oldest alongside Leah and Ari, all bundled up in ski jackets and snow pants, lined up on a long toboggan. Michael Bregman was sitting at the front, ready to guide it down the slope, and Dan was at the back, poised to push off, before jumping on behind Rachel. The children had each leaned out behind Michael so every face was clear.

Ari was suddenly much less calm and not smiling. He grabbed the picture out of Tovah's hand. "See," he said. "You said someone's Daddy died. I'm someone, and that ..."

here his small finger punctuated his sentence, stabbing at the spot where Dan stood poised. "He's someone's daddy. He's my Daddy. Anyway, he can die 'cause we don't love him anymore."

"Ari," Tovah said. She tried to say more, something comforting and reassuring, but she couldn't get a single word out. She couldn't help it, her tears spilled over.

Her children looked at her with consternation. After a second or two Leah tried patting her hand, obviously an effort to comfort her. Very gently, Ari handed back the picture he'd pulled from her grasp.

"We don't not love him all of the time," Ari said.

Tovah pulled a crumpled tissue from her purse dabbing at her eyes while trying to smile apologetically to her children.

"It's okay to cry when you're sad," she managed to say. "I'm sad because my friend died. Wouldn't you be sad if your Daddy had really died? Rachel will be very sad, and Doron too. They'll cry too."

"Just like you," Leah offered. "Anyway, we do love Daddy. Except he said, 'see you soon,' on the phone to me, but he didn't come. When is soon? That's why Ari's mad. What if he comes now and we're not there."

"I promise you he won't come while we're at this funeral," was all Tovah could manage. "Let's look at these pictures again. This man – very carefully she pointed to Michael -— "this man is Rachel and Doron's daddy. You knew him. His name is Michael. You remember going on the sled with him, don't you? Anyway, Michael got very sick. So sick even the very best doctors couldn't help. It doesn't happen very often to mommies or daddies; practically never. But this time it did happen. And he died. That's why I was crying, and why Rachel and Doron and Amir will cry. What will you do when you see them crying?" she asked. She was totally adrift. She had no idea if she was handling this subject in an appropriate way. They didn't teach this sort of thing at the seminary, and becoming a parent didn't automatically provide expertise either.

"If they cry, we will give them Kleenex," Leah said. "We will hold their hands, too. We will tell them not to be sad."

"We will tell them our Daddy went away, too," Ari said.

# CHAPTER TWENTY-THREE

After Tovah got the children settled at her parents, she walked over to Ilana's, where her friend was waiting out the time before the funeral for her husband.

Of all of Tovah's friends, Dan had picked Ilana Braun for his friend Michael. "A rabbi would be too much for Michael," he'd said, sounding a little smug. Tovah thought Michael could handle anything Dan could, if he'd wanted to. But, he and Ilana were so wonderful for each other. Like Ilana, Michael had been raised in a traditional home.

Tovah and Ilana had been friends most of their lives. For years they'd been the only two girls in the small Madison Jewish community from observant homes, a powerful bond. They had both studied with Tovah's father and brothers. Ilana had had a crush on each of Tovah's brothers in turn.

Ilana was the only child of older parents. She needed a friend. Tovah, with five older brothers and no sisters, needed a girlfriend too. They were different in temperament, Ilana quiet and thoughtful, Tovah much more aggressive. Perhaps for that reason they had made a good team all through school.

The only time they'd been somewhat out of touch was when Tovah went away to University and to Seminary.

Ilana had never felt free to leave Madison. She couldn't leave her parents. She'd gone to the University of Wisconsin in Madison, living at home, not in a dormitory. Eventually she'd taken a job teaching at a private school in the area.

Ilana and Michael had married only a few months after Dan and Tovah. They had started a family right away. Once both couples were settled, they'd been able to weave the stands of their individual relationships into one of those rare friendships that connected all of them. Later, they had a made a good start at extending their relationship to their children. Dan and Tovah always saw the Bregmans when they visited Madison and they were always in touch.

Tonight Ilana's calm and gracious home, all in shades of cream and blue, seemed nothing more than a stage set, as though the play had not yet started, or, worse, as though it had just closed for the last time.

"This is so hard," Ilana said. She pulled herself out of Tovah's embrace. She groped for a tissue in the pocket of her sweater. Not finding one, she tried blotting her tears on the back of her hand.

Tovah took a moment to get up, cross the living room, find a box of tissues and place it on the coffee table. Ilana plucked a tissue out of the box, rendering it useless at the same time by wadding it tightly in her clenched hand.

"We should have had the funeral today, but we couldn't get everyone here fast enough. We should have moved faster," Ilana said.

For the first time in her life Ilana looked older than her years. She was a little taller than Tovah, but very small-boned, and she had always retained something of the look of an adolescent, despite the fact she was the mother of three. Her long brown hair was parted at the side and pulled back, fastened out of her way with a large barrette. Her daughter, six-year-old Rachel, wore her hair the same way, heightening the strong resemblance between the two.

"You couldn't possibly have done more than this. And you can only move as fast as people could manage. Like Michael's father. The earliest he could get here is tomorrow morning."

Tovah took both of Ilana's hands in her own, hoping Ilana would relax her fingers a little. Tovah couldn't tell which way the comfort between them flowed. She needed to be with Ilana, to try and help. She kept talking, trying to engage her friend's attention.

"Even if you'd known something was wrong, you could never have imagined that Michael would ..."

Tovah couldn't finish her sentence. She tried again, "Even though you were always rock."

"And you were flint," Ilana said, repeating the next line of a little routine that had been a ritual between them when they were much younger.

They recited the last line of their old formula. "Together, we make fire." The memory made one precious moment of laughter between them.

Tovah had resolved to draw on her training as a rabbi, to be calm and helpful. She couldn't quite manage it. All it took was Ilana's plaintive wail, "I can't believe I'm going to have to say that I'm a widow," to start Tovah crying, too. She couldn't tell Ilana how she had resisted the word 'deserted,' or how angry she had been. Thank God, she'd never admitted to anyone expect Robin that she'd wished Dan dead. Now she could see her troubles were nothing beside Michael's death.

Ilana kept going over things, trying to make sense of the last few days.

"It was as though he knew something might happen. He wouldn't even consider going to Rochester until all his papers were in order, insurance, everything. He'd had his will updated; even though it was re-written when Amir was born, less than two years ago."

Tovah said, "Michael was being careful. He loved you. He was like that." It occurred to her that she'd been alone almost three months and hadn't given a thought to changing her will, or to making some kind of formal custody arrangements for the children. What if she'd died? What if it had really been Dan, not Michael?

Ilana looked around the room somewhat wildly, as though searching for an escape. Of course she didn't find one. She clutched Tovah's wrist. "How can you be a widow in your thirties?"

Usually, Ilana's fragile pink and white complexion gave her a glowing look. Today her eyes were shadowed from crying, and she was pasty pale.

The two of them clung together again. Tovah knew there was nothing to do but put her arms around her friend. No matter how hard this time of waiting might be, what came next would be harder still.

# CHAPTER TWENTY-FOUR

The next morning Tovah awoke in her old bedroom in her parents' home. For just a moment she luxuriated in the most delicious sense of absolute safety. But, as she peeled back the warm blankets cuddled around her, all the hurts of the last two days layered over her.

Dan. Thank God she'd managed to leave a message for him on the cell phone he now carried. But, she could not lie in bed worrying about herself, or even about Dan. Next to Ilana's suffering they were like small children squabbling.

For once the calm of her parents' home felt fragile. She had pushed back the blankets slowly, trying to get out of bed silently. If she moved too quickly, she might shatter the peace.

Had she heard someone moving around after she'd gone to bed? Maybe Ben and Hillel had arrived. She would preserve every possible moment of silence, just in case her brothers and her children were still sleeping.

Her nose told her there was coffee waiting in the kitchen. She peered into her old closet for something to wear over her sleep-shirt. She never bothered to pack a robe when she came home. There always seemed to be some orphan around that she could borrow. She found the old chenille robe she had owned while in high school. It was short and bulky, but very warm, the fuzzy pale blue fabric decorated with yellow and white stars and moons.

She wrapped the robe tight, belted it, also putting on an old pair of slippers. The house was always chilly in the morning.

Downstairs, both her parents were already gone. It was past eight o'clock. Her father would be at morning *minyan*. Her mother would be running errands for her own home, for Ilana, and for Ilana's parents too.

She was heading toward the kitchen for coffee and orange juice when the doorbell rang.

It must be her mother, her arms encircling bulging brown paper bags full of groceries. She'd have rung the bell instead of struggling with her key, since she'd assume someone would be awake. Or, it might be a delivery for her father. If FedEx didn't find him at the synagogue they automatically brought his packages to the house.

Tovah adjusted her robe closer around her, tugging on the tie. She opened the door.

Dan stood there.

At the sight of him, Tovah had the overwhelming sensation that she must still be upstairs in bed, asleep and caught up in a dream.

No, she must be awake. In a dream she would never have let him appear wearing exactly the same clothes he'd worn the night he'd disappeared. Because this was Dan, he managed to look elegant, even dressed in brown corduroy pants, a shirt and a sweater, with his parka layered on top. She felt something like a stab to her mid-section, and pulled her robe even more tightly around her waist. It didn't protect her. Seeing him felt like taking a blow. He was wearing the Chanukah gifts she'd selected. The dark red scarf, hat and gloves were still perfect for him.

He smiled; tentative, testing. Tovah was quite unable to imagine what the buzz in her ears could be, or what caused the cold, clammy feeling at the back of her neck. She stared at him. She saw Dan's eyes widen in alarm. He understood immediately she might faint, even if it took her some seconds longer.

He took a step forward and dropped his old duffel bag just inside the front door. He pulled off his glove, taking her hand. With his free arm around her, Dan guided her to a chair in the nearby living room. He had just come in from outside; his hand should have been cold and hers warm, but the reverse was true. His hand warmed and supported her. The grip of his arm around her meant that even if she fainted she would not fall.

She sat down in the familiar wing chair. Dan put one hand – how could it feel so warm and alive to her? – on the back of her neck and gently forced her head down toward her knees.

When she struggled to sit up straight the room was full of people. Her mother appeared in the open front door with grocery bags in her arms. Her brothers, Hillel and Ben, were there too. As she'd guessed, they had arrived from Chicago. Both of them ignored Dan. They marched from the stairway across to where Tovah sat. They leaned down to kiss her, one on each side. Dan was forced away, shouldered out of his spot by Hillel, who looked as though he might like to take a punch at his brother-in-law.

Even though she still felt faint, Tovah saw her mother immediately size up the situation. Hadas had her mouth set in a prim, straight line. Either she was feeling particularly grim, or, more likely, she was trying not to laugh at the young men posturing in her living room. Whatever Hadas was thinking, she diverted their attention with one of her familiar string of tasks.

"Dan. You're still dressed for the outdoors. The car is full of groceries. Hillel, don't hover over Tovah as though she's a maiden in a tower. Go and get her a glass of juice. Ben, take these." She handed her eldest son the bags she was carrying and watched him obediently take them into the kitchen. Dan, clearly relieved to have been assigned a job as though nothing unusual was happening, glanced quickly at Tovah. He could see she appeared somewhat recovered, so he went to unload the car.

Hillel stood his ground despite his mother's directions. He balanced on one arm of Tovah's chair and kept an arm curved protectively around his little sister. Her brothers might have tormented the life out of her when they were growing up, but it was a right they reserved for themselves. In a situation where there was any possible danger, Hillel would stand guard.

Hadas didn't argue with her son. She went through the front hall, past the living room, clearly heading in the direction of the kitchen without stopping to take off her black car coat, or remove her snow boots. In a moment she was back with a glass of orange juice. She handed it to Hillel. "If you're going to be her Lancelot, please make sure she drinks this. Tovah, sweetheart, you've had a shock. Do you feel faint?"

Tovah could only nod. With shaking hands she took the glass, drank a little, then handed the glass to her brother. She had to fully collect herself, so she could face the day, and Dan. Thank God the children were still upstairs either sleeping or playing. There would be quite a scene when they saw their father.

There was another flash forward in time for Tovah, and they were all together in the living room. Dan must have brought the groceries into the foyer, and taken them through into the kitchen. She'd heard cupboard doors opening and closing. Dan always did the whole job, putting everything away.

She held an empty glass. She'd finished the juice. Maybe that was why she felt better. Both her brothers were again hovered near her. She felt grateful enough to cry. But she wouldn't allow herself such a luxury. Her mother sat in a wing chair too, the mate to her own. Dan came in from the kitchen. He stood in the archway between the living room and the dining room. For the first time since his arrival he looked ill at ease, embarrassed.

Hadas said, "You boys will have to sit down. It makes me nervous to have you all towering over me. I know you want to make a grand gesture of some sort, even if you don't quite know what it could be. There isn't time. The funeral is later today. I've got jobs for everyone. Our own *mishugas* will have to wait. Believe me, there will be plenty of time for it later."

Dan spun around one of the dining room chairs and straddled it. Ben and Hillel sat down on the floor near Tovah, as though they were still teenagers, not men with children of their own. Their mother's lists of chores were familiar. Besides, she had just labeled their behavior as foolishness, *mishugas*. For the moment they would put aside their tensions with each other.

"Ben, Dad wants you to go to the airport to meet Michael's father. He's due in just after ten. Please take him straight to Ilana's. He's a very elderly man; all of this is going to be very hard on him. Perhaps he'll have some time to lie down before the funeral. Please take along one of your father's warm jackets for him, and gloves, a hat and a scarf. He may not have the correct clothing, coming from Florida.

"Hillel, I need you to stay with me. I'm going to have to get ready for *Shabbes* today, not leave anything for later in the week. You're the best cleaner. You'll do that, please, and I'll get food ready for here, for the Bregmans and for Ilana's parents. We'll probably all eat together."

Hadas paused for a minute. Her children knew she was silently working her way through a lengthy and very complete mental checklist.

"Dan, Tovah, I'm glad you're both here. Please, you'll go to Ilana's this morning and take the children out for a while. If you take Leah and Ari with you they can play together. It's not too cold today. Ilana's children know you two the best, and of course Ari and Leah will be a big help.

"Ilana won't go outside until the funeral, and then not again until *Shiva* is over, but the children need to get some air and some exercise. After they've played a little, you can take them home and give them all lunch. Try to get Ilana and Mr. Bregman to eat something."

She stopped for a moment. "Will the two of you be able to do this without arguments, without tripping over each other? I suppose Leah and Ari will help there too."

Dan and Tovah responded identically, nodding yes. Even if Tovah had felt she couldn't be in the same room as Dan one moment more, she would not have disappointed her mother. And, truthfully, she didn't feel angry at the moment.

Hadas smiled at them as though they were especially well-behaved children today. "A limousine will come for Ilana and her father-in-law at one-thirty. There will be room for all the children too, and for both of you. Ilana wants the children, except for Amir, at the funeral, including graveside. Amir is just too little.

"The funeral will be at half past two. Your father would like to have us all back at the house before the heavy afternoon traffic becomes a problem. We have to go to the east side, to the old cemetery. Some ladies from the Sisterhood and the *Bikkur Cholim* committee will be at the house at one o'clock, to get things ready for the meal of consolation and the first *minyan,* after the funeral. A lot of people have already sent over food. *Minyan* will have to be no later than four-thirty. The committee members will stay until we get back, so they'll also look after Amir. He should be napping a good part of the time. He knows the ladies from *shul,* so when he wakes up, there shouldn't be a problem."

Hadas paused once more. "You can help Rachael and Doron dress for the funeral. Ilana will need some help too, I'm sure. Please take your own clothes for the funeral along with you. I don't think you'll get back here to change. Now, all of you get some breakfast quickly, and please get to work."

Slowly, but determined not to look needy or shaky, Tovah stood up. Unwillingly, Hillel started to edge away from her, then stopped, because Dan took a tentative step in her direction.

Ben broke the impasse by saying to Dan, "I'm glad you're here, brother. We'll leave you two to sort things out on your own." He nudged Hillel with his elbow and the two of them retreated.

Tovah took advantage of the few seconds while Ben was speaking, heading for the stairs. She could take refuge in her mother's assignment. This felt like other times when funerals or some other crisis brought Hadas Feldner's formidable organizing skills to the fore. If Tovah focused on what needed doing, she could handle Dan's unexpected presence.

She started up the stairs, not turning to speak until she had gained the advantage of standing above everyone. For a moment she realized that her hair was a mess, that she must be pale and drawn looking, and that the chenille robe she'd grabbed from the closet probably made her look blimp-like. Firmly, she dismissed those thoughts as unworthy.

When she'd gathered sufficient breath, and was able to call on her pulpit voice, she said, "Dan, you can bring whatever you'll need to Ilana's. I'll be in the kitchen in fifteen minutes for breakfast. No, it will take me a half hour. I think I hear the kids. You'll want some time with them, I'm sure."

She was going to recite her morning prayers, *daven,* no matter what. Dan didn't have to know. "Since we won't need a car later, we can all walk over to Ilana's right after breakfast."

She only waited until she'd seen Dan's almost imperceptible agreement. Then, hearing the children approaching the stairs, she went to meet them, calling out in an especially cheerful voice, "Leah, Ari, there's a great big surprise waiting for you downstairs."

Later, walking over to Ilana's, with the children between them at first, Dan said quietly, "Thank you for leaving that message. Otherwise, I wouldn't have known. I called my parents and got their machine, so I didn't have to explain, or tell them where I was. I just left a message about Michael. I'm sure we'll hear from them later."

Then he was silent again. Tovah didn't really need to supply any conversational openings since the children had a hundred things to tell their father. She didn't know what to say, anyway. One part of her was happy to be walking alongside Dan. Another part was on the defensive in his presence. A very large part was still very angry.

Dan tried to start a conversation, but Tovah waved him off, saying, "I'd like to talk Dan, but it has to be later."

He nodded, and instead said to the kids, "Let me show you how to make the best soft snowball in the world. We can show Rachel, Doron, and Amir, too."

As they walked up the sidewalk to Ilana's home, the children now walking together in front of them, Dan managed to say, "Tovah, I have to tell you, when you answered the door, I was so glad ..."

"Dan. I don't know why I was so shocked to see you, but I was. For some reason it didn't occur to me you would come." Then she had to add, "It's a horrible reason to be together, but I guess we'll have a chance to talk, and that's good."

"Michael was my friend," Dan said. "I had to come. And, I have to admit it. It was a good ..."

"Excuse?" Tovah said, with a tiny flash of bitterness that she immediately regretted.

"It was an opportunity. It was a very good, and a very sad reason to come home," Dan said.

By now they were at the front door, and thankfully there was no more time. Tovah echoed Dan, "A good reason. I suppose." Then they were swept up in the demands of a difficult day.

# CHAPTER TWENTY-FIVE

Tovah found the day of any funeral a crazed kaleido-
scope of images linked to each other by something
more potent than time. And, this was Michael's
funeral. Because she'd shared so much with Ilana, each
image echoed on and on even longer than usual, following her as she moved from one painful vignette to
another. Whatever took place earlier seemed to still be
happening, always added to the newer event, ampli-
fied, undiminished.

After the morning at Ilana's and the actual funeral
service, they were all at the site of Michael's grave. Dan
kept one sturdy arm around the elderly Mr. Bregman and
he never put Doron down. The little boy had attached
himself to Dan, clearly selecting him as a surrogate for
his father. Tovah and her mother had stationed themselves on either side of Ilana's parents, with Ari and
Leah standing between them. The Brauns were at least
a decade older than Tovah's parents, in their late seventies, both frail. They had seemed elderly to Tovah even

when she and Ilana were growing up. Mrs. Braun and Rachel both leaned against her. It seemed to Tovah she could feel the little girl's heart and her grandmother's heart beating right through their heavy winter coats. Two distinct rhythms: Rachael's body vibrating wildly while a slow labored effort kept Mrs. Braun upright.

Then, in what seemed the same moment, Ilana wanted her children beside her as she recited the *Kaddish*. Except for actually filling in the grave, they had reached one of the last ritual moments.

Rachel's fingers were tightly entwined in her own so Tovah moved forward with the little girl, her mind flashing dark secret thoughts. This would have been her had Dan died. She would have had to say *Kaddish* with Ari and Leah beside her. But Dan was there, so warmly alive, with one arm around Doron as the little boy joined his mother and sister. She knew she should feel unutterably grateful she'd never faced what Ilana had to do now, practically kneel in the snow at the edge of her husband's grave, so her children could follow her shaking finger as she showed them the words of the memorial prayer in her prayer book.

Hours later, back at the house, Tovah could not rid herself of the picture. It reverberated through her soul, a silent bell tolling.

It had been the hardest day of her life, and she was only a friend, not the widow, not the orphan. She'd been the rabbi in situations something like this before. Much easier. Why did people under extreme stress always proudly proclaim at least they could still work? Work was easier, far easier, than most of real life. Maybe Dan had known she was hiding from life, taking refuge in her work, all those hours in her study.

The idea that Dan had figured it out before her, while she'd needed a friend's death to drive the lesson home, did not make her feel more kindly toward him.

By the time all of them returned to the Feldner's house in the evening, long after the funeral, exhaustion had made any meaningful conversation impossible. Tovah and Dan, her parents, and her brothers were together at the kitchen table sipping hot tea, but there were long lapses between their few desultory remarks. Every sentence seemed a *non sequitur.*

Finally Tovah's father looked up at the clock. It was just past eleven. "I'm leaving for *shul* tomorrow morning before eight. Is anyone coming with me?"

Ben volunteered immediately. "I'll meet you downstairs at a quarter to." Clearly he'd given himself permission to stand up and say, "Good night. That's it for me."

Hillel stood up at the same moment as Ben. They both looked very much like their father, tall and slim with thinning brown hair.

Hillel stretched, hugely. "I don't know, yet. Not likely. I'll need to make a few calls. I booked off for two days, but I don't know what's happening over the weekend. I'm not sure when I'm assigned again."

Hillel left the kitchen a step behind Ben. "I'll say good night. I'm totally exhausted. Funerals are worse than jet lag any day."

Hadas took the empty teacups and deposited them in the sink. "Tovah?" she questioned.

Dan cut in. "We need to talk."

Tovah bristled internally. He had no right to make any claim on her. But, she spoke as calmly as she could, to hide how she felt.

"I suppose we do. But it can't be until later, maybe tomorrow. We need to be at Ilana's all day."

She went upstairs wondering what she and Dan might eventually say to each other.

Throughout Wednesday and Thursday Tovah found reasons to avoid serious discussion with Dan, although she knew they would have to face each other. It felt very strange to go home to her parents' house every night, to put the children to bed and go to her own room as Dan went to what had been her brothers' large dormitory space on the third floor.

On Friday they all ate Sabbath dinner at the Bregmans'. There were so many food offerings, more than enough for the Brauns, Michael's father, and other family members who'd stayed on. There was no *shiva* Friday night or Saturday morning, since all mourning stopped for the Sabbath. It would begin again after sundown on Saturday, with a *minyan* at the Bregman home, and continue with morning and evening *minyanim* and with people visiting, until the seven days of this first, intense mourning period were completed.

Once the Bregmans' long dining room table had been cleared after dinner and the children were in bed, they all left Ilana's home. Tovah and Dan had trouble keeping up with her parents, even though Ari and Leah were with their grandparents.

By the time they arrived home everyone was upstairs. Her parents had obviously spirited the children away to give the two of them time together.

Tovah sat on the sofa in front of the living room's large window, primly folding her hands in her lap. She immediately regretted her choice of a seat. Dan would come and sit beside her. She didn't want him that close.

To her surprise he seemed to understand. He came and remained standing before her. "This isn't really a conversation for *Shabbat*, I suppose, except that every other moment you find some excuse to avoid me and any discussion at all."

How dare he attack like that! The warm feelings she'd been trying to hold down for the last few days fled, and she was instantaneously angry, as angry as when she'd realized that he'd deserted her.

"I don't think our future is ever off limits," she said, every word stiff and correct. She had to concentrate on not looking up at him.

Since the moment Tovah had heard Michael had died, she'd been half ready to forgive Dan. Watching Ilana say *Kaddish*, standing in the snow with her children around her, the idea it could have been her had been profoundly shocking. The fact she'd actually told Robin it would have been better if Dan had died had been preying on her, even infiltrated her uneasy sleep in Madison. How had she come to be sleeping in her old bedroom in her parents home, with her children in the guest room down the hall and her husband upstairs in the boy's dorm, as though a stranger? Every footstep above her head had been Dan's, even though she knew Ben and Hillel were sleeping there too. Now Dan was telling her how she ought to feel. She was the rabbi. He was the one who'd left them.

He must have understood something of what she was thinking. He stood there looking down at her.

"So, Tovah," he said, "What's next?"

From the moment at the front door of the house when Dan put his arm around her because he knew she might faint, she'd been afraid to talk to him because it seemed to her that a request to come home had been hovering on her lips. Now she couldn't imagine saying those words. So many other things had to come first. "Dan, how could you have left us?" she said.

As soon as the words were out of her mouth she wanted to retrieve them, but of course it was too late.

Dan looked around desperately. He clearly didn't feel he could sit beside her on the sofa. Finally he walked over to the matching loveseat set at a right angle to the sofa and sat down. He didn't say anything. Instead, he reached over and absentmindedly moved every ornament on the square end table. He even shifted the lamp, as though it was blocking their view of each other. Tovah had to restrain her instinct to reach out and slap his hands into stillness.

Instead she waited, and finally Dan clasped his hands in front of him and leaned toward her.

"I should have told you I needed to go," he said. "I see that now. I knew right away, right after I left. I should have tried to share my need to find my mother with you. Somehow, I couldn't. I didn't think you'd let … I didn't think you'd want me to go."

"Of course I wouldn't have wanted you to go. But, if you'd absolutely felt you had to I would have tried …"

"Would you have, Tovah? When I left we were hardly talking to each other. I couldn't see a way … I couldn't seem to … So, when the doctor told me that Leah might have Dystonia not C.P. I thought: I have to find my mother. I have to know if it's familial, my family. If it had been your family we would have known."

Tovah stood up and walked across the room, away from Dan and his halting explanation. She didn't want to hear it. It seemed such an attack. She didn't want Dan to know how she felt, how feelings of regret, rage and jealousy kept her in turmoil. Still facing away from Dan, she said, "Suppose I said: forget it all? Come home. Suppose I said that?"

There wasn't a sound from behind her. What was Dan thinking?

Tovah felt his hands on her shoulders. He turned her around so she faced him.

"First I'd say "thank you." But, I'd have to point out that you don't mean it. Finally, I'd say I can't come home yet. Will you wait until I've finished what I'm trying to do and ask me again?"

"Dan," was the only word she could choke out. His hands were still on her shoulders. Without being fully aware of her body's response she tried to shrug them off.

He let go of her and she almost ran across the room to the archway to the dining room. "Are you telling me you don't want to come home," she said. "How dare you?"

The dimly lit, pleasantly furnished room they stood in hardly seemed a background for such feelings, Tovah's anger and pain, and what seemed to be Dan's reluctance.

Dan straightened up to his full height and slowly lowered his hands that had rested on Tovah's shoulders only a few seconds before.

"Tovah," he said. "I just said that when the doctor said Leah might have Dystonia, I grabbed on to the idea it meant I had to find my mother. I might just as easily have decided that I had to go to Chicago to talk to the Dystonia foundation. I could have decided they would be able to tell me everything I needed to know. But the thought didn't even cross my mind, even though I did exactly that kind of research when they said Leah had C.P.

"I don't understand exactly, but obviously I've needed to do this all my life, all my adult life. I handled it for years by denying it and running away. I was running away when we met. I know that now."

Dan took one step toward where Tovah was standing. She moved back the same step.

At an impasse, Dan tried again to explain, "But somehow this time the balance tipped. I'm older, maybe it made the difference. You hated what you were doing, but wouldn't talk about it. We weren't … We were so out of touch. I don't know. But, I made the choice to go. Now I want to finish the job. I also want to understand why I made the choice. I have to."

"No matter what the impact on me and the kids," Tovah said.

"It's not a case of what it causes. It's already caused the pain. It's already caused this rift." Dan gestured across the space between them as exemplifying the rift.

"I'm in New York. You're in California. Whatever else my leaving did, it got you to act. You should have done this a year ago. Two years. I knew it. You say your father knew. How come you didn't know?"

"How could I know? It was my first job. I got there so late. I couldn't imagine ever catching up. And, there was Leah too. You were so willing to take on her care."

"I thought Leah's condition was my fault. And I didn't really have a choice, did I? Of course I wanted her to be healed. You couldn't take it on. You couldn't do it. Not that and do your job, too."

"Why do we keep blaming Leah?"

"No one is blaming anyone. Except, in not blaming each other we were hardly talking to each other. You've never wanted to look at changing a decision we made three years ago. As far as you were concerned it was working. At least the crucial things were getting done. I didn't want to deal with my issues, so, on some level, it suited me too. I've always thought I was the luckiest man in the world to get you. I was willing to do anything to hang on to you."

"Then you didn't want to do that anymore."

"I couldn't do it anymore. What's worse, I didn't really know it. Give me some credit for self-discovery since then. I only figured some of this out when I realized I didn't quite know why I found myself in New York chasing my mother's ghost, while you moved to California with the children. Then Michael died. That was just moments after Jo and Father Art told me where my mother was in the months before my birth."

Tovah made a noise somewhere between a moan and a cry of despair. She wasn't the only one to find a profound lesson in Michael's death, but she hated what Dan was saying. She hated that she'd just said, "Come home," and he'd rejected her, again.

As though he was reading her mind, Dan said, "Please, please, don't take this as rejection. Take it as love. Take it as a gift of awareness of what our life ought to be. It's been wrong for a long time. We have to fix it. I have to fix what's wrong in my life first."

He crossed the room to her and he took her hand. Tovah willed herself not to pull away, and Dan held on, even though he must have felt the tremors of rejection in her fingers.

"We've paid such a high price for this, Tovah. And, I hope when I've finished my job you'll say it again, you'll say 'come home.' I'd have thought I'd give anything to hear those words. In fact hearing them gives me the greatest hope that we will be able to make this work again, the way it should.

"For once in my life I have to finish what I've started. Without it, our marriage, the best thing I have, you and the kids, will never be right. If I came home now it would be just like before. You don't want me just like before."

"You don't want me at all," Tovah said, actively trying to pull her hand away.

He didn't let go. "Oh, yes, Rabbi Tovah Feldner, I do want you," he said. "You are exactly what I want. But you deserve more than we've had lately." He dropped her hand and they stood there, only inches apart, staring at each other. "I do, too."

His saying 'I do, too' rankled a little, but she let it pass.

"So, what happens now?" she said instead.

"Now," Dan said, as though he'd been waiting for her question. "This is what we do. I think … I've been thinking about this since the moment I saw you at the door. Tomorrow morning I explain to the kids as much as possible, and to your parents, so they won't hate me, I've set myself this task in New York. I tell them what happened just before Michael died. I got a really solid lead. I explain I'm going back to New York to pursue my lead."

He was talking to himself as much as her, Tovah realized.

"I have to pursue it," he said, as though to convince himself.

"When *shivah* is over I go back to New York, you and the kids go back to Orange County." He spoke in the same strong voice, but then he he fell silent, as though actually hearing his own words frightened him.

If they followed his plan they would be putting more than 3,000 miles between the two of them, and between him and his children, with no guarantee that they would ever be able to bridge the distance.

Dan moved away from her. He sat down on the love seat, looking so distressed that, although Tovah was still angry, she felt compelled to go and sit down on the sofa nearby. Mutely they stared at each other.

Dan took a deep breath and went on. "I go to New York, you to California. We set a time limit. I'll take another month, six weeks at the most. I'm almost out of communities of nuns to meet with, and Father's Art information wasn't very specific. My mother might be in France. But, I have to keep doing what I've been doing. I'll try to think of other ways to search too. Passover is in about six weeks. By Passover I'll come home, if you'll have me."

Somewhere deep inside Tovah was almost in awe of her husband. She'd never imagined Dan would risk so much. But she couldn't help asking, "What if I don't ask again?"

He looked up sharply. "If you won't ask again, I'll have lost everything," he said. He stood up, moved toward her. She froze, but he only bent down and kissed her cheek.

"I'll have lost everything," he repeated, before turning away and going upstairs.

# CHAPTER TWENTY-SIX

Tovah and the children were home only three days after their traumatic trip to Madison when she awoke in the middle of the night to a low, loud rumble on all sides, a rumbling both heard and felt. Her bed quivered and shook. Against the all-enveloping, deep background noise she heard fearful orchestration; the high-pitched bell sounds of breaking glass and a single deep kettledrum 'thunk' as a heavy object somewhere at the front of the house struck something.

For about one second, heart in mouth, she thought of staying in bed, supposedly the safest thing to do.

She couldn't. She had to get to Leah and Ari. She stood, felt the building and the earth shimmy in a combined up, down, and sideways motion that should have been impossible. She managed one step as though on roller skates, and after what seemed a fearfully long time, another. Finally, the motion of the floor beneath her ceased and the noise faded rather than simply stopping. As though suddenly freed, she ran into the hall, wrenching open the door to Leah's room. Total peace reigned.

True, Leah's dresser had spun almost sideways to the wall, but had been prevented from sliding into the bed by the cable securing it to the wall. All of Leah's favorite toys, normally stored in a tall bookcase, were scattered, as though some giant hand had thrown stuffed animals, dolls, and books across the floor in an evenly dispersed pattern. The colorful new youth bed Leah had selected all by herself had moved a little, but she had not awakened. She was still warmly covered. Tovah stood for just a moment, reassured by her sleeping child.

She couldn't take the time to enjoy the feeling. She raced back into the hall to find Ari.

She almost tripped over him; he was standing in the hallway outside his room.

"Where's the bathroom?" Ari said, seemingly confused. "Did it move?"

"Actually, sweetie, everything moved." Ari didn't question her remark. The earthquake must have awakened him, and then he'd decided to go to the bathroom.

With one hand lightly on Ari's shoulder she guided him the few steps down the hall. At first glance the bathroom looked the same. Then she realized the clear glass panels that made up the door of the stall shower had jumped from their track. Amazingly, they had not broken. They leaned casually against the tiled back wall of the enclosure. The mirrored sliding panels covering most of the wall and the medicine cabinet had slid one behind the other. Everything on the unprotected side had fallen out onto the counter or into the sink. When Ari, still on automatic, went to wash his hands, he found the sculptured marble sink full of the bottles. He looked up at Tovah in confusion.

"Small earthquake," she said briefly. The word didn't register and that was fine with her. He didn't need to have nightmares. She tried the tap for him, never mind the bottles for the moment. No water.

"We're going to wash your hands this way," Tovah said. She grabbed a bottle of waterless hand cleaner from the jumble in the sink and rubbed it on briskly. "Just as though we're at the beach."

The sink had pulled away from the wall a little. She had better check the water all over the house. What if one of the bathrooms, the laundry room, or the kitchen, was flooding?

She guided Ari back to bed. As she tucked him in a tremor passed under her feet. It seemed to take a detour up her spine. She waited for worse, but the sensation stopped. She told herself a little aftershock probably meant it had just been a little quake.

In Ari's room his chest of drawers had swung away from the wall, but again, the earthquake cable had prevented any violent dislocation. Ari's room also had a tall bookcase that had stayed firmly in place because of the restraints, although every book stored in it had spewed out.

Bless the Steins. They had insisted she not delay bringing in the specialist who did earthquake-proofing. He was a retired engineer from Chicago who obviously loved his California job.

"Course I haven't stopped a quake yet," he'd said, obviously his favorite joke. "But, once I've been through a house there'll be as little damage as possible. And, especially, there will be as little danger to people. I don't want you, or any one else, killed because some stupid thing falls on you. People from the east always want me to hang a big picture or a mirror over their bed. They assume I can do it safely. I tell them it can't be done. I can't do it; not any more than I can control the quake. But, I can make the preparations that allow you to get out of the house if it's necessary. Beside nothing falling on you, the main thing is to have a clear path."

Tovah had asked him how to keep her Coca-Cola memorabilia and her other collectibles safe. He'd looked over the tin trays, glasses and china, clearly not impressed.

"Well, anything you don't use too much," he'd said, indicating the china and glass, "You keep in a cupboard with a ship lock.

"This other stuff," here he'd flicked one finger on a tin tray, "you can glue down to those fancy shelves of yours with museum wax. You won't like the fact you have to get the wax off if you want to use a piece. I'd suggest you just duck if you happen to be in the kitchen when it quakes. This stuff is tin. It won't hurt you. If it dents, it's just more antique."

He'd put ship locks on several cupboards and suggested Tovah learn to store cereal and cracker boxes in the high cupboards, and dishes down low.

Now, with both children safe, she decided getting outside was not a priority. Ari was asleep again. But there had been a loud, deep noise from the front of the house, and glass breaking. She ran back to her bedroom and put on heavy socks and thick-soled sneakers. The phone rang.

"Rabbi, are you okay?"

Teddy Stein.

"I seem to be. The children are asleep. They're okay. I was just going to check the rest of the house."

"Just remember, don't light a candle. Don't strike a match, or turn on the stove. The water heater should cut out automatically, and it's properly strapped. Just don't risk any kind of flame. There could be a gas line break somewhere. Don't try to cook anything. You've got bottled water. If you can't get to it, call me. Don't move anything back in place; it all has to be documented. Is your clock working? Do you have flashlights?"

"Yes. Yes. The alarm clock is battery run. I've got a flashlight in my hand this minute. It was right where you told me it should be, in my night table drawer. Are you all okay?"

"We're fine. There's a bit of a mess here. The girls are hysterical; they want to check on the horses. They'll have to wait. It's people first, property after. As far as I'm concerned the horses are property. The girls think they're people."

Tovah could hear high-pitched voices behind Teddy. He said, "Just a minute, Rabbi." He must have only half turned away, because she could hear him clearly. "Honey, we're all okay. That's the important thing."

He came back on the line, now speaking very fast. "Janice hates earthquakes. We've been in four of them. She didn't tell you, 'cause it might have frightened you. I tell her it's okay to be frightened, under the circumstances. She's been through so many. She'll be all right. Are you sure you're okay? Do you have our cell phone numbers? This wasn't the biggest quake, but it not a real small one either. They'll be lots of coverage on the news, non-stop, days of it. There'll be aftershocks. Don't be surprised. Do you have lights? You must have, the phone works. It might not later. It might cut out. Don't be scared. Keep your cell phone for emergency use. If it's charged, don't let it run down."

"I'm not scared. Not yet," Tovah said, a little surprised because it was true. How would she feel after four earthquakes? "I'm – it's sort of exciting, actually."

Then she asked, "What about the synagogue?"

"We wait to find out. It's property too. The ark is bolted to the wall. The Torahs are in their special racks inside the ark. The prayer books will be all over the floor. The water cooler will have made a mess and the coffee maker too. I don't know about the copier. But there's no one there, so no one is hurt. The alarm will be going crazy. I'll call you later. Don't be frightened by the temblors you feel, the aftershocks. Try not to worry." Teddy hung up.

With flashlight in hand – although the electricity was working – and still in her sleep-shirt, but with the protection of sneakers on her feet, Tovah ventured to the front of the house.

All of Dan's acrylic cases had fallen over and two of them had split. The model of Solomon's Temple was broken; the Ark appeared to be whole. Tovah picked up every piece in turn, but in each case she realized there was no safer spot, so she ended up with each piece on the floor again.

The one unanchored piece of furniture in the dining room, the massive mahogany table, had been responsible for the deep noise she'd heard. The table had gone for a walk, tumbling several of the chairs standing around it. It had only stopped when it smashed into the sideboard. Her silver candlesticks were in disarray. The contents of her china cabinet had toppled one onto the other. She'd have to think about what damage had been done, but she could do that later.

The kitchen was another story. Water fountained from behind the faucets, going straight up in the air and missing the sink completely as it came down. The kitchen counter had pulled away from the wall which had displaced the sink and ruptured the plumbing connection. Tovah could see the granite counter had moved enough so the trash compacter had opened, detached itself and traveled across the floor.

Every piece of Tovah's Coca Cola memorabilia that had been on display had fallen. The term "Coke float" suddenly had an all-new meaning, because as Tovah stood there with cold water beginning to seep into her sneakers, she saw a good part of her collection being carried along by the flow.

Several of the cabinets without ship locks had opened and the contents had marched out and fallen on the counters. She hadn't thought about where she ought to have stored drinking glasses. Out of habit she'd put them in an upper cupboard to the immediate right of the sink. Every single glass had shattered on the granite counter top or on the floor's Mexican pavers. Glass shards afloat in water would make for a hazardous clean up.

Several of her spice bottles lay scattered on the counter. She had a habit of not closing them well after she used them. The kitchen smelled like an Israeli *falafel* stand: cardamom, coriander and garlic predominating. She'd never detect the odor if natural gas was seeping.

Resolutely Tovah went over to the cupboard under the sink, reached in and turned off the flow of water with the valve. That wasn't so bad, she thought, proud that she knew exactly where that detail of plumbing was located.

Her portable phone rang.

"Yes, Teddy," she said, trying to sound as lighthearted as possible. She didn't want him to feel he had to leave his family to deal with hers.

"This is not Teddy. Who in the hell is Teddy? This is Dan." His voice barked in her ear. "Tovah, are you all right? I just turned on the TV."

"You probably know more than I do. Teddy is the president of my synagogue. You know that. I was just headed for the TV to see exactly what happened. But, we're fine. The kids are sleeping. It didn't seem to bother them. I've got a bit of a flood in the kitchen, and some of … some stuff is broken."

"I'm coming out there today," Dan said.

For several seconds she couldn't think of any response.

"Tovah, did you hear me? I said I'm coming out there."

As though hoping for assistance, some suggestion as to what to say to her husband, Tovah looked around the flooded kitchen and into the other rooms. For the first time she realized all the windows at this end of the house had broken, all in exactly the same horizontal plane. Where she and Dan broken too, in the same places? The comparison seemed apt.

For a fleeing moment it seemed her only response to Dan had to be, 'Yes, please come. I need you here so badly.' Surely wanting him there beside her, to deal with an earthquake on top of a new job and looking after their family, was legitimate.

But, it was not what she said. Instead, speaking slowly, trying to pick her words carefully, she said, "Dan. No. Don't come. We've got to stick to our plan."

"Damn the plan. I haven't found another shred of evidence of my mother, and almost all my meetings are done. Is this your way of telling me you're never going to say 'come home' again? Tovah, you need me there."

"Yes," she said. "Yes. You'd be … you'd be invaluable. You'd be … You'd be the same as before. You said you didn't want to be the same as before. I don't want that either. Here is another crisis, like when Leah was born. You'll rush in and fix it. But in Madison we decided, I think we were trying to say – you said – things had to be different. This has nothing to do with saying 'come home.' This has to do with sticking to the plan. There's no special crisis for us. Everyone is the same boat. Ari, Leah and I are fine. You finish what you have to do."

"You don't want me to come, is that it? You don't need me."

"I don't want you to come right now," she admitted. "Not that I don't need you, or ever want you here. I think it's important we stay …"

"The plan was my idea," he interrupted. "You wanted me to come home, but I said 'no'. Now, you're going to punish me. I can't believe it. Obviously, that's what this is all about. I'll call you later, to make sure you're really okay, and to talk to the children."

"Dan," Tovah started to speak, but the phone in her hand had gone dead.

She heard a small noise behind her. Ari stood looking at her from a few feet away. How much had he heard? If he'd understood any of the conversation between her and his father, he didn't admit to it. But, he looked far more angry than frightened.

"Something woke me up," he said in an especially querulous voice. "You were talking very loud. The room shook too. I don't like this."

"Oh, sweetheart, it's okay," she said, hurrying to him. "It's called an aftershock. It's just like the earthquake going back to sleep. There won't be another big…"

Ari stopped and looked her straight in the eye. As always during such a moment, Tovah had the disconcerting feeling of looking into her own mind. It was her look of intensity in Ari's dark brown eyes, and the tilt of his eyebrows telegraphing the same anger she felt when things did not go as she wanted them to go.

"I think you ought to tell Daddy to come here, to this house right away," Ari declared. "He can fix this. He can fix anything. You can't."

Her son may have been only five, but he knew an exit line when he had one.

"I'm going back to bed now," he said. Without looking back at her he walked down the hall and into his bedroom, closing the door behind him just a trifle too firmly.

Tovah could only hope he wouldn't remember much of this when he got up again. Obviously he'd heard enough of the conversation to get the drift of what had been said between her and Dan. She'd have to tell Dan that too; so he could help her deal with it. Also, she had to convince Dan he'd been right back in Madison. He had to finish the job he set himself, no matter what.

Did she really need Dan just to function? Being without him was frightening, but needing him, needing anyone so badly, was also scary.

Just then, as though to test her resolve, a new temblor passed under her feet. She could only gasp, and grab hold of the doorframe. It seemed longer and much stronger than the first aftershocks. Could there be more than one earthquake?

She waited, but Ari didn't come out of his room again, and, when she checked on him, he was sleeping.

Oddly, when the children finally woke up for the day neither of them asked many questions; as though they'd made some sort of a pact. But, no matter what task she was busy with, every time she checked on them they stared back at her, huge eyed.

"No school today," she'd said, as she put together a simple breakfast. "And probably not tomorrow either." Both children were very quiet.

Tovah felt she had to prompt them to talk, although she didn't really want to jog Ari's memory of her early morning phone conversation. But, she didn't want nameless nightmares either. "Can you tell me what happened last night?" she said.

"A cave-in?" Leah said.

"A six point six earthquake," Ari corrected, precise information he'd garnered from the endless television reports.

Those reports had told Tovah the earthquake had been centered in a nature preserve some miles inland. Although the preserve was ringed with new communities, no one lived at the epicenter. Tovah had congregants in many of the surrounding suburbs, but when she tried to reach some of them by phone there was no response.

Later she learned that the phones and the power had gone out in a wide swath through inland Orange, Riverside and San Diego Counties and into Mexico.

Since the children seemed to be okay, if somewhat subdued, Tovah went to recite her morning prayers. This was not the moment to lose the rhythm. Normally the children ignored her during her prayers, preferring to watch television or play. Today they followed her like well-behaved ducklings, actually sitting and listening. Morning prayers usually took her about twenty minutes. Today she took a little more time, adding the prayers for when one has escaped danger, translating the words from the Hebrew for Leah and Ari. She was amused, and very touched when she heard her son follow up her explanation and the prayer with a very energetic "amen," Leah joining him the barest part of a second later.

According to reports there was actually less damage in Dana Point than in some of the areas to the south and east, in parts of San Diego County and to the far south, in Mexico.

Fortunately the quake had taken place in the middle of the night so there had been very little traffic. One or two roads thought to be earthquake-proof were not, but there had been no deaths.

The television interviews with geologists frustrated Tovah terribly. They kept trying to explain the nature of aftershocks. No wonder they kept repeating those segments. Tovah couldn't follow their logic. She wondered if people who'd lived through more than one quake understood what they were saying. Aftershocks should get milder and milder, diminishing over time. But, apparently that wasn't the case. They simply continued until they stopped. It seemed the last aftershock of an earthquake could be the most severe, or the least severe. It could take place days, weeks, even months, later. Tovah wanted to argue violently again that logic. It seemed to make the world precarious, even more than the original earthquake. The earthquake itself was easy enough to understand, since every expert had diagrams and computer simulations of the underground faults honeycombing California.

She was watching yet another report on the subject of aftershocks when a familiar white SUV pulled up and Teddy Stein vaulted from the driver's seat.

"We're fine here. Go find someone who really needs help," Tovah said, as she let him in.

"I'm being a responsible landlord. I have to document damage as soon as possible." Teddy said.

He'd brought one of his foremen with him, who nodded hello to Tovah, then began walking around the house, making notes while taking pictures of the damage with a disposable camera.

"Thank you for all the earthquake preparations," Tovah said. And, thanks for taking the time to phone this morning. I don't know if I did everything right, but we really are okay. I lost a few things. A couple of my husband's models broke too. He'll be upset."

"If he made them, he can fix them," Teddy said briskly. Teddy and Janet had both admired Dan's models when they were unpacked.

The Steins and the board of the synagogue knew Tovah and her husband had recently separated. No one during the interview process had commented on their separation, except for an attorney on the board who'd asked if she had the freedom to take the children out of the state of Minnesota. Tovah had no idea if people were just being supportive and discreet, or if separation and divorce were such an everyday part of life in California that no one gave it any thought.

# CHAPTER TWENTY-SEVEN

Tovah was in the master bathroom getting dressed for the trip to the synagogue Teddy had just suggested, when she heard the phone ring. Teddy would answer it.

"Your Dan and I just met. Not exactly under ideal circumstances," Teddy said. Tovah was holding both children tightly by the hand.

"I tried introducing myself, but I don't think he was listening. He said there are no planes landing here, so he can't come today, but he'll call you back to talk later."

"He's a little anxious about us," was all Tovah offered as an explanation.

They left Tovah's quiet street. In one backyard a storage shed had collapsed. Two of the cottages on the street listed badly. At one point quite near Tovah's house Teddy had to back up his van, because a landslide blocked at least thirty feet of road.

Teddy drove very slowly through Dana Point, weaving through side streets whenever possible.

"Is this what they mean by light damage?" Tovah asked. It looked bad to her. Most buildings had broken windows. Uprooted palm trees were everywhere, across driveways, on rooftops. One large one had squashed the back of a station wagon parked in a driveway. Some of the prettiest bougainvillea-covered retaining walls had slumped. The colored vines must have been pulled up by their roots because they were wilting in the hot sun.

All over Dana Point traffic lights were out, blinking red or yellow. Drivers seemed to know how to proceed, taking careful turns at the busier intersections. At two locations police were directing traffic.

"I don't know why they can keep the highways from falling down, usually, but the traffic lights always go out. There ought to be some kind of back-up battery system, or solar panels. I'm sure it can be done. We shouldn't really be adding to the traffic problems, but I want to make sure we don't have a flood or something at the *shul*."

At the site Teddy drove into the synagogue parking area and parked directly in front of the building. The metal structure looked slightly different, but Tovah couldn't figure out why.

"Some major seams must have separated," Teddy said with a sigh. "The whole building is out of plumb, so every window is going to be broken. It'll have to be repaired or even replaced. The insurance company will pay, they have to, but it'll take forever to get it settled. There's such a high deductible, and I hate to spend any more money on this tin can."

Just to get inside they had to struggle with the jammed main door. Then they had to turn off the alarm. Those things accomplished, they found things pretty much as Teddy had predicted. The water cooler jar had only had a couple of quarts left in it, so there wasn't a flood, only a wet spot on the flat industrial carpeting. All the electrical and plumbing connections seemed to have held. But, once inside the building the fact the walls no longer met at right angles was clear.

"We aren't going to be able to meet here at all. It isn't safe." Teddy said.

Tovah went over to the ark. The sliding doors were half open, and jammed. It was easy to see the track had twisted. The congregation's three Torah scrolls were all safe, each one cradled within the stand securing it to the wall. Tovah reached in and around the jammed doors and brought out each scroll. She took a few steps, intending to put them down on the readers' desk at the front of the sanctuary's *bimah*.

"The floor is safer," Teddy said. "I know you don't usually put a Torah on the floor, but falling off the readers' table during an aftershock is worse."

Tovah moved the three scrolls to the floor, first wrapping each one in a prayer shawl.

"I suppose you think I'm being silly," she said to Teddy, using another prayer shawl to cover them, with a gesture almost identical to covering a sleeping child.

"No, it's not silly; it's a custom, and a sign of respect. But a lot about earthquakes is counter-intuitive. Like the business with the aftershocks. Like the Torahs are safer on the floor. Would you like me to put them in the car right now? They can't stay here. Nothing valuable can. Even if we get the front door shut, the lock isn't going to hold."

"When we leave, we'll take them," Tovah said.

"Is it true that if a Torah falls to the ground the whole community has to fast?" Teddy asked. Tovah figured his question was just meant as a diversion, but she welcomed it.

From where she was kneeling in front of the scrolls, Tovah said, "Yes, true, there is still such a custom. But, only if someone drops it, not because of something like an earthquake."

Tovah was getting to her feet when another temblor passed under them. She ended up, surprised, back on the floor, sitting flat with her legs straight out in front of her. Teddy grabbed the ark. Tovah could see it pull away from the wall, then move back gain. He'd been concerned that it might topple over on them. This time the quaking went on and on.

"Long one," Teddy said when the motion finally stopped. "Not so bad. Maybe four and a point or two, but very long."

"Surely they must get weaker and weaker, even if the guys on television says it doesn't happen like that?" Tovah gasped, from her spot on the floor. The whole out-of-control nature of the aftershocks was beginning to seem like a personal assault.

Leah and Ari, one on each side of her, had seen her fall and they'd clearly felt the aftershock.

Ari's eyes were like headlights and Leah looked down at her feet as though she would never trust them again. They both started to cry.

At the same moment Teddy's cell phone rang. His grimace was an apology to Tovah as he left her to calm and comfort both children. Even from a few feet away Tovah could hear Janice's voice coming sharply through Teddy's phone.

"Honey, honest, I'm sure it's not a new one. Well, you know they can be as strong as the original. But it wasn't that strong. Just very long." Tovah could hear Janice keep on talking through Teddy's attempt to comfort her. It wasn't like Janice. She was usually the calmest person in a room. But, obviously that wasn't true during an earthquake or its aftermath. Tovah reminded herself to make the time to talk to Janice, as her rabbi and as her friend.

Teddy was still trying to comfort his wife.

"Janice, sweetheart, I can't control it even if you'd like me to.

"No, I've said I don't want the girls in the stables, no matter what. The horses rode out the first quake, they'll ride out the aftershocks too. They'll be fine."

Tovah had to assume that Teddy was more excited than he seemed and so didn't realize how odd it sounded to be talking about horses riding anything.

"The paddock is open to the horses. They're smart. You'll probably see them from the window in a couple of minutes. There's nothing to be done, and I don't want the girls trying. They are to stay with you."

There was a pause as he listened. "I know you're scared honey. I know. Leah and Ari are here and they're scared too. But, you're all okay."

"I'm not scared," Ari insisted the minute he heard Teddy's remark. He stood up, shaking off Tovah's embrace. "I was just very surprised."

"Me too. I'm surprised too. I'm not crying." That was Leah of course. She stood up beside her brother, also shaking off her mother's encircling arm.

Teddy was speaking to Janice and he had walked over to one of the broken windows on the far side of the sanctuary. He glanced outside.

Suddenly he made an odd, choking noise, and began gesturing violently to Tovah to come and see. His urgency suggesting a fire or a landslide must be rushing down on them, except he had an enormous smile on his face.

"Janice!" Teddy interrupted his wife. "You'll never believe what I'm looking at. This whole thing might not be so bad. The place next door – *Chicken Feathers* – it's down, flat. Isn't that awful?"

Tovah had never heard any one sound so insincere.

# CHAPTER TWENTY-EIGHT

*hicken Feathers* hadn't crashed in a dramatic way. Rather it seemed to have folded up like a house of cards. The triangular panels making up the building had piled up fairly neatly, one upon the other. At the back of the building, the kitchen no longer existed. All its cement blocks were lying on the ground, very few of them bonded to a mate. It looked as though a child had scattered a pile of blocks with one sweep of a hand. Several parts of a commercial stove, a grill, and some large pots and pans, were visible in the midst of the debris. There was a glass-fronted, double-door commercial refrigerator lying on its back.

As Tovah and Teddy watched, a battered red truck with an open deck pulled on to the lot and stopped. The man who owned the land, the chicken restaurant and the car wash hopped out. He walked over to what had been his building. He nudged the pile of panels sharply with his toe; not quite a kick, but close.

"I'd go out and offer my sympathy, but he'd kick me too," Teddy said.

"Well, he won't kick me," Tovah said. She gave Teddy the children's hands to hold and said, "I've got to make a neighborly and pastoral call. You wait for me."

Tovah and her neighbor had never met, although she'd seen him. He was a tall, nice-looking man in his fifties. He had long, white hair receding at the temples. He wore it neatly tied back in a low pony tail. Today he was wearing his usual outfit: worn jeans, a t-shirt, and heavy sandals over thick socks.

Tovah walked across the boundary of no-man's-land.

"I'm sorry, but I don't know your name. I'm the Rabbi here, Tovah Feldner. I want to say how sorry I am your building collapsed. You must be so upset."

"Not so much. Kind of expect it, you know. But,come into the shade, before we broil here," her friendly neighbor said. He led her over to a fallen tree next to the synagogue; obviously unafraid to cross what Teddy had told her was no man's land.

"So, you're the Rabbi," he said when they'd settled. He held her hand after having pumped it far longer than the duration of a normal handshake. They were stitting right under the window Teddy was near, although they couldn't see him.

"I kept watching for you, but I thought you'd be a guy. Didn't know they made lady rabbis these days. Good idea. They didn't do it when I was a kid." He finally freed her hand, but still smiled at her.

Tovah was nonplussed. "Then, you're...I mean..."

"Don't you know a *lantzman* when you see one, Rabbi?" the man said.

"George Berg. Used to be Goldberg or something like that I would imagine."

"Well, Mr. Berg, one day you might like to ..."

She paused. Inviting someone to worship just then seemed odd.

"No thanks. I'd have come already, if I was ever going to," he said with irrefutable logic. As Tovah watched, her neighbor got up, walked back to the pile of rubble that had been his building. This time, despite the fact he was wearing sandals, he kicked it hard. That must have satisfied him somehow, because he crossed over the low bushes again and sat down beside Tovah, leaning against the synagogue's back wall.

"Had to do something," he said. "I wouldn't hardly have felt that, even if they'd all landed on me. Felt like I ought to return the favor."

He turned toward Tovah. "Is the guy who bought the land you're on, Stein, hiding in there?" George Berg bumped his hand against the synagogue. Tovah could imagine what Teddy, hovering over them, must be thinking.

"Why ... why ... do you ask?" Tovah said, unable to think of any other answer.

"You go and tell him I've got a deal for him. I've got a twenty minute, blue-light special for him. If he wants this piece of land for your group, he can have it. Tell him I want the last price he offered me, less a few percent – tell him ten percent – although I suppose I ought to negotiate. But, I just can't bring myself to do it. I'm only taking the reduction so the insurance won't argue on the value of the building. They'd like to claim the building isn't really worth anything, but I want them to pay for it. It's insured. It being down already is a bonus for you. I ought to charge Stein more 'cause God did the work for him. But maybe he expected it; you being a synagogue. Anyway, he's saved the trouble of demolition. He's still got to promise he isn't going to put even one of his God-awful houses on this lot. I was going to tell the new rabbi that anyway, sooner or later."

George Berg clearly didn't think Tovah had any blame in the war between him and the developers.

"I'd have stuck around, just to slow him down, but now I can't afford it. I'm going to get out of here, away from all these people showing up, and lady rabbis who'll want to civilize me. Not that I take it personal, or anything." He favored Tovah with another smile before he continued.

"Go and tell him. Tell him the clock is running. I'll wait right here."

"I'll go … I'll deliver your message," Tovah said. It wasn't dignified, but they'd never covered a situation like this in seminary. Nor could she think of a single precedent in her father's long career that helped her at this moment.

"Oh, Rabbi, there is one more thing."

"Yes?" Tovah asked, turning back to this man who seemed to be entirely amiable, no matter how he felt about Teddy Stein, and despite the fact his property was in ruins.

"I could use someone to say *Kaddish* for my folks. You'll do it? Before I go I can give you the dates and their Hebrew names. You need their parents' Hebrew names too. Right?"

"Yes," Tovah said. "I hope these aren't recent losses for you."

"Nope," George said. He didn't seem to feel the need to explain any further. He just nodded, apparently satisfied with the agreement they'd just made. Without further comment Tovah headed around to the synagogue's front door.

When she was back inside, she didn't have to say a thing. Not only had Teddy heard every word, now he was relaying it all to Janice.

"Yup!" Teddy said. "We're going to buy it, absolutely. I'm going to do give him a good-faith binder right now. Then we'll worry about financing. The board has always said we ought to take the land when we can get it. I'll get it okayed. We'll meet this week. No, we'll meet tomorrow afternoon. I can get the word out by email and phone today. Not everyone has email yet. It's only a little past noon. Fund raising, here we come. 'Join the building fund.' 'Own a piece of the action!'"

Over the phone, Tovah could hear Janice's voice again, high and shrill. She was undoubtedly trying to restrain Teddy's enthusiasm, but that wasn't possible.

"Well Rabbi," Teddy said. "What do you know about building synagogues?" Got any ideas about any of this? What do you know about raising money? There will be some from insurance. We'll have to use it to fix up this piece of junk, I suppose, although I sure hate to waste it." He kicked at the wall of their building. George Berg had made a special point of kicking the detritus of his building. It must be a guy thing. Tovah felt absolutely no desire to kick anything.

"I wouldn't want us burdened forever with a huge mortgage just to buy the land," Tovah said. "That can be so disheartening. We would have to pay it off before we could put one stick in the ground. I do think we have to do this. I guess we do it on faith."

Teddy gave Tovah a big smile. "That's your department. All I know is I'm going outside right now and talk to Berg. Why didn't he say he was Jewish?"

"He obviously doesn't think it's relevant," Tovah said. "And, I don't know anything about design. My husband knows."

"Right, all those models of his. Well, if we ever get to building, I'll be able to put him to work. He seemed to think he ought to be able to get here fast. I don't know how, with no planes flying. He'll manage it, sooner or later, if that's what you two want."

Teddy looked down at Leah and Ari who were watching the adults, eyes swinging from one to the other, as though a championship tennis match was going on in front of them. "Do you two know you are witnesses?" Teddy said.

He squatted down so he was at their eye level. "When you're grown ups you'll say, 'I was there the day they bought the land that made the new synagogue possible; the day of the nature preserve quake.'"

The children kept looking at him steadily, as though their concentrated gaze would make what he'd just said comprehensible.

Teddy stood up, bowed ceremonially to the children and to Tovah, and said, "Excuse me. If you'll just wait here for fifteen minutes or so, I'm going to shake hands on our deal." He pushed the door open energetically, and walked out. When he tried to push the door shut behind him it would not close fully.

For the rest of the day at home Tovah cleaned up, picked things up, swept up broken glass, and took phone calls from Dan.

# CHAPTER TWENTY-NINE

Dan had an evening appointment with one of the last communities of nuns. At one time, in response to his troubling conversation with Tovah and his concern for his family, he might have cancelled. This time he didn't even consider it.

He'd already stood this group up once, when Michael died. He thought that what Tovah said, that he should follow his own plan and finish the task he'd set, had sounded like a dare. He was certainly going to get to California, no matter what Tovah said. But, for the moment, planes weren't flying, so he might as well keep his appointment.

He had nothing else important on his agenda. His conversation with Tovah hadn't told him much. Tovah, and Teddy Stein, even the children, actually sounded excited to be part of an earthquake, one making the purchase of the rest of the land around their industrial building possible. Well, no matter what transpired, he needed to see all of them, touch them, put his arms around them and know with every fiber of his body that they were really okay.

It was dark when he took the subway uptown to a location quite different from any of the other community apartments he'd visited already.

He found himself in front of what had once been a small commercial building of brown brick. The massive front door had to be original. He felt unreasonably pleased that someone had taken the trouble to preserve it. It had inset glass panels of old wavy glass in place long enough to have turned a lovely pale blue.

The original cornerstone said 1810. Above that was a new brass plate recording the year the building had become the official Motherhouse of the Sisters of the Star of Jesus' Birth. The Old English script they'd used was so elaborate the sign was almost impossible to read. Other than the cornerstone plaque, the only other identification was a second brass plate set over the front door. The Maltese cross engraved on it was so ornamented it looked more like an Asian pictograph than a Christian symbol.

The exterior of the building had been renovated fairly recently. All the windows, the gutters and new downspouts were painted a rich, dark red. There were beautifully wrought guards on the windows of the lowest two levels. Two weighty looking concrete urns filled with cut pine boughs flanked the door.

It was a building that didn't want to call attention to its presence, but also wanted to be correct in every detail, so it would fit into this affluent East Side neighborhood.

The nun who opened the door was one of the really young women Dan had met in a religious community, not more than twenty. Given that she was Vietnamese he expected a heavy accent, but her greeting was one hundred percent New York.

Once inside, he saw the interior of the building was special, where the exterior had just been trim and tidy.

There was an extraordinary chapel located to the right. Several rows of pews made of deeply colored rosewood, banded with brass, were in place. He had a glimpse of the altar, located on the back wall of the building, inspiring in its simplicity. The crucifix over the altar had been rendered in an almost abstract manner, with the tension in the figure of Jesus making it especially poignant. The Stations of the Cross were in the form of exquisite traditional scrolls. A tiny confessional had been placed at the rear of the chapel, directly opposite where Dan stood. In any other setting it might have been taken for a curtained model of a tea pavilion.

The young sister must have been accustomed to curious visitors, because she let him absorb the details of the chapel before suggesting he follow her.

She led him away from the chapel, to the left, through a perfectly neat, conventional office with at least ten work stations in the open area, and a series of small individual office along the back and far side of the large space.

Half-way back, they came to a set of stairs. Stairs should be ordinary. But, he realized the stairwell running down from the floor above, was only one half of a structure.

"The other part of this stairway is in the chapel?" he guessed.

"Oh, you figured that out so quickly," she said. "Would you like to see it?"

He followed her around again. This time they entered the chapel. The stairwell on the inside wall was a work of art, not simply utilitarian like its twin in the office. Instead of balusters, there was fretwork matching the confessional. Cleverly, the fourth stair widened into a platform and functioned as the pulpit. Stairs from the pulpit led back toward the altar.

"Very nice," Dan said. "Your architect made wonderful use of the space. The stairs allow the priest to come and go from the altar."

Yes. Our designer even provided a small vesting room, a sacristy, for the priest. It's a half-floor up." His guide seemed happy he enjoyed the details of her home. "But it was not an architect who designed all this. It was one of our sisters."

They were going to leave the chapel again, when the young nun's smile broadened, if that was possible. As though they were both slightly naughty children she said, "Why don't we go up this side?"

Clearly the trip was meant as a treat. The chapel stairs joined its mate in a lovely seamless fashion just below the level of the second floor.

Dan had assumed that the second floor would be the convent's living space, but instead they ended up in a hallway almost as exceptional as the chapel and the staircase.

There were four, old, wonderfully detailed doors, paneled walls and moldings that had the weight of wonderful furniture, because everything had been painted in colors reminiscent of the chapel, and there was brass banding like the pews.

"That is our dormitory floor," his guide explained, leading him to the third floor where it was immediately obvious they were in the convent's living space.

Sunshine would stream in here all day, and the large windows provided wonderful views. Yet it all felt serene, removed from the busy city below.

He was facing the rear of the building, the dining room, the sisters' refectory. It had been furnished with Shaker-inspired pieces: a long harvest table and many chairs. There were Shaker pegged hanging racks running all the way around the room as a dado, some of the pegs holding navy blue cloaks and dark gray veils. They were also storage for pairs of long white ecclesiastical candles, hanging by joined wicks. A few bouquets of fragrant herbs mixed with small roses hung head down, drying.

Dan finally turned to face the front of the house and found an entire community waiting for him.

The nuns were ranged like a small army, in four rows, about fifty sisters in identical habits. He had been told many of the sisters worked in the community where he imagined they wore ordinary, secular clothing. In their own home each sister dressed in a neat gray and white habit; a mid-calf-length gray dress covered with a white scapular and alb. Each sister also wore a headdress of stiff gray linen shaped like a nurses' coif of First World War vintage, securing their veils. The same elaborate black Maltese cross appearing on the plaque over their front door centered each headdress.

Dan looked around for his guide, but she had disappeared. He saw the flash of her white veil as she stepped into position in the last row, next to two others wearing white veils; the youngest in the community, postulants.

Three of the most elderly nuns, clearly those in charge, sat on a small white sofa pulled into the middle of the room. There was a small tea table in front of them. The nun in the center had to be the abbess. She was dressed just like the others, except around her neck she wore a heavy silver chain with a silver crucifix suspended from it. It was a perfect miniature of the crucifix he'd seen in the chapel. She stood up. She was not much taller than a ten-or-twelve year old, but she managed to radiate great authority.

"Welcome," she said, in a surprising strong voice, very much like Tovah's pulpit voice.

"Please," she said, inviting Dan into the room. He came and stood in front of her. Her face had an ageless quality, but the hair showing at the edge of her veil was white, and at close range he could see her face was a fabric of fine wrinkles.

"I am Mother Abbess On-Lei," she said, extending her hand. Dan had learned ecclesiastical manners in his weeks in New York. He knew she would not expect a Jewish person to kiss her silver and black opal ring. Shaking hands with this personage didn't feel quite right either, so he took her hand in his, and bowed deeply. When he looked up she smiled in a way suggesting his compromise gesture pleased her.

He'd been afraid this community was greeting him in such a formal manner because he'd failed to show up for his first appointment. But, he could see every nun was smiling at him.

The Mother Abbess introduced him formally, first to the two lieutenants flanking her. She also walked him through the ranks, naming each sister. It was all so orderly, the military metaphor persisted.

When they returned to the front of the grouping, an armchair had been placed for him directly across from the Mother Abbess. She sat down. So did Dan. The rest of the Sisters moved in, but remained standing.

Then he knew. He'd found his mother.

Immediately his eyes went back to the group of nuns behind the abbess, flickering across each face, mentally comparing every nun to the face he knew from his drawing.

"She is not here, Mr. Goldin," said one of the two senior nuns sitting beside the abbess. "Our Sister Adele passed away more than three years ago. I am sorry to have to inform you. But, she left you this."

Sister Adele. She'd kept the name, a link to him. Mother Abbess put one small hand on a large, heavy envelope lying on the tea table. Words written on it sprang into focus: *For My Son*.

He didn't ask how they knew. Of course they knew. They had been waiting for him. He felt a wave of regret so powerful it was as though he was being pushed back in his chair. He should have come sooner. He could have met her.

"She never thought you would come when she was alive. She said you would have to be a man, grown, before you'd want to come. For the last years she was so ill. It concerned her greatly, because it was cancer. She felt if you had children they would need to know. You would need to know. Her medical records are here." The sister tapped her finger on the envelope.

"This also contains family information, her family, and your father's family too. There is a memoir she wrote for us. Plus, there is a record of her work, at the U.N. and on this building."

"She was your designer," Dan said, the realization a gift. Now he had a place where he could visit, one his mother had an important role in shaping. He would bring Tovah, his children, and his parents to this building.

"The Reverend Dr. Waggoneer told us of your interest in buildings. Perhaps you have this gift from her." Dan had never heard Jo referred to in such a formal way.

"I also understand that this is one of the very last places you had to visit," the abbess said.

"Jo knows about this?" Dan said.

"No, we have not told her. Only we asked about you when she called. We immediately thought it would be you; Sister Adele's son. We were almost one hundred percent certain. We also knew you had to come to us. You had to ask. Perhaps you had not come up to this point, because you were not ready."

"I've been in New York for more than two months," Dan said. He didn't want finding Adele, finding his mother, invested with mystical implications. It had been persistence and his willingness to take a huge risk that allowed him to find her.

"Believe, me, I was ready. I'm sorry I didn't look earlier, five years earlier."

But the sisters didn't seem to share his regret. Rather they had the air of having completed a task left to them. One of the abbesses' two lieutenants, clearly a spokesperson for the group, said, "Sister Adele came to us for sanctuary after you were born. She had intended to go to France, to join an order there. By the time she recovered, she decided to stay amongst us. She was able to go back to her work at the U.N., not as a translator on the floor, which would have been too risky. She worked only on documents, and she did her work here. The couriers came almost daily. She held the highest level of security clearance."

"And, her designing this building; how did it happen?" How wonderful his interest and talent might come as an inheritance from his mother.

"Both of your parents had this ... ability. Although she feared your father for many years; she acknowledged he was a man of many talents. A military engineer. Her talent seemed to manifest later, when we began to make this building our mother house, after all of us arrived from Vietnam."

The nuns standing behind the sofa had finally broken ranks and were clustered around the sofa. At the word 'Vietnam,' several of the older sisters, obviously remembering, looked somber.

"I … I have so many questions, and I also have to go, to leave New York very soon. My wife and children are in California. They've just been through the earthquake there." He couldn't believe he could feel torn about leaving. More than anything he wanted to be with Tovah and the children. More than anything he wanted to hear every word he could about Adele, his mother.

"It is the living who have first claim," the abbess said. "When you have been through all the papers Sister Adele left, you will come back to us."

The Abbess seemed to speak in brief, pithy sentences, as though to preserve her strength. Her second-in-command took over when a longer speech was needed.

"Anything more you want to know can wait. And, many of your questions will be answered by these." The younger woman held out the large, heavy envelope to him.

"Each of our sisters writes a biography, a memoir, when she comes here. As our sisters grow older, or before their deaths, if they know when it is coming, they each complete their story. Your mother knew long before most people do. Hers is very complete. She believed, absolutely, you would come. Many of us were not so convinced. I'm very glad she was right."

She smiled at Dan, tears gleaming in her eyes. The look on faces of all the sisters standing clustered around the sofa made it clear she spoke for all of them. "When you have been through all of this you will come back. Later you will bring your family to see this building, and to hear our stories of our beloved Sister Adele, your mother."

# CHAPTER THIRTY

Just as he'd promised, Teddy Stein had an emergency board meeting called for the very next day. He'd sent out a rapid round of email, and activated his established synagogue-wide phone system. All their congregants were safe, although a few homes were damaged. Almost every single board member said they'd attend his emergency board meeting.

"I think it's a welcome distraction," Teddy said. "Synagogue business is better than their concerns. I caught most of them before their jobs really start up again. And, it's a daytime meeting. I've noticed people don't like being out at night right after a quake"

"I think the aftershocks feel worse at night," Tovah agreed. The earthquake itself — about sixty seconds of quaking earth and objects falling – wasn't the worst part to Tovah.

Very early that morning, hours before Teddy's meeting, Tovah realized she had to get a hold of herself. She took the children down to their nearby beach. She was sitting on a blanket watching them play when the sand around her shivered and shifted. She'd never seen anything like it. She hadn't thought what an aftershock could be like at the beach. She stood up, grabbed the beach bag and ran down to where the children were digging in the sand. She was ready to grab Ari and Leah and flee.

The children looked up at her, all smiles. Had they even felt the little tremor? If they noticed, they paid no attention. They just thought their mother had come to admire their sand castle.

After she'd listened to them outline their construction plans, Tovah walked back to their blanket, embarrassed by her panic.

Pretty much the same thing had happened last night. She'd been visiting one of her neighbors to find out if they were okay. A tiny ripple of an aftershock ran through the house. Tovah stood up, ready to run, but the woman she was with looked around, said, "Two point nothing," and continued to make tea for both of them.

So, determined to be at least as calm as her children, Tovah took out the board-meeting agenda Teddy had sent her to review. There were only four items.

1. Rabbi's *drash*

2. Earthquake report (damage and emergency response)

3. Offer to purchase the land on The Big Divide

4. Passover

"I don't know that we'll get to Passover" Teddy had said. "As for reports, we already know everyone in the synagogue is all right. There can't be a real emergency. It's okay though. It still feels like an emergency. We'll want to make a decent donation to the earthquake relief fund. It's the offer to purchase that's getting them to the meeting. A lot of them want to meet you again too, as our rabbi this time, not just as a candidate."

Tovah had been unreasonably concerned she hadn't done anything noteworthy for her community. Now she had a real worry. How could she support people shaken by earthquake? People like Janice for example.

She'd made talking to Janice her earliest priority. Once prompted, Janice talked for almost two hours, recounting all the earthquakes she'd lived through: Silmar, Whittier, Northridge, and the first one she'd ever experienced, a small earthquake in San Francisco no one else ever talked about anymore. That was the quake Janice remembered the most clearly.

She and Teddy had been newlyweds living in a rented house on the edge of the Castro area, "You could still afford to rent there when we got married," Janice said. "That day – it was early on a Saturday morning – there was a smallish temblor, maybe a five. But the kitchen had been renovated from some kind of sunroom. It had a glass solarium ceiling, which collapsed. Plus, every dish and glass we owned was smashed.

"We weren't hurt, sort of a miracle. We had just gone outside to spray the roses because they were bug infested. A minute or two later, or a minute or two earlier, and I'd have been in the kitchen when the glass ceiling caved in."

Even as Janice told her story her eyes widened with fear. They were sitting out on one of the many patios attached to Janice's home. Their surroundings were so beautiful, seemed so safe.

When Janice finished retelling the story, she seemed to feel a little better. She said to Tovah, "We've learned a lot. We never live in a house that isn't up to code. We know how to hang things, and to tie things down. But, when I have earthquake nightmares, it's about the first one. And when there's a new quake, I flash to the first one. It certainly isn't the most dangerous one I've been though. But I go straight back there."

She'd looked stricken. "I don't mean you'll have nightmares or flash on this one. Honestly. Not the children either."

"Of course we won't," Tovah said, reaching over to touch Janice's arm, to reassure her. "Remember, we had you. You made sure we would be safe. Without you we would never have been prepared."

That seemed to help.

Talking to Janice made Tovah felt better. She hadn't yet dealt with Dan's expected arrival, even though she was pretty sure that by Friday at the latest, airplane landings would have resumed.

She still didn't know what she'd say to Dan. And, would he move into the house when he came? Or, did she want him living somewhere else?

She couldn't imagine directing him to the nearest hotel. Even temporarily it would be so … so … Her imagination failed her.

Well, she had other things to think about. She had to consider what to say to the board of her synagogue later in the day. Never mind thinking about what to say to Dan when he got a flight.

The board would be expecting her to open the meeting with some sort of *drash*, a teaching, something appropriate to the moment.

Traditionally she'd have said something about the *Parshah,* the portion of the Torah read in the synagogue that week. Currently the readings dealt with purity issues. It was all fascinating in a scholarly way, but not a subject she thought people would want to hear about, given their present concerns.

Tovah knew you could tell a lot about a society by the categories they selected. In ancient Israel pure and impure were categories that were considered essential. She just didn't think of anything relevant on the subject when the only two categories making sense right at the moment were: damaged in the earthquake or not damaged in the earthquake.

What could she say to people who might be feeling very traumatized, just as rattled as she felt? It seemed to her she could feel quake-like tremors in her soul, ripples not yet stilled.

Reading up on earthquakes had to humble you. After the Northridge earthquake, the whole San Fernando Valley was actually a different size and shape then before: narrower by inches, with its northern border several inches farther north. And, it had all happened in less than a minute. From somewhere came energy that moved mountain ranges. In the face of such power, could she come up with THE answer to people's problems, or her own?

No, not THE answer, she told herself, just an answer – one approach.

She was working on the coffee table at home, still unable to get into her study. The broken windows had been taped. Teddy and his foreman managed to tip back her china cupboard then eased open the door. Surprisingly, most of the things inside were intact.

This morning at the beach, she'd looked up at the cliffs that towered above the highway just across from where she sat. She had thought of them as a bulwark. But even those sustaining cliffs showed the after-affects of the earthquake. Rivulets of lighter colored soil showed against the dark earth and rock surface of the cliffs. Some of the tough-rooted creosote and cacti had fallen. Even though powerful forces had been at work on the cliffs, they had not fallen.

They had not fallen? Of course! They had not fallen.

She knew exactly what she would say to the synagogue board.

She got up and went to dress for the meeting, deliberately selecting a new suit, unlike anything she'd ever owned before, far more chic than anything B.C., before California. Wearing the suit's gray and red pinstriped knee-length lightweight fitted coat over the sleeveless dress, just barely longer than the coat, she left the house to drive to the Steins'.

Okay, she though, this proves it. I know what to say. Nothing, not this move to California, not the earthquake and its aftermath, not even the troubles she and Dan faced as a couple, would prove to be too much. Her problems, their problems, were going to be solved, even if she didn't yet know how.

If she felt this way, just because she'd solved the problem of what to say to the board, okay. She would take full advantage of how good she felt at this moment.

Problems had to be used, faced, even if they couldn't all be solved. If you didn't confront your problems, you found yourself backing away from life.

She'd been doing that before in Minneapolis. She had not tried to solve anything. She'd just worked to defend herself from more loses, even from the realization she'd made some terrible and fundamental mistakes.

In Minneapolis she'd actually feared Dan would find something he wanted to do. If you'd asked her, she would have said she only felt that way because it was better if Dan was willing to be at home, looking after the children, taking special care with Leah's therapy.

But limiting someone else's life was no basis for building your own. If she wanted to be with Dan, there had to be room for his choices too. She'd exacted a cost from him he'd never said he was willing to pay. She would never have paid that price either.

She pulled into the Stein's compound and got out of her car. As though Dan, far away in New York and still trying to get a flight, knew she was thinking of him, the new cell phone in her coat pocket rang.

Before she could really say hello, Dan was telling her planes would be flying the next day, Friday. "Tomorrow morning, first thing, I'll be on a flight," he said in a tone of voice that suggested he was trying to convince himself, and her.

Tovah's response probably surprised her as much as it surprised Dan. Clearly he was ready to argue, but she said, "Dan, you're right. When you can get a flight, please come home. We're never going to solve anything this way."

There was a long silence at the other end of the line and finally Dan said, in an emotion-chocked voice he was obviously struggling to control, "I agree. I'll try to make it early tomorrow, before Shabbat."

Oddly, there wasn't much more to say. Dan concluded, "I'm going to call for a reservation on the first flight out of here."

Tovah said, "I have a board meeting. I guess I should go inside."

"You're not meeting in that shaky building, are you?"

"No, we're at the Stein's home."

"Well, at least you're not in a tent," Dan said. They both laughed and hung up.

Only a few minutes later, feeling oddly relaxed, Tovah began her *drash* at the board meeting. "I'm going to fall back on an old tradition today and tell you a story. A story from the Talmud, which I think I may finally have understood in a whole new way. This is the story:

*There is a famous debate in the Talmud, one of the first things you study.*

*There was a certain kind of clay oven in ancient Babylon that could be taken to pieces or, might come apart. So, regarding such an oven, the question the great Rabbi Eliezer asked the* rabbonim, *the leading intellects of the Babylonian Yeshiva, was this: If the oven is taken apart, or somehow falls apart, and then is put together but has touched something that is unclean, is the oven unclean or can it be used?*

*Rabbi Eliezer himself said the oven could be used. But, all the other* rabbonim *said it could not.*

*Rabbi Eliezer knew his judgment was true, so he said, "If I am correct, let the carob tree show you."*

*A carob tree uprooted itself and walked 100 paces. The other* rabbonim *were not impressed. "A carob tree cannot rule on such things," they said.*

*"Let the water in the stream show that I am correct," Rabbi Eliezer said. The water in a nearby stream flowed backward, uphill not downhill. The others said, "Water has no standing in such matters."*

*Rabbi Eliezer tried to bring his argument even closer to home. "Let the walls of the house of learning, this Beit HaMidrash, show I am correct." So, the walls surrounding them leaned in.*

*The other rabbis were neither frightened nor impressed. "Who are you, walls, to think you have any say in such matters?" they said. Showing no fear at all, they admonished the leaning walls surrounding them. The walls moved back. But, while out of respect for the* rabbonim *the walls straightened up somewhat, at the same time, out of respect for the great Rabbi Eliezer, they did not straighten out completely. They remained leaning in at an angle. But they did not fall."*

Tovah looked around. Of course no one had missed her point. She asked a totally rhetorical question. "What does it all sound like to you?"

"An earthquake," Janice said promptly. "All those things can happen during an earthquake."

"Right. It could well have been an earthquake that broke the oven apart. We've all seen trees uprooted. Our climate is even something like the climate in Babylon, so we could even find an uprooted carob tree that might have moved right here. And, although I've never seen it, people tell me water in small streams and rivers sometimes flows backwards for a while as the result of a quake. Goodness knows we've seen walls leaning. Our own walls.

"But, just as those ancient walls did not fall, ours did not either. No one was killed by the walls in the Talmud. That's also true for us.

"Our walls have leaned in, but they have not fallen. We might even need new walls, still to be built by us, but they will stand."

There was actually a little ripple of applause around the room, something Tovah had never heard after any *drash* she'd delivered.

"Now, I must tell you there is not one word about an earthquake in this story from Babylon in the Talmud. But earthquakes are common in the area. I checked today. And, because people are used to them, unless they're greenhorns like me, they would hardly be worth mentioning if the damage was limited to water running backward, or a tree or two being uprooted. Also without stringent building codes to worry about, as long as the learning could go on uninterrupted, the Yeshiva staff and members would have been content to live with leaning walls.

"So, I think we can own this story, make it ours in this way, adding our interpretation to the thousands of interpretations in the last two thousand years."

She sat down. She'd had made an impact.

Still basking in the sensation of how well her story had been received, Tovah made herself pay attention to what Teddy was saying.

"Two churches in the area, the Lutheran one, Holy Redeemer, and First Congregational, have offered us space. I've said thank you, and that we would very likely take them up on their offer. We have to make both short and medium term plans. Certainly we aren't going to have a building immediately. I know it's going to be frustrating, having the land, not being able to use it, but there's nothing we can do about it. We'll just…"

He stopped because Tovah stood up.

"Rabbi, are you all right?" Teddy said.

"What we have to do is pitch a tent." Tovah said.

"A tent?" The whole room responded simultaneously, a single chorus of confusion.

"Yes. Whatever we eventually do about a place for services, until we have a building, we ought to pitch a tent. It ought to be a great big tent, right on the property. It's a gesture – you could even say it's a gimmick – but, whenever possible we ought to meet in it. We're coming into the warmer, dryer weather. We wouldn't even have to heat or air condition it at the moment. And we ought to have one congregational *Seder* there too, on the second night of Passover. It's an important symbol. Like Moses and the children of Israel during the Exodus. It'll get us noticed. It'll get us members. It's a symbol people, our people and everyone else in the area, will understand. And, the more members we acquire, the faster we'll have a permanent new home."

There was total silence in the room for a several seconds. Tovah waited. She was going to hear a chorus of dissent. Why had she thrown out such a ridiculous idea, just when she had a success? Then, from a corner of the room, one woman, someone Tovah had never met before, said, "A tent is a great idea. We're going to do it, Rabbi. We're going to put up a tent."

The protest Tovah expecting never happened. It was as though faced with two women who thought a tent was a wonderful idea, any opposition simply evaporated.

Tovah's unknown supporter said, "Look, one of our members owns the Abby Rents out here. I rented a tent from him for my daughter's wedding.

"If we put up a tent, it'll get us a rush of new members, you watch. This isn't the time to be cautious. Naturally, we have to keep those new members, but our biggest problem has never been keeping people, it's been getting them in the first place. Getting them to know we exist. This will do it. We have to do it right away. Any news coming out of the earthquake is important. Good news is the most important. We have to set up this tent right now, and really use it for the time being. Why not? Later on it doesn't matter what other arrangements we make."

"I vote yes to a tent," she concluded, even though no vote had been called for. Then she added, blessedly pragmatic and generous, "My husband and I will underwrite the cost for the first three months."

The whole board waited while Teddy called the man who owned the tent. He came back to the meeting saying Abby Rents would have the tent set up first thing in the morning, six a.m.

"It's a very big tent," Teddy said. "It holds a seated dinner party of two hundred. So, it'll take a whole lot of seats, theater style."

Somewhere along the line, between Tovah's off-the-cuff suggestion and the call to Abby Rents, Teddy had become a convert to the idea of a tent. No one would have guessed Tovah was practically faint with relief, and, at the same time, vowing that not one more spontaneous remark was ever going to pass her lips.

"Pitch a tent," Teddy said, actually chuckling. "Who'd have thought of it? It's one hell of an idea. It'll put us on the map. And, we'll announce a new name too, at the same time. We can link it to our old name, so people will know who we are."

"What new name?" several people, including Tovah, asked at the same time. Teddy hated when people criticized the synagogue's name. Tovah thought the lackluster name deserved all the criticism it got, but she'd never said a word to Teddy.

"I know no one likes the name any more, except me," Teddy said.

"It was a good name for the beginning," Janice said, making a wifely effort to be diplomatic. Tovah knew Janice didn't like the name either.

"You mean, even if it's boring. I've always thought you don't just change your name; your name is your identity."

"Oh for heaven sakes, Teddy," Janice said, waspishly, now obviously done with her attempt at diplomacy. "Women change their name all the time. When they get married, or divorced. Men don't, but that's not everyone. When someone's status changes; their name can change too. And that goes for organizations as well as people."

Teddy looked a little hurt that even Janice had become impatient with him, but he clearly wasn't going to admit it. Instead, very dignified, he said, "I'm quite willing to admit if we have to have a new game here, and if we're going to have to change our name, it ought to be right now. Rabbi, the Hebrew word for tent is Ohel, right?"

No wonder they keep electing Teddy president, Tovah thought. Who else would have thought of changing the name at this moment, in the middle of a crisis? He'd even thought of using the idea of part of their solution, a tent, in their name.

"Tent is Ohel," she confirmed. "It's a nice idea to use it. But, we have to think about it a little. Will it wear well? We have to think about what we're doing. What attribute do we want attached to it. What's our identity? Will it be Learning, Charity, Prayer, or Study? We won't want to change the name again. We could be *Ohel Shalom*, or ..."

Tovah might wax philosophical over a name, but Teddy would not. "Nope, not *Shalom*," he said. "*Shalom*, peace, is a great idea. But, every second Reform synagogue is Temple *Shalom*. I don't want to be confused with any of them. So, how about 'hope, *Tikvah*?' We hope for peace anyway, so hope includes everything. Putting up the tent is an act demonstrating our hope for the future. Also, it's an name easy to say. We don't want such a difficult name no one can say it in English. *Ohel Tikvah*, Tent of Hope. The 'tent' part is for our past, when our people were wanderers living in tents. But it's totally relevant to our currant problem and it speaks to the solution we've found. *Tikvah,* hope, is for all those things we hope will happen in the future, including our hope for peace. Plus, the national anthem is Israel is *Hatikvah*, The Hope. That's another important link."

A buzz of agreement flowed around the room.

"I like it."

"Wonderful symbolism."

Somebody ventured, "*Ohel Shalom* sounds good too."

But the group had already adopted Teddy's idea. He obviously knew exactly when the buzz of voices meant agreement, like the sizzle that tells a good cook when the skillet is ready.

"Okay, people," Teddy said. "Let's get this done. Then you can all go home and I'll get out another emergency mail and phoning. We're going to recommend *Ohel Tikvah* to the membership at a full meeting tomorrow. It's so perfect: the new land, the tent and the name, all of it at the same time. We won't need the usual notice period for an emergency meeting."

# CHAPTER THIRTY-ONE

By the next morning they had a tent. Tovah couldn't believe the earthquake was less than two full days in the past. Here they were meeting together on their own land, in a tent, an idea coming spontaneously from Dan's remark. Teddy had not only called a membership meeting, he'd also called a press conference to follow.

"It's good all this is happening so fast," Teddy said, exultant. He stood at his temporary podium, a folding table from the synagogue building, echoing his theme of the day before. "People aren't really back to work yet. The press, the media, will kill for an earthquake story that's not a landslide, or a flood, or a picture of some store with all the stock on the floor."

He was grinning from ear to ear. On the table in front of him he had a fistful of faxed proxies, the backing of members who couldn't get to the meeting.

By eleven a.m. synagogue business was out of the way, with the tent and the new name now official. The media arrived in force for Teddy's press conference, a better turnout then expected.

Teddy didn't miss the opportunity to introduce Tovah to the widest possible audience. He even handed out her biography; something he must have put together himself.

Reading solemnly Teddy said Tovah's father, "the revered Rabbi Eliezer Feldner, will officiate at the installation of his daughter, Rabbi Tovah Feldner, as Senior Rabbi of Ohel Tikvah. The service will be held later this year in the synagogue's tent. Also, honoring their new rabbi, the synagogue will sponsor Rabbi Eliezer Feldner as a scholar-in-residence for the whole community; in their tent, and at other locations to be announced."

It was a great idea, and Tovah knew her father would be delighted. Tovah realized all this was as good as a vote of confidence. She could almost feel the last of her job tension flowing out of her. She was home. *Ohel Tikvah* would be her home, spiritual and actual.

Teddy was beginning to address the subject of the synagogue's building. He started quite formally, "Our congregation has had a nasty shock," he said.

However, the reporters didn't have time for speeches.

"Is this a gimmick?" one of the TV newsmen asked, breaking in.

"Yes. It is." Teddy's admitted readily, surprising his audience. They looked pleased too, as though they now had the quote they needed for their story. But, Teddy had more to say.

"It's a gimmick. It's a pose. We desperately need a new, safe building. Our old building," here Teddy gestured toward their old building visible through an open tent flap. It had sagged since the earthquake.

"That's the illusion of safety. It's too dangerous. We need to know our building is safe. In all else we're secure. We're secure in our tradition, our real security. The building is just a detail, but, an essential detail. Like brakes are one detail on a car; but an essential detail. We need a building. But, for the moment, we're safer in a tent than in there."

Teddy shrugged toward the old building so dismissively Tovah half expected it would fall down from the blast of mental energy Teddy had sent its way.

"And, we've got even more; we've got the promise of as much help as we'll need. Holy Redeemer, our Lutheran neighbor, has kindly offered to house our *Torah* scrolls for us. We'll pick them up every Friday, and one of us will keep them for the weekend. The church will take them back on Sunday. And, since they'll be guarding our *Torahs* we're talking about a joint bible study project, run by their Minister and our Rabbi, with texts from both Testaments." Apparently Teddy had an unlimited supply of ideas touching on every aspect of synagogue life.

"When are you going to build?" one of the reporters hollered.

"I have absolutely no idea. It depends on membership," Teddy shot back. "If you or anyone else is interested in helping, we would love to have you. Come and join us. Come back for services every Friday night and Saturday morning. Join us here the second night of Passover; we're going to hold our *Seder* right here, the Passover meal and ritual. Metaphorically, we're in the desert. However, not only will the tent be here, there will be another addition for the *Seder*, one our forbearers might well have liked to have along on their crossing."

"What's that?" they chorused.

"A caterer's truck," Teddy said.

He got a laugh, and one reporter, showing off, Tovah thought, asked, "Will you be serving *manna* or *matzah?*"

As the two of them walked away after the formal press conference, Tovah said to Teddy, in an aside, "I didn't know you did stand-up. Can you actually get a kosher caterer out here to do a *Seder* on short notice? Mind you, I can't think of a better way to invite people. Almost as good as the repartee. You were going to have both *Seders* at home. I was invited."

"Janice will arrange it. She can arrange anything, and it'll give her something important to think about. It'll help her get over her scare. You're invited to this one too. You just have to come up with the great – and not too long – version of the *Haggadah*, stressing our situation.

I didn't know I could do stand-up either. Someone told me once to always leave them laughing." Teddy bent over, scuttled sideways a little and flicked an imaginary cigar, doing a very bad imitation of Groucho Marx.

The Los Angeles Time reporter, the one who'd made the *'manna'* joke, came up to them, with two of the television reporters and their cameramen trailing behind him. "Rabbi, I'd like to know how you really feel about this circus?"

"Do you think it's a circus, just because there's a tent?"

"Fair enough," the reporter responded. "But, did they have to force you into this rather undignified – at least I think it's undignified – way of doing business?"

"You and I differ in that," Tovah said. She would have thought the cameras would make her self-conscious, but she just wanted to refute what the reporter said.

"I certainly wasn't forced into anything. You just heard me say that the tent was my idea, inspired by something my husband said."

Tovah could feel Teddy bristling beside her. He exploded. "We don't force our rabbi to do anything. She just said the tent was her idea, for God's sake."

"As I said, my husband inspired the tent idea," Tovah said with one hand on Teddy's arm. He seemed to understand the "I can handle this" message of her gesture.

"I certainly don't see why a tent is undignified," she said. "Not having any building, not even a tent, is an awfully high price for dignity. Real life is messy, and it can be a bit of a circus. Resting on our dignity would keep us standing still. We can't afford it. We are a group of people dedicated to creating a vibrant religious community. Genteel poverty and dignity can keep religious institutions invisible in this high-tech age. It won't do. We have too much to say about modern life."

They were listening, so she went on, "I wasn't forced into anything. I'm delighted to be a part of this. I regret the earthquake. But, in the long run, maybe it's the best thing that could have happened."

She could sense what was coming next so she hurried on, "And no, before you ask, I don't think God visits earthquakes upon us. They just happen. We probably should have thought of this before. I think we're going to have plans for a building in two years, maybe less. If it means two years in a tent for *Ohel Tikvah* when the weather cooperates, and in the fellowship halls of one of our church neighbors, or in a hotel, when the weather is bad, that's fine as far as I'm concerned. When we get the building, we'll understand what a gift a home can be."

Beginning with the very next news broadcast, all evening, and in the newspapers the next morning, there was complete coverage of the newly named *Ohel Tikvah*, the synagogue in a tent.

The headlines made Tovah part of the news.

"Woman Rabbi says life can be a circus."

"Woman Rabbi lauds her congregation's vision"

"Woman rabbi says hubby inspired tent."

"Woman rabbi," Tovah said with distaste when she saw the first TV coverage, only hours after the press conference. "How can it still be news the Rabbi is a lady?"

"The lady is a genius, as far as I'm concerned," Teddy said. "We've had twenty-four calls from people who want to join. They all say they want to bring friends. They all wanted to know how come no one ever let them know we even existed?" He made a face.

"Teddy, you didn't give them your lecture, about how they should have known about us?" Tovah said, mock stern.

"I did not. I said I was delighted they'd take time from cleaning up after the earthquake to come to services. I also said we were having special services tomorrow, on Friday evening, and Shabbat morning, too.

"We are?"

"Didn't you say something about prayers, the kind you say when you've escaped a danger."

"Yes. I guess I did. I guess I'd better get busy."

# CHAPTER THIRTY-TWO

"Look, the earthquake was almost four days ago. The planes are landing again in California, and need to be on one of them. My family is there. I have to get to them. I've got to get home."

The airline clerk looked at Dan as though she'd be delighted to put him on an airplane if she could, any destination, just to get rid of him.

"Mr. Goldin. The earthquake was three days and a few hours ago. I know planes are landing again. We just got permission. And, no matter what, I don't have a seat for you."

"I made a reservation."

"So did a lot of other people. The flight you were supposed to be on happened to be the last one that couldn't land. I told you. I can get you a flight tomorrow, no problem."

"No. It's a big problem. My wife and kids are alone out there and I need to get to them. I need to get there today. I need to be on a plane to L.A., Riverside County,

Santa Barbara, San Diego or Orange County. Just get me within driving distance. I'm not unreasonable."

The expression on the young agent's face made it clear she didn't agree with him. He'd seen the same expression on the face of the first ticket agent he'd accosted at five a.m. in the morning He'd even threatened to stage a sit-in with a sign saying "This airline unfair to earthquake victims."

The clerk had motioned to someone, a man dressed in the same uniform as the other clerks, but suspiciously beefy-looking. The man took him aside. "Mr. Goldin let me spell this out for you. You are flying on points, not a high priority ticket. We've got people backed up because there were no airplanes landings anywhere in Southern California since the earthquake. You might get lucky in the terminal trying for standby at one of the gates. I'll give you a pass, for today only. If you raise a ruckus, we will have you arrested. I only need to mention the words 'security concern,' and you're out of here for a very long time. Then you'll have to take a train, a bus, or walk to California."

Clearly the security guard meant exactly what he said. Dan took the pass offered and went back into the departure area to see if he could get on stand-by. He could not believe he'd been successful in his search, Tovah had invited him — actually invited him — to come home, but he could not get a seat on an airplane.

He was at his third departure site of the day, still behaving perfectly. He'd been talking to the same young agent for quite some time. She'd just had a flight leave for San Diego. He'd really wanted to be on that flight. Neither pleading nor charm had worked. He was trying to think of a new tactic for the next flight when he heard Tovah's voice.

He spun around looking for her, or for whoever sounded so much like her.

It was Tovah, although not in person. There she was, on the News Channel that ran interminably on the airport's television sets.

She was saying her synagogue had pitched a tent and would be holding services in it. In fact, she was standing in a tent, at a press conference. They were going to have a *Seder* in their tent. The man beside her – who had to be Teddy Stein – seemed to be inviting everyone who saw the broadcast to their S*eder.*

"That's my wife," he said in amazement to the young woman behind the desk. She was busy closing the gate, obviously planning to get away from him. She looked at Dan as if to say, "You're claiming a woman on television is your wife? You really are desperate."

"She just happens to be your wife?" was what she actually said.

"Yes," he said. "Why would I say that, if it isn't true?"

"Listen, you'd say anything to get a flight to the West Coast. You said as much a few minutes ago."

"Her being my wife might get me on a flight? If that'll do it, would you like to hear about our kids, or see pictures?" He pulled his wallet out of his pocket. At least the gate agent was now somewhat interested. He had a picture of his whole family, all four of them smiling hugely, taken less than a year before.

The young woman looked closely at the picture then up at the TV screen again. For some reason Tovah seemed to be an excellent credential.

"Okay, it's the same person. She's a smart lady. I've been watching her through most of this shift. I've got a couple more flights, and then I'm off for two days. I guess I can believe you on this one."

"I swear it. I swear it," Dan said, raising his right arm, even though it meant putting down his precious backpack. "Why would I have her picture otherwise? Her name is Rabbi Tovah Feldner, right? She's a rabbi in Dana Point, California, right?"

"Okay, rabbi's husband. I believe you. If she's a rabbi, I guess you really need to be there by the beginning of Sabbath. Why didn't you say so? Don't worry; it's three hours earlier there. I'm Jewish. I wish she was my rabbi. I've got one more flight to L.A. I'll get you on, even with that ticket of yours. It's the best I can do. It's for her, not you. In honor of you being her husband."

She looked at Dan, a lot friendlier now then when he'd been just another scruffy traveler carrying a backpack and pulling a suitcase on wheels. She said, "Here are the rules. You don't move until then. You don't talk to one living soul in this airport and tell them you're on the flight. My luck it'll be my supervisor, or some hotshot businessman who doesn't get off standby because of you. Not one word, to anyone. Swear it?"

Dan raised his right hand again. "I swear, by everything I hold holy."

"Okay, Rabbi's husband. I'm going to hold you to it. And, remember, I know where to find your wife if you fink on me."

"Can I call her?

"You can call her, but from a quiet spot, where no one else will hear you."

Dan found a quiet corner and got Tovah on her cell phone.

"Where are you?"

"I've just dropping the kids at day care. Then I'm going to the synagogue to get some stuff, so I can work at home. Where are you?"

"I'm at the airport."

"Dan, you should have been here yesterday. I wish you'd been here. We had a press conference. You don't know what an idea you gave me when you said … "

"I know, I know. I just saw you on TV. I couldn't believe it. It was great, it just got me …"

"You saw it! Where? I can't believe …"

"Yes I did. Right there on the airport news. There you were …"

"It was actually on the airport news? You actually saw it? Wait until I tell Janice and Teddy. They'll be thrilled. They're running around getting copies of every inch of coverage, every moment on television. You know, good news from bad, earthquake brings inspiration. It makes people feel as though they have some control. It makes me feel that way, at least. They say when we hold the synagogue's tenth, fifteenth, twenty-fifth anniversary; the tapes will be a wonderful memento. I think they're going to give out copies as awards for big gifts to the synagogue fund."

"Now that you're a star, they'll want to make a movie of your life, *California Rabbi.* They'll even have real footage to use."

She laughed, joyous, and uninhibited, the old Tovah's laugh. "*California Rabbi.* I like it. It's good. Maybe they'll call it, *The Rabbi's Husband,* since you inspired this whole wonderful idea. I always said you looked a little like Lou Diamond Phillips, but better."

"Thanks," Dan said. "I think."

"But who will they cast in my part? Someone once told me I look a little bit like Janine Garafalo, except taller. No one has ever mentioned Nicole Kidman, or Cameron Diaz."

# CHAPTER THIRTY-THREE

He only told her he was ready to come home. No details. Not that he'd really found his mother. He wondered if she thought less of him because he'd quit. When he'd insisted he was coming, she hadn't argued. She'd said, 'Come home.' In a subsequent call he'd been thrilled to hear her admit he was right, the kids needed to see him.

She had even said, "I need …" She hadn't finished her thought but he was willing to wait for the thrill of her concluding that sentence.

He didn't want to tell her about finding his mother's convent over the phone. He wanted to see her face when he handed her the heavy envelope of material his mother had left for him.

Last night at his apartment, all he had looked at was one small packet of pictures. He wanted Tovah there when he went through the documents and examined the pictures. It would be almost as good as introducing her to his family.

Sitting in the corner of the airport waiting for his flight, he pulled out just one of the pictures he'd looked at the night before, a wedding picture of his parents.

No one would ever have to find some standard remark to repeat endlessly, to wonder that he didn't look like his family.

Now he had two families, one he loved deeply and one he might come to love. And he looked just like one of them. It was enough. How wonderful to find his birth family, tall, handsome, exotic looking.

Despite any antipathy he felt toward his birth father, he saw he resembled him more than his mother. For the first time in his life, he could look at a photo of people who'd come directly before him and see his face emerging. Leah looked so much like his mother.

In naming Leah, Tovah had been prescient. In the first moments after Leah's birth, she'd said they should name her Leah Adele. He'd let her do it, humoring her in the face of their very sick baby. In those days he'd been unwilling to make any claim on his birth mother. Now he knew she'd have welcomed any claim he might have made. The packet of things she'd left for him was proof.

Neither Leah or Ari, nor any other children they might have, would ever have to feel as he had. He would never feel that way again, although it might take him some time to be comfortable with this new sensation.

Just to know Leah could look at these pictures and see a part of herself would give her the kind of foundation he'd always lacked. He was receiving that gift very late in life. He might have to work for years to fully understand what it meant. His children would always have it as their birthright.

Tonight, in their new home, when the children were asleep, with the earthquake in the past, he and Tovah would look at all this material together. Eventually it might help make a new marriage between them, a bond even stronger than the first.

He eased the wedding picture of his parents back into the envelope, then he put the whole package flat against the back of his pack where it would lie safe, close to his body. It would take months of study to understand it all. She'd gathered a lifetime of information for him. One thing was clear. She believed in their bond, had never doubted he would come looking for her. All her life, even a few days before her death, she'd updated her memoir. Not for her sister nuns, but for him. She herself had written those words, 'For My Son,' in the graceful black letters resting against his back; the closest thing to a caress from his mother he'd ever felt.

For the first time he realized his not talking to Tovah before he left had been a kind of holding back. It wasn't clear why he'd been afraid to make demands on her. Had he been afraid she'd leave too, if he'd actually voiced his needs?

Probably Tovah had never thought of leaving. It wasn't her way of dealing with problems. Somehow, because it had been his way, he'd projected the idea onto her.

Dan glanced at his wristwatch. Finally, it was time. The last thing he did before he went to the gate was take the plastic-covered original of the sketch he'd carried throughout his trip out of a pocket on the side of his backpack and add it to his envelope of family memorabilia.

# CHAPTER THIRTY-FOUR

Once Dan was in L.A., he remembered Tovah had said Friday afternoon traffic from L.A. south to Orange County could be awful. One car accident on the 405 or the 5 could result in hours of backed up cars. But today the cars flowed freely, as though to especially accommodate him in his rental automobile.

The landmarks Tovah had mentioned flashed by: the oil refinery near the L.A. airport, and then, it seemed only moments later, the cut-off to the Long Beach Freeway, the 710. He'd been driving for more than an hour when he passed the exit for South Coast Plaza on the edge of Santa Ana, but it felt like only a few moments had passed. Then he was at the El Toro Y, where the 405 and the 5 meet.

During Tovah's first trip to Orange County, she and Janice had been stuck there, moving only three miles in a half hour.

He whizzed through the area, traffic more than twenty lanes across, counting on and off ramps, truck lanes and the diamond car pool lanes. Dan couldn't use the car pool lanes, because there had to be two in the car to qualify. It didn't matter. Today regular traffic seemed to be there only to carry him along.

Any other time Dan would have been fascinated by the complex highway design, by the concrete pylons like great dinosaur limbs supporting the upper levels of the freeway. Today the roads only had to get him to his family.

He didn't get lost looking for Tovah's street or the house once he was in Dana Point. He'd looked at the map of the area so often he felt as though he'd been there before. He turned into the small, quiet street knowing the fourth house from the corner would be a large, white, Spanish-inspired mansion. It had a gate leading to a courtyard before the front door. As a result of the earthquake, there would be a crack running right across the home's stucco front and through every window on the façade.

He parked and sat in the car for a moment, exultant. He'd made it in time to join his family at *Ohel Tikvah's* first official Sabbath service in their new tent.

He'd parked near the house, across the street. As if their old sense of timing as a couple had come back, Tovah pulled into the driveway. He'd have thought he'd leap from the car the moment he saw them, but he didn't. He was so entranced by his family he actually couldn't move. Tovah went around the far side of the mini-van to help Leah and Ari out of their car seats.

Just seeing them was as great a pleasure as he could ever recall. He watched Ari heft a big bag of groceries for Tovah, saw Leah walking confidently, managing to carry her own school gear and her brother's things too.

Her gait was almost perfect. Then they were gone, disappearing into the house.

He had to sit there for another moment. He didn't want to break down the first time he saw their faces or spoke to them. It seemed only a second, but when he checked his watch he realized he'd been sitting in the car for almost twenty minutes.

Finally he told himself: you have to do something. Don't you want to be there for *Shabbat*? Of course! And, just as Tovah had described to him, it was getting dark more rapidly than he'd have believed possible.

He took his backpack from the front seat and slung it over his shoulder, but carefully, so the precious packet of material from his mother wouldn't be disturbed.

As he walked past the big house he could see straight into the dining room through the arched windows. Tovah stood in front of the sideboard. He could see the shine of silver in front of her.

He hurried to the front gate. It yielded easily, not locked. Grateful he didn't have to knock or ring the bell, he could only hope the door to the house would be unlocked too. It was, opening quietly and closing behind him, equally silently.

Could he possibly be as fortunate with the door to the apartment? Should he? He didn't want to frighten them. The door with the patterned etched-glass inset Tovah had described to him opened quietly too.

They didn't hear him come in. He only dared to take one step inside. Then he stopped.

Tovah had gone back to the traditional, sunset moment of candle lighting, as her mother had always done. Tovah, Ari and Leah were all in the dining room, at the sideboard, with their backs to him. Tovah held

Leah on one hip and Ari stood on a dining room chair next to her.

It was like a play. But, he shouldn't be in the audience. He should be part of the action, alongside his family.

A small point of light flared in Tovah's hand, one of the long wooden matches she used to light candles. It moved, once, twice. The light wavered. Why did she hesitate? Time slowed for Dan, almost stopped. The very air between him and his family seemed to catch, to impede the candles' light. He watched, frozen. Tovah's hand moved forward again, agonizingly slowly. She lit the third candle. Again, she stopped. Dan felt blood drain from his face. His backpack slipped from his arm to the floor. Would she only light three candles? Had she only lit three candles all these weeks?

It took only a second, although it seemed forever, as long as the whole time he'd been away from his family. Tovah had stopped because she'd sensed he was in the room. She must have heard something, or felt his presence. She turned to look at him, the most wonderful smile on her face.

Unlike the frozen seconds of time he'd just experienced, things moved quickly. Tovah's smile, the joy on the children's faces, flashed across the room to him. In an instant both children would be clamoring to get to him. He needed to get to them first.

So many times Tovah had told him the rooms in their new home were very large. It didn't seem true just then. Dan felt as though he crossed the distance to them with one step. Something like their old understanding flowed between them: *before we do anything else, we'll finish the candle lighting.*

Tovah turned back to the sideboard. There were four candles. Of course there were four. How could he have been so fearful again, even for an instant?

Tovah handed him a match, lighting it from the remnant of the one she'd been using. The light flared, illuminating each face. Leah reached her hand across from her perch on Tovah's hip to hug him. Ari leaned back against him so easily, as always. Dan put one arm around Leah and Tovah, and, reaching around Ari with his other arm, he lit the last candle. Before he and Tovah had to face all the hard work, the issues still before them, they would have this Sabbath. Together the four of them sang the blessing.

*Baruch atah adenoy, elohainu melech ha'alom. Asher kiddishanu b'mitzvah-tov, vitzevonu, l'hadlich ner shel Shabbat.*

*Blessed are you, Sovereign of the Universe, who has commanded us to kindle the Sabbath lights.*

### THE END

## Some Topics for Book Clubs to Ponder

I am long-time and ardent book club member having belonged to at least one club in every city I've ever lived in. I've never found the "questions" at the back of a novel helpful, since they always sound as though they are written by a grammar teacher or an academic, hell-bent on impressing the readers.

Rather than formal questions, I'd like to suggest a couple of viewpoints to consider in your approach to *The Rabbi's Husband.* A couple of them are phrased as questions, the English language not allowing otherwise.

*The Rabbi's Husband* addresses aspects of contemporary religious life in America. I have long been active in interfaith and Jewish communal activities. I've always found that people of faith, any faith, have a great deal to say to each other.

So, first, consider *The Rabbi's Husband*, against the background of your own faith, or lack thereof. If Jewish, does *The Rabbi's Husband* ring true to you? If Christian, Muslim, Ba'hai or any of the major Eastern religions, do you see parallels or major differences in your own community.

Tovah is a rabbi, a field that was once exclusively male. Do you think women coming into such a field – one that was fully or heavily male – have special problems or issues to deal with? Have you had similar experiences in your own professional or personal choices?

Are those issues religious, feminist, cultural or some other category that you think is important?

Finally, do you like the characters: Dan, as he behaves at the beginning or when you come to know him better? Tovah? Tovah's parents, children or her neighbor Robin? The Reverend Jo Waggoneer? Teddy and Janice Stein? George Berg?

In my first novel, *The Binding*, Rabbi Tovah Feldner has a small but crucial role. In *The Rabbi's Husband* she is central to the action.

Do you like novels where people from other books make appearances or are a continuing presence?

And, finally, was this guide of any use to you as an individual reader or a member of a book club?

I am always available to phone into book club meetings, and to attend book clubs in person if distances allow.

Please check my website www.brendabarrie.com for my schedule. All my contact information is available there.